Still A Marine

STILL A MARINE

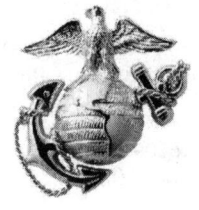

Donald F. McKenna

Still A Marine Press

Disclaimer: While fiction, this narrative comes from real events in the Korean War. A few of the characters in this story are composites of two or more actual people. The names of those characters were chosen from a copy of the actual roster of Baker Company in September 1951.

Herman Sobel, Sal Mollo, Frank Morales, Frank Pagano and Sgt. Raymond Goetsell are more than real.

The concept "Still A Marine" is real.

IMAGE CREDITS
Cover
Upper: Department of Defense Photo, National Archives, NWDNS-127-N-A156882
Lower: "Winter Trail," ca. 1951, copyright Donald F. McKenna
Cover Design by Glenn C. Wong
Inside
p. 42, Department of Defense Photo (USMC) A170084; p. 48, National Archives Photo (USMC) 127-N-A2888; p. 54, National Archives Photo (USMC), 127-N-A156882; p. 55, National Archives Photo (USMC) 127-N-A8866; p. 57, Department of Defense Photo (USMC) A155692; p. 71, National Archives Photo (USMC) 127-N-A6869; p. 75, Department of Defense Photo (USMC) A167091; p. 76, Department of Defense Photo (USMC) A8868; p. 146, National Archives Photo (USN) 80-G-429642; p. 149, National Archives Photo (USMC) 127-N-A155354
Otherwise, all photographs copyright Donald F. McKenna

Copyright ©2007, The Prescription Shop, Inc.

All rights reserved. No part of this book may be used or reproduced in any manner whatsoever without written permission, except in the case of brief quotations embodied in critical articles or reviews.

Published 2007

Printed by Still A Marine Press in the United States of America

StillAMarine.com

ISBN 978-0-9799990-0-0

There is no such thing as an ex-Marine.

www.StillAMarine.com

CHAPTER 1

It is one of those moments in life.

Crouched down, there I am looking through my binoculars out of the dirty window of a second-story window of a dilapidated South Tucson building, scanning the empty lot below. To my right, another gray-haired man is peering through the scope of a high-powered rifle.

It is one of those moments in life when you stop and wonder, "What twists and turns in my life put me in this place, at this time?"

Chapter 2

I can't remember—were you in the Navy or Air Force?

Not that long ago, I was looking out the window of my second floor office above my pharmacy, absentmindedly moving papers around on my desk.

"Fifty years in business and I have hated paperwork every day of it," I complained aloud to no one in particular.

My office door opened and an attractive Hispanic woman entered. "Stop muttering and do some work."

"I like to mutter and I don't feel like working."

Fifty years in business and Alma had been with me well over half of that time. From day one, even fresh out of high school, she had been indispensable. We made a perfect team—she always seemed to know what I was thinking. Sometimes I thought she made my job so easy, I could stay home and the small pharmacy chain would do just as well, despite the tough market they faced. Over the years we had also become good friends.

"Hey Alma—help me to understand this internet search thing."

"If I teach you that, I will never get any work out of you. A computer is a tool, not a toy." After a pause, she relented with a small grin. "OK—What do you want to search for?"

"Someone told me that there was a site on there for my old unit from the military. They formed some sort of club or something."

Chapter 2

After a deep sigh, Alma moved a chair up to my computer and proceeded to open a search Web page. "Why is it you have never talked much about your time in Korea? Why haven't you tried to contact any of your old buddies?"

I should have been used to it by now—Alma always did have a way of getting to the heart of things. I leaned back a bit in my chair and cleared my throat. "Good questions. First question. I guess the answer is that the only people who could talk about it and understand would be the guys who were there with me. To someone who had not been there and felt it, it would be just another collection of musty old war stories."

I leaned back a bit more in my chair and crossed my arms thoughtfully. "The second question is tougher. To be honest, I have never thought about it until now. My true feeling is that those of us who were there together just separated and headed off in different directions, but we never really parted. I know that we were a lot closer than any of us knew at the time." After a moment of silence, I looked back at the search page Alma had opened. "You know what is funny? I realize now that I have always seen them in my mind as they were then. Young, tough and together. Thinking about it today, it is hard to imagine that they are old guys with grey hair!"

Alma knew now was the time to go with the lighter tone. "Lets see," she teased. "I can't remember—were you in the Navy or Air Force?"

"Come on Alma! One smart ass in this operation is enough!"

She grinned. "Of course, I know you are an ex-Marine. How could I miss it when some dirt bag walks into the store with some kind of Marine hat or the 350 pound gorilla with a Marine tattoo and you treat them all like long lost rich uncles. Or—remember that old man with a simple Marine pin who looked like he was in the Civil War and 4000 years old? Once he told you that he had been on Iwo Jima, you called him a 'boot-assed Marine.' He lit up like a Christmas tree and the two of you talked forever. I have also seen you with my two uncles who are ex-Marines. The three of you act like you were born of the same mother at the same time. AND you refuse to work on the Marine Corps Birthday every year because you have lunch with Gabe Sanchez."

"First of all young lady, there are no ex-Marines. Once you are a Marine, you do not escape. The pilot light will always burn. It really doesn't matter what era you are from. Give me a World War II Marine, a Korea Marine, a Vietnam Marine, and an Iraq Marine and I will give you a fire team from hell. Send us out and the job will get done. Secondly your uncles and all of those other South Side Mexican Marines were the first friends I had in Tucson. At 13, I was a scared, lonely east coast kid. They accepted me from the first day I hit town. And, they are the reason that I chose the Marine Corps."

"Well, whatever it is, I have seen it with you and my uncles. Just what does the Marine Corps do that none of you can shake?" Not really waiting for an answer, Alma turned back to the search page. "Tell me the name of your old military unit."

"1st Battalion, 7th Marines, 1st Marine Division."

Five seconds later, Alma had a web site up titled "First Battalion Seventh Marines Korea 1950–1953."

"Goddamn—Alma you are good!" I drew my chair back towards the desk. "I may just keep you on the payroll after all."

Alma rolled her eyes playfully and put the extra chair back against the wall. "I have work to do . . . call me if you get stuck," she called over her shoulder as she went back to work.

The site offered a roster of its members. I scrolled down the list, reading the names one by one. My eye lit on a familiar name . . . Herman!!!!!!

Out my office I went and down the hall to Alma's. "I found a name on the list, I recognized. How can I get his phone number?"

"Where is he from?"

"New Jersey"

Alma crossed her arms across her chest. "OK, but it will be a really hard job to find the phone number. Here's the deal. If I do it, you will find the time and we will sit down and you will tell me

—5—

CHAPTER 2

about the year you spent in Korea and why Marines are like they are. I have never figured it out."

I was barely listening. "OK. OK. Deal. Just get me a phone number."

"Wait a second." Alma turned her chair to her own computer. Within seconds she was writing a phone number down. She handed my the paper. "When did you see or talk to this guy last?"

"Must have been either late 1951 or early 1952. Let's see, Holy Shit! That is over 50 years ago!"

I headed out the door. Then, remembering my promise, I turned back a bit. "Hey, Alma, come on down to my office, I will put the phone on that speaker thing and you can hear the conversation."

In a few minutes we were both back in my office. Alma took a chair by the door.

I put the phone on speaker, dialed the number, and a couple of rings later a male voice politely answered on the other end. "Hello."

"Is this Corporal Herman, super Marine and the first man to the top of hill 673?"

There was a slight pause on the other end, then the voice changed. "Smart Mouth—you Son-of-a-Bitch!!!!"

By the door, Alma began erupting in uncontrolled laughter. She caught her breath and got up to step closer to the speaker phone. "Herman, I am Alma and I have worked for Don Mackinaw forever—so I understand the Son-of-a-Bitch thing. My life will not be complete until I hear the part about Smart Mouth. I'd listen now, but I do all of the thinking AND all of the work around here, so I'll leave you two to catch up."

Alma headed down the hall to run the business saying to herself, "Smart Mouth—I love it!!" Two old Marines, our conversation went on most of the morning. We had over 50 years to catch up on.

Alma did not forget the promise. It was not, however, until the next three-day weekend rolled around that she reminded me

I owed her some stories. As we were closing the store that Friday, she said "Time to pay up on your promise to tell me about the Marines and Korea."

"True. How about Monday at the El Salto for lunch?"

Alma nodded her head. "Deal. By the way—I knew we had the right number when I heard Herman call you 'Son-of-a-Bitch,' but the 'Smart Mouth' thing must be added to the story. I will pay big money to hear that."

Lunch at El Salto

Alma and I were seated in the corner of El Salto. "Are you sure you are up for this Alma? It is going to be a long lunch!—maybe a bit more than you bargained for . . ."

"I am more than ready. Let's get started."

CHAPTER 3

"Fuck you, Goat Breath"

It was April, 1951, and Harry Truman was the president of the United States. The American military, including the 1st Marine Division, were part of the United Nations forces fighting against the communist armies of North Korea and China. North Korea had invaded the Republic of Korea (South Korea) nearly a year before—June, 1950. China had entered the war as the U.N. Forces came near their border in November, 1950. The outcome of this conflict was still far from clear. Fighting had taken turns moving up and down the narrow Korean peninsula. By April, 1951, the United Nations forces were working their way north.

Somewhere north of the 38th parallel in the Republic of Korea.
. . .

Three trucks came to a stop in a huge cloud of dust kicked up by the crude Korean dirt road. Once more the convoy had made it safely into the company perimeter of Baker Company, 7th Marines, 1st Division. The drivers knew that today's ride had been one of the better ones. The raw replacement Marines in the back of the trucks were unaware that on most trips into this area the convoys had received intense shell fire. Not today.

A squad of Marines sitting on an embankment by the side of the road casually watched as about thirty clean, freshly shaven, fully equipped Marines unloaded from the trucks. Back from a long

STILL A MARINE

day on patrol out of the company perimeter and deep into Chinese territory, they had just returned and plopped down their tired bodies. The last hill up from the valley was a 1500 ft climb with full equipment. Though dirty, tired, and hungry, today had been a good day because they had encountered no one and everyone had made it back safely. The members of the patrol had little to say as they quietly eyed the new Marines unloading.

The 1st Division had been under-strength since the start of the war. As fast as men could be trained in the United States, they were being shipped over to Korea. These were the replacements of newly trained Marines that had been promised. Fresh bodies to fill the ranks.

A Corporal from company headquarters arrived and took charge of the new group.

"OK guys, line up in three rows. You are now with Baker Company, 7th Marines."

"Weapons guys, go with him." The Corporal called off a few names, and those men followed a helmeted Marine off toward the company command post. More names were read off—these headed to the 2nd and 3rd platoons. Only one new Marine was left; he appeared to be the runt of the litter.

I stood with my pack and rifle and waited.

"Ok Mackinaw. You, go to 1st squad, 1st platoon."

I barely met the Corps' minimum size requirement. These were tough times. The first Division Marines needed warm bodies—every man they could get their hands on. Korea had come up suddenly. When World War II was over, the Marine Corps had been left for dead and was grossly undermanned. Harry Truman had even talked about doing away with the Marine Corps completely.

Chapter 3

I was one of those helping fill out the ranks of the 1st Division.

The Corporal gestured and said. "Mackinaw, that is the lst squad of the 1st platoon crapped out there on the side of the road. They don't look like much, but there they are. You belong to them."

By now, the first squad was stirring on the small incline by the side of the road, quietly talking among themselves. One voice came out of the group loud and clear. "Fuck, they sent us a boy scout in place of a Marine!"

Standing alone on the road, I stiffened, but shot back just as clearly.

"Fuck you Jack!! I didn't come here to take shit from some goat fucking Okie."

Setting aside his equipment and weapon, the Marine who had spoken from the side of the hill didn't simply stand up, he unraveled. He was one big boy—huge. He started towards me, making several comments as he moved toward the road. Each utterance revolved around physical abuse.

As he approached, I pulled himself up straight, but that did not add enough to my size. This was not going to be pretty. Nonetheless, I prepared for the boarding party. Off came the clean new pack, I set my jaw, and carefully put my rifle down. I was thinking, "There will always be a penalty for having a big mouth." It appeared as though this might be that day.

Up close, the big guy stared down at me. Before he could say a word, I disregarded the momentary warning I had just given myself about my big mouth. "You even have goat breath—you ugly goat fucker!!!"

"Look you little 98-pound smart mouth son of a bitch—one more word and I . . . . ."

A voice came from behind the monster Marine.

"Try me first Snyder. He's mine."

From the side of the road another Marine from the patrol had come up behind the oversized Marine. Snyder looked back at him, stopped dead in his tracks, and backed off a step or two.

"Shit Boost, what do you want with this little smart mouth shit?"

Boost said, "He's my new rifleman and I want him in one piece."

With that, the confrontation ended.

Walking off with Boost, I looked over my shoulder and came up with one more verbal shot. "Fuck you, goat breath."

This was not without a response from the huge Marine.

"Fuck you, you smart mouth little shit."

By now, the group on the side of the hill had loosened up and was chuckling at the feisty new member of the 1st platoon walking away from its largest member. They found great luxury in laughing at the gigantic Marine, knowing that he was not going to beat THEM to death.

From that day and forever, in 1st platoon, neither of us would ever be called by our given names again.

"Goat" met "Smart Mouth."

Chapter 4

"Welcome aboard"

It didn't take long for Goat and I to get better acquainted. Two hours after our warm and friendly encounter, the squad leader, Sergeant Peterson, otherwise known simply as 'Pete,' aroused the squad from a brief nap with a terse order. "Saddle up."

"First squad has been picked to go back up north toward Yangu. Activity has been reported by one of the spotter planes and Division wants to know how many people are up there and what they are doing."

Pete gave Boost instructions to check me out for equipment, ammo, grenades, and water. He then took me aside and told me to stay loose, keep my eyes open, and stay with Boost. "Do exactly what he tells you, no more, no less." Pete also gave Endo, the fire team leader, instructions to keep an eye on the 'rookie.'

First Squad headed out through the company perimeter, down from the high ground, and began the hike north. The grumbling about the abbreviated nap and other assorted subjects stopped abruptly on Pete's command. "Knock it off, NOW!!" Quieted, we continued north at a brisk pace.

After an hour or so, Peterson signaled the patrol to take cover. "We'll break for ten minutes." We automatically spread out and formed a rough perimeter. We each found a well-spaced and protected spot and faced outward.

Pete pointed at me. "Snyder, take the new guy up to that little ridge and see what is on the other side. Be back in 10 minutes. Take my binocs." Goat grumbled at me, "Come on eagle scout. Stay on me and keep your skinny little sorry ass low. Stay about 15 to 20 yards to the right of me. Keep your eyes on me all the time. Hand signals only. No talking."

Goat and I moved out as instructed. Creeping and crawling over the rough ground, we quickly arrived at the top of the small rise Peterson had indicated. Goat took the first look over the embankment and found himself face to face with a startled a Chinese soldier. A chance encounter that surprised the hell out of both of them.

In that instant, Goat did the only thing possible. He tucked his weapon, dove to his left and hit the ground rolling. I came to the top of the rise and cranked off three shots into the chest of the enemy soldier. From this position I spotted another group of four more Chinese soldiers who were starting to move from where they had been sitting and resting. They were not expecting company and were totally unprepared to respond. I cleaned up the group with rifle fire from about 30 yards. . . . None were moving. I reloaded and put a couple more rounds in each.

The Chinese soldier that Goat had encountered had been loosely carrying his Burp Gun over his shoulder. A truly scary weapon. With a rate of fire of 750 rounds per minute, it made an eerie ripping noise, frightening to hear even at a distance. Lucky day for Goat.

Less than a minute had elapsed since Goat had first peered over the ridge. Goat recovered most of his composure, moved to

Chapter 4

the top of the ridge, and surveyed the damage. His instructions for total silence were forgotten.

"Follow me, we are getting the fuck out of here! We made way too much noise. You are in big trouble because we were supposed to get a prisoner on this patrol and you—you dumb shit—killed them all."

There wasn't much creeping and crawling as we returned to the place where the rest of the squad had formed their defensive circle. Basic hauling ass.

When we got back to the perimeter, Pete was there waiting. "What happened?"

Goat explained how he "almost fell over a Chinaman with a Burp. The kid dropped him before he could get off a round. Then he trashed the entire group with his M-1."

Pete quickly gathered the men and gave orders to form up and begin the return trip. "We need to report what we found." Leaving the area seemed like an excellent idea. No need to hang around and encounter a much larger group of enemy soldiers. Most likely the rifle fire had attracted attention.

I trudged along behind Goat at the end of the patrol. The thoughts passing through my mind were jumbled. Mostly I was wondering why Goat had eaten my ass out for doing what I thought I was supposed to do—shoot the enemy.

Nobody told me about prisoners. What would you want a prisoner for?

About halfway back through the valley, the squad stopped for a break and automatically formed another perimeter. As we moved out again, there was another chastisement from the Goat. "You dumb shit. You are walking too close to me. Didn't they teach you not to bunch up! Get farther away from me. Give me more space."

The next time we halted and started out again, I was assigned the spot behind the fire team leader, Corporal Endo. This time spacing was kept at fifteen or twenty yards between each man and the line moved quickly and carefully through the valley.

Then it happened. A gigantic explosion interrupted the moving line and Endo went down with his hands over his face. The rest of the group spread and hit the ready-for-action position. Someone yelled, "A god-damn trip mine!" A tripwire had been stretched across the trail. Endo must have touched the wire and triggered it. The 'Bouncing Betty' type mine jumped to about shoulder level and exploded, causing pieces of metal to fly in every direction.

Endo was down on the ground. His face, chest, and dungarees a bloody mess. Pete and I, being the closest, moved towards him, with Pete yelling for the Corpsman. As soon as Doc got close, he brushed me aside. I promptly moved behind a tree where I hoped no one would see me throw up my guts.

As Doc's magic hands got Endo's bleeding under control, others moved in to pick up the extra load of Endo's weapon and equipment, and the patrol quickly moved out. For the rest of the long hike back, my smart mouth was temporarily silenced—the experiences of the day making even more of a mess of my thoughts. "Some Marine you are!! A little blood and you ralph. This is only one day. This is going to be a long fucking war!!"

The line finally passed thru the perimeter and headed for the Command Post. Pete sent Goat and me to the command post to brief the company commander on what we had encountered. As Goat went over his description of the patrol to the Commanding Officer, I stood quietly. The company commander asked "Was there any chance for prisoners?" To my surprise, Goat lied his ass off. "No sir. If this replacement guy hadn't done them in, they would have gotten us both. He had no choice but to wax them all."

The Skipper replied, "Good job men. I need to call battalion with a report of the activity. Dismissed." As we returned to the squad area not a word was spoken between Goat and me. I dropped down beside Boost—physically and emotionally drained by the day's activities. Goat started to walk away, but stopped and turned to Boost. "Hey Boost, you had better keep and eye on that Smart Mouth little mother fucker. I may need

Chapter 4

him again. For Christ sakes, he greased about half of the Chinese army and didn't change expression. Boost—I have always thought you were the coldest man I ever met. I'd hate to meet you two in a dark alley. It would scare the shit out of me."

A casual observer of the scene might think that the large Marine had said—"thank you and welcome aboard."

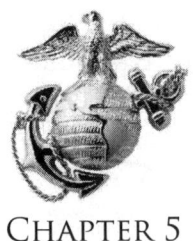

Chapter 5

"Properly led Marines are a force of nature"

—Sgt. Got Balls

The first meeting with Raymond was the same eventful day I became acquainted with "Goat Breath" and Boost.

As soon as I had settled in and gotten my equipment squared away, Boost had been instructed to deliver me to the platoon sergeant. Sergeant Gotshall was apparently aware of the new arrival in the company and also the account of the patrol. He had certainly heard about the introduction ceremony with one of the perfect gentleman in his platoon—Snyder, who had by now been permanently christened Goat. Word traveled fast.

Per orders, Boost soon had me standing in front of the sergeant in his tent. "My name is Sergeant Raymond Gotshall. That is Sergeant to you until I tell you otherwise," he quietly began. "I have earned these three stripes and you will respect them."

He continued. "From what I have heard, you are either the dumbest person I have ever met or the luckiest. Maybe both. I am from Texas and I truly believe that Corporal Snyder—the one you addressed as "Goat Breath"—is the meanest man I have ever met. He has put two army guys and one Marine out of action with his bare hands. All each did was give him a little lip. You may not know it, but the only thing that kept you from being stuffed down a shitter head first, or worse, is that you have been assigned as assistant BAR man to Frank Bustamante—Boost."

Chapter 5

"Boost is the quietest REAL Marine you will ever meet. Most of us in this platoon owe Boost for something. He has pulled Corporal Snyder out of deep shit at least twice and the respect he has for Boost is all that saved your boot-ass butt. You are a lucky boy."

"The man that invented the BAR would pay good money to watch Boost in action with it. He is SO damn effective using it under fire. My strict rule is that the BAR is rotated equally among the four fire team people. If you remember anything you learned in training, that sucker weighs 20 pounds and each magazine weighs a pound. Your M-1 is only nine and one-half pounds."

After this speech, I snapped out of the silence I had been in since Endo was hit. "Hey Raymond, I think your rule sucks if he is that good."

Sgt. Gotshall got up from his seat on the wooden grenade box, walked around a bit, and quietly looked at his new replacement. As he examined me, it reminded me of the looks my mother had given me as a child when something I had said did not require a verbal response. The same look also said "you are truly pissing me off."

At 6'-3" and 195 pounds of solid Marine, Raymond Gotshall, Sgt. USMC stood over me, barely the reported 5'8" and, after a full meal, I might have been lucky to tip 130 on the scales. Being examined by this man was intimidating enough. With a modicum of wisdom, I decided not to blurt out to my new leader my thought about the sergeant reminding me of my mother. Possibly he would not take it in the manner in which it was offered.

"Again, that is Sergeant Gotshall or Sergeant to you. But, I will answer your question. Because of who he is and what he is Boost is exempt from the rule."

"Hey Raymond," I offered. "I don't want to carry the BAR. How do I tell him that it is OK for him to carry it?"

The sergeant shook his head in exasperation. "Snyder was right. You are a smart-mouth little shit. Here I am with five years in the Corps and thinking about making it a career and they send me—YOU. If that is not bad enough, I also owe Boost for getting

me out of tight spots and I thank him by giving him—YOU. Go find him and extend my apologies to him."

"Smart Mouth," he continued after a pause, "if you have a half brain, you will get Boost to talk. Listen to him and remember everything he says. He IS good at what we are doing here. Now go!"

"OK. Raymond. To make you feel good about yourself, I will try to live up to your high expectations." This earned another penetrating look. With a small dose of wisdom, I left the presence of my new leader.

I would hear and see much more about the man in command of this platoon. When Sergeant Gotshall was out of hearing, he was called Sergeant Got Balls. Raymond hated that name. He did not want to hear it and never did from members of his platoon. We knew that if we were going to explore the limits of his wrath, it would be best to find another way.

His appearance and bearing commanded respect from everyone. The platoon knew that our leader was special. In the coming months I would see a man who displayed courage as if it were a given. Somewhere in history it has been written, "Courage is not the absence of fear, courage is overcoming that fear and getting the job done." That would sum up Sergeant Got Balls. Under fire he always looked as though he had a pre-written script and he was merely acting it out. It really didn't matter if it was a heavy

Chapter 5

fire fight, a full scale assault, or being overrun by the Chinese—he was always a composed complete leader. This man dragged back wounded, brought back bodies, gave directions, and coordinated things under fire as if he were managing an office.

His real talent was in the managing of people, the prime example being the young men that made up his platoon. First platoon could best have been described as a collection of motley, sorry, society misfits. Not one "pick of the litter" was to be found in the group.

Under Sergeant Got Balls 1st platoon looked and acted like Marines . . . most of the time.

CHAPTER 6

Los Hombres

Aside from Boost and Goat, a nod, a grunt or a slight wave of the hand seemed to be the maximum welcome I got from the members of 1st platoon.

Boost advised me, "Keep quiet for a few days. Just listen." This eloquent speech turned out to be the way this man communicated. Boost was a listener and a watcher. Obviously from the encounter with Goat and the message from the platoon Sergeant, the others paid careful attention to what Boost had to say. OK, I told myself, "be quiet, watch, and see what comes next."

Getting into the shooting and ducking that first day had come pretty fast. Keeping my mouth shut for a few hours offered me a good chance to absorb the sights. . . . Korea was a beautiful country, if you could overlook the stinky rice paddies. Even they were a pretty green. The paddies appeared to be stacked or layered with one higher than the other so the irrigation drained naturally. The hills and mountains were covered with pines and other pretty trees, while the valleys had all kinds of rivers and streams.

When I arrived in Korea that April, the Division had been on the move north. It had been ten months since the North Korean Army had surprised the world by storming across the 38th parallel invading South Korea. After only one day with me on the job, the division started to pull back, and was moving south to something that was being called a main line of resistance.

Chapter 6

Whenever Marines move in the field—or even when they were not moving—patrols were sent out to see what was going on around you. Whether they were moving as a unit north or south, the ridges, valleys, river beds, and mountains on all sides needed to be fully investigated to eliminate surprises. This meant patrols of various sizes were always in motion in all directions.

"Get it together, 1st Squad—you have a patrol"

"What do you mean? We just came back from patrol!"

"Yeah, but you didn't bring a prisoner, so you get to go again."

I chose this particular moment in time to execute the foreign concept of listening. It was time to duck the head, appear nonchalant, and hope no one remembered that the need for this patrol would have been solved if some dummy had not shot all the potential prisoners the day before.

"We are moving farther south and we need to go over that river and see what is going on. Battalion headquarters wants information. Be ready to go in 20 minutes."

Boost gave me another of his 'long' speeches. A quick briefing consisting of "Stay on me and carry this along with your stuff." 'Stuff' meant the full load of a Marine going on patrol—including, but not limited to, rifle, grenades, and extra bandoleers of ammo for the M-1. 'This' turned out to be a full load of magazines for Boost's BAR. Each BAR magazine weighed 1 pound and fit into a pocket of a webbed canvas belt. The belt held 10 magazines. Because of the weight, there were also suspenders that went over the shoulders.

Yesterday Boost had told Goat "He is mine." The impact of that statement was beginning to sink in. If I had not been commanded to stay quiet, I could have informed Boost that they had done away with slavery years ago.

Best left for another time.

I had little fear about what we were starting to do—partly because I lacked experience and had little understanding of the situation, and partly because Boost had a unique demeanor—he exported calmness.

As the group came together for patrol, there were four guys hanging together. When I looked closer I noticed that they were all Mexicans, off in their own world like the Mexican kids I knew back home in Arizona.

I parked myself near the four and listened. They were jabbering among themselves in Spanish, which made me homesick. Just like in high school, no matter what was going on, Mexican kids drifted into the language most comfortable to them. It had nothing to do with anything else, or anyone else and it really had nothing to do with exclusiveness. Just the way it was.

By the time I had arrived in Tucson at 13, I had lived in a number of different homes. I had not lived long enough in one place to form friendships. Once again I was in a new school in a new town. My locker had turned out to be near a congregating place for the Mexican kids. Almost all conversations were in Spanish. In time, the language became understandable—including all the bad words.

Pete and Raymond had plotted the direction of the patrol. Raymond had told Pete, "We really need prisoners. Two would be great, but one will do. The big guys at Battalion are concerned about what the Chinese are going to do. They do not want surprises."

First Squad headed out into the Korean countryside for the second time in two days. We were spread out in accordance with the principle of plenty of room between each Marine. Suddenly there was a loud report from one of the squad's weapons. The patrol hit the deck immediately. I was a moment slower than the rest dropping down into the rice paddy. Forget the smell and getting wet. Down, boy!

The guys on the far right of the line had made contact with a group of Chinese. My eyes stayed on Boost who was moving to the right looking for a good firing position. I remembered those instructions Marines heard a million times. "Don't bunch up, one grenade will get you all." I also remembered my pre-patrol instructions from Boost. "Stay close to me." Moving quickly Boost found a spot about 15 yards up an incline. Heavy fire caused all but four

Chapter 6

of the Chinese patrol to take off. Three were wounded and one had decided that this wasn't his argument. He was laying on the ground away from his weapon with his arms and hands fully in sight.

Boost pointed to Jose, one of the four Mexican Marines I had been listening to earlier, and me. "Grab the guy on the ground." We scrambled down the side of the bank and grabbed the Chinese soldier. For some reason, at the last moment, he changed his mind and wanted to struggle. He tried very hard to pull away from us. As we worked to control the prisoner, I let out a "chinga su madre" (a Spanish "fuck your mother" expression I had learned in high school).

After the long hike back to the company area with the four prisoners, Boost and I were sitting on the ground cleaning weapons. I was questioning him about what had happened—mostly looking for assurance that I had done an acceptable job. My request for a performance evaluation was met with a simple "OK."

Jose came over and asked Boost in Spanish about my "chinga su madre" comment during our wrestling match with the Chinese soldier. "Did you teach him that already?"

Boost responded in his usual eloquent manner. "Nope." They chatted as much as Boost ever did and Jose started to walk away. I took the opportunity to speak to Jose's back—"Que suave, pendejo." 'Que suave,' meant 'Pretty smooth. . .' To all but those you knew well, pendejo was definitely not a nice word. Jose stopped, turned, looked, and stood silent for a moment, then shook his head and walked off.

The four Mexican Marines were a great team. Under fire, they were the same as when they were just hanging out. They moved as one, got the job done, and then hung out together again.

You had to love Jose Villegas, my partner in capturing the prisoner. He was quite possibly the happiest man in Marine Corps history. A world class smile and always happy to see you. He had not a mean bone in his body and absolutely no pretensions. Naturally, he was questioned on his demeanor and why he was always in such good humor. His answer was simple—he was from what he described as the smallest town in Texas on the Mexican border, without even a post office. Jose was one of a large number of children. The parents had re-located from Mexico. He would say with his big smile. "We were not 'wet-backs'—the river was dry that time of year." The parents and the older children did the back-breaking stoop labor in the fields, but Jose was his mother's baby and favorite and she put him on a bus to school every day. When there was no school, he was back in the field. After high school, Jose found a home in the Marine Corps. "Why wouldn't I be happy?" He would answer those who teased him about his cheery demeanor. "You try a couple days of that bracero stuff."

Rivas and Escamilla were Los Angeles Mexicans. Two big tough kids—straight from the streets. Without asking, I assumed they belonged to the large number of Marines who had stood in front of a kindly judge and had heard something like "Son, I see some good in you. I have to make a decision here. For what you have done the law tells me I can send you to prison. As a judge, I am given some choices, where and how long? As a person, I see something in you and I do not think prison is the best place for you. I want you to help me with my decision. I will hold off on a decision until tomorrow at this time. Down the street is a Marine Corps recruiting station. You come back tomorrow with papers that tell me they want you. If you make

Chapter 6

that decision, it will be mine also." A judge would have been right with these two. Both were smart and basically good kids that really hadn't had much of a chance.

The last of the four, Eduardo Villareal, was the quiet one. A bright kid, he had been an excellent student in high school in New Mexico, but did not have the money to go to college. Eduardo was smart enough to know that after World War II the government put in a GI Bill so those that wanted to could go to college. He joined the Marine Corps hoping that after his time in the Marines and the Korean War they would do the same for him.

I hung their fire team with the name 'Los Hombres.' It stuck.

CHAPTER 7

Musical chairs

Spring of 1951–1952

The division headed south to the 'No Name Line.' The good news was that positions on 'No Name' had been constructed. A combination effort of Army Engineers and Korean laborers. Our current assignment was to hold firm and give our sister regiment, the 1st Marine Regiment, the time they needed to withdraw over a couple of rivers.

It didn't take a think tank of geniuses to figure that we were getting ready for a big push from the North Koreans and Chinese. Our new positions did not suit Raymond. Sgt. Gotshall had different ideas about what constituted a satisfactory defensive position. He worked his platoon constantly to be sure that all of the elements needed to defend our area on 'No Name' were the best they possibly could be.

We knew the Chinese army was getting ready to test us. Patrols, patrols, patrols. Every patrol found lots of Chinese moving between us and the river.

Artillery was constant. All day and all night. Both sides trying to weaken the other.

In mid-May, after we had been on 'No Name' for about 10 days, it started. The proverbial shit hit the fan when the Chinese

Chapter 7

moved with heavy forces in a southerly direction, hitting an Army division and a couple Republic of Korea (ROK) divisions with everything they had. Many of those units became disorganized, were overrun, and fell back many miles.

The sudden onset of the Korean war found once proud Army Divisions in disrepair, with entire units ill-equipped to stand and fight. When the Chinese Army entered the war in full force in November of 1950, it accentuated the problems of the United States Army.

The frailties and failings of the Army and ROK units put the 1st Marine Division in one tough spot after another. Units of our Division were constantly moved off 'No Name' to a variety of places trying to shore up the United Nations front lines. The resulting state of affairs on the front lines was chaotic.

Baker Company was among those taken off 'No Name' and put into positions to back up the Army and ROK divisions in an attempt to slow the Chinese offensive. Baker didn't stay in any one place for any length of time. We would get one situation under control then it would be "Good job Marines. Pick up your toys and move again."

To the men on the ground, everything felt like the musical chairs game kids play–except here on the peninsula of Korea we had no choice of where to sit when the music stopped. The game was to simply move when and where you are told.

Finally, the Chinese were stopped. Patrols were discovering almost no activity. Everything looked like they had had enough and had headed back up the peninsula to the north.

Guess what?

How long did it take to figure out that the brass would have us chasing them? In the last week of May, the entire 1st Marine Division was headed north again.

CHAPTER 8

They can't have the Moose!

How or when they became friends, no one knew. John Harrison from Minnesota and Harold Bernstein from Bayonne, New Jersey. In appearance, they were just two Marines with a gigantic size difference. A full 12 inches in height and at least 100 pounds. It wasn't Mutt and Jeff. It was more like a midget and King Kong. A giant of a man, John Harrison was Baker Company's 'Moose.' If he had not played offensive tackle in high school football, it was a waste. Moose was a gentleman—and friendly as a pup.

Harry Bernstein was typical New Jerseyan—with the accent, the self-presumed vast knowledge, and the attitude. Another recruit who cheated the Marine Corps height requirement, Harry Bernstein was the tallest short man you could ever meet. Eleven feet tall. Among Marines there will always be discussions about the legend of the Marine Corps, 'Chesty Puller.' Along with a million other medals, Chesty had about 13 Purple Hearts and 4 Navy Crosses. For our money, Harry Bernstein was the closest thing we had.

Harry wasn't from a nice part of Bayonne and had not given up the habit of carrying a mean looking switchblade. Watching Harry under fire was like watching a fierce demon. In any childhood game that involved choosing teams, Harry always would have been everyone's first choice. The same was true in Korea. Harry was a keeper.

Chapter 8

Harry and Moose. You rarely saw one without the other. Moose was always quiet when he was with Harry. Of course, Harry did not give him much opportunity to talk, but that did not seem to bother Moose. Whenever he spoke to or about Harry Bernstein—Moose always called him by his given name, Harold. Unusual.

The two did have one thing in common. Both were from families that operated businesses. Moose's family had a couple dairy farms while Harry's ran a pawn shop. Harry was sure he knew everything there was to know and offered up his knowledge routinely, whether anyone asked or not; and Moose, who knew plenty about many things, shared it only when asked. For one thing, Moose was recognized as the platoon expert on all weather subjects. Being a farm boy, his specialty was also the goddamned barbed wire. He elected himself project director whenever that ugly task presented itself.

One day, a yell came down. "The listening post patrol stepped in shit and are surrounded in the valley—1st squad move it! We go in 5 minutes."

Down the line there was pretty much of a conditioned response. Ready, go. Harry was heard saying, "Oh fuck—Moose is out there on that listening post. Move it you assholes !!!"

The listening post was at the end of a knob overlooking the valley and the river. Their radio was in action and they had informed the company that they had been discovered and were under heavy small arms and mortar fire. The Chinese were closing on them.

Our squad gathered quickly and headed down the trail toward the valley. Raymond took the lead with his radio guy trying to keep up the pace. He informed Raymond, "They are pinned down, holding their own, but pretty much cornered and trapped on the nose of the ridge."

As we moved rapidly down one hill and into the valley below the listening post, Harry Bernstein took over the point position, making a flat and determined announcement, "They can't have the Moose!!"

As we reached the bottom of the hill, Raymond assessed the situation quickly and began yelling commands to spread out and to pour on covering fire. All the while, Harry was talking rapidly to Raymond and gesturing. Raymond nodded to him as he pointed the rest of us to positions. Harry was seen taking off alone, to the left along the river bank and then disappearing around the bend.

We continued with heavy fire. The responding fire from the Chinese seemed to have slowed. Raymond called to Moose up on the small ridge, "Stay down and hold your position until I give the word."

Suddenly across the river there was a series of grenade explosions. . . . Then quiet. After more silence, a voice came from across the small river with Harry's unmistakable New Jersey accent. "Moose, take the others and move up the trail and then down that slope toward Raymond, I have this side covered. Raymond—send me three big guys. I have a wounded prisoner. We can carry him up the hill."

Soon three big guys made their way to Harry's spot on the other side of the river. They found a very frightened young Chinese soldier, bound with a belt and wounded in the leg. Harry gave them an order, "Grab him and let's get the fuck out of here." As they made their way to the wounded soldier, they saw three dead Chinese soldiers. One of the big guys dropped into one of the holes to check if there was another who might still be alive. He staggered back a bit and promptly threw up. "Shit, these guys have had their throats cut!!" Harry, however, was still in command mode. "Look fuck brain, wipe that slobber off your mouth and get the wounded guy. I have important things to do up on the hill. They interrupted my nap. Move it."

As the squad climbed the trail back up the hill toward the company position, the conversation was a thing of beauty that you would have paid a fortune to watch and listen to.

Chapter 8

Harry Bernstein did not shut up. "Jesus Christ, Moose, do I have to go everywhere with you?" . . . until we got to the barbed wire and into the trench line. Moose was blasted on every possible shortcoming in his entire life. The little fucker Bernstein had a real mouth. A small smile said everything Moose had to say.

"Well God-Damn it Moose," Harry said again. "Do I have to go everywhere with you?"

Moose quietly answered, "Yes, Harold, that would be nice."

The three big guys carried the Chinese kid back to the command CP and received plenty of praise from the Captain for bringing in a prisoner. The patrol had not really been out looking for a prisoner, but who cared. They were back with everyone in one piece and a prisoner to boot. That would keep the brass happy for awhile.

Prisoners were always the object of patrols—part of the shaky term 'Marine Intelligence.' How likely was it that this Chinese kid was going to know the battle plan for his whole division? Not very! He surely knew no more than we did about our own battle plan.

The real focus of those who reported to the Skipper after that day's patrol was the wide-eyed version of the cut throats. A month later no one in the platoon or company would know who someone with the name Harry Bernstein was. They would deny that there had ever been anyone in the company with that name.

'Harry the Hack' was born, soon to be shortened to just 'Hack.'

CHAPTER 9

Charlie Shishido is a fucking U.S. fucking Marine!

From the beginning in boot camp, all objects got a new name. Navy names. A simple wall became a 'bulkhead,' undershorts 'skivvies,' and the billed fatigue hat was a 'cover.' Commanding officers of rifle companies were to be addressed as 'Skipper.' The atmosphere in boot camp was too intense to worry about why. Go along with the joke.

In a Marine front line company the name thing changed completely, beginning with the complete refusal of everyone to use both first and last names. One name and only one. It might be the first name or the last name. You might be next to someone named Herman for several months fighting the bad guys, but if you asked around the platoon to find out if it was his first or last name, you would get a blank stare and "beats the shit out of me."

Even the first or last names could be thrown aside. A single event in the field could earn a Marine a new name.

People who arrived with the multi-syllable names that ended in -ski always became 'Ski.' Period.

Our platoon had the problem of having three 'Ski's.' This was easily sorted out by our collection of 'intellectuals.' The first one was dubbed 'Killer Ski.' An awesome mean little shit. One day on a patrol in May a pretty good sized group of Chinese jumped us. 'Ski' had the point (the lead guy in the patrol column) and charged them all by himself. His BAR cut loose a massive number

CHAPTER 9

of rounds. The rain of automatic fire startled not only the Chinese, but everyone in the patrol as well. In less than a minute, the balance of the Chinese patrol tucked tail and moved back north as quickly as they could, leaving behind about six KIA (killed in action). No one else fired a shot. Thus, 'Killer Ski.' What else? When two more 'Ski's' arrived, one became 'Little Ski' and the other 'Big Ski.' Problem solved.

Once the group had fastened a name to an individual—it stuck. Nothing else was used and after a while if someone did use a first name or a family name they might not get a response. If a guy was tagged with a name he did not like—tough. He got no vote in the matter. Those of American Indian descent, always were 'Chief.' Automatic. No amount of explaining about the structure of his particular tribe and the ascension to the rank within the tribe counted. 'Hey Chief.' That was it.

Charlie Shishido was different. Charlie did not have a nickname. By the usual standards there were plenty available due to his ancestry or to the complete lack of an ounce body fat on his body. Charlie was a tall skinny kid from Hawaii. No question about his ancestry—Japanese— American. A gentlemanly and polite young man. As soon as Charlie joined our platoon, he fit in well. Everyone liked him and he was especially good under fire; a combat-tested Marine.

Charlie took cheap shit from Marines from other units on a regular basis. Everyone but 1st platoon seemed to be confused about whether he was a Korean, North Korean, Chinese, or whatever. First platoon protected our own. We damn well went after anyone who leaned on Charlie. A perimeter would quickly form around Charlie and the offending party heard " Fuck you, Jack. His name is Charlie Shishido and he is a fucking U.S. Fucking Marine and leave him alone." No nickname for Charlie.

Company B's other Charles demanded to be called Sir Charles. Or we could call him just Sir. Probably as our way of ignoring his demand, it was just plain Charles for him.

For most of us, coming from Texas was considered to be the worst thing that could happen to any person. The Texas demeanor is to be proud of something invisible to everyone else. There was no question that they made good Marines, but there was that swagger that went with it that the rest of us did not understand. For that reason, those from Texas were not automatically given the title of 'Tex.' Our platoon did our best to just ignore the Texas issue. If any of us had to interact or refer to a fellow Marine from Texas, it was considered better to act as if we did not know where or what Texas was. For some reason, being from Texas, they took no offense.

During the Korean War, the Marine Corps drew heavily from the densely populated areas of South Boston, South Philly, and New Jersey. Those Marines were mostly from the lovely parts of those big cities where 'The Country Club' is Joe's Bar and Grill. What was hard to understand was how 'The Knowledge Fairy' found them in those highly populated areas and managed to touch them with his magic wand. As far as they were concerned, they were the smartest people in the world. Maybe it was just a big city thing, but there was nothing they did not profess to know, including their own interpretation of geography. They knew that the Red Sox were from Boston and the Yankees from New York, but for their money the rest of the United States was simply somewhere else and its residents just plain yokels.

Still, having grown up in the streets fighting for their lives from day one, there was no question of the inner strength of the big city enlisted men.

CHAPTER 10

No Name Line

April-May, 1951

Apparently Raymond did not listen to rumors; it was all business in his platoon. We all wanted to believe the stuff we heard about the peace negotiations. Raymond was more disposed to believe in something when he saw it. Once we arrived at our assigned place on 'No Name Line,' we went right to work.

'No Name.' Defensive positions sought by every army since the beginning of time, were found at the highest place possible. Make the other guy come up a hill to get at you. When our sergeant saw the positions the Army Engineers and South Korean laborers had built, he told us that they were better than some. Of course, 'better than some' was not good enough. Everything had to be done to Raymond's quality specifications. That meant he observed every position using its view down the hill as the criteria. Each position and its field of fire overlapped with the one next to it. Then we removed any visual obstructions such as trees or bushes. The fighting holes and the bunkers were either re-created from scratch or the existing ones brought up to his standards. All were connected by a trench at the standard depth of about 5-6 feet.

As we worked on improving the positions, nights were not for the exclusive purpose of sleeping. Every night an order would come down the line giving the percentage of watch for that night—25 %, 50 %, or 100 %. From dusk until dawn, we manned positions accordingly. Since each position was a two man partnership, 50 % meant that one man in each position would be awake and watchful; 25 % meant one in every other position. The one-hundred percent order meant that the shit was supposed to hit the fan that night. Everyone stayed awake to watch and listen. Not as hard as it sounded. If you thought someone was coming, you couldn't sleep anyway. Regardless of the percentage watch, listening posts were placed out in front of the lines and patrols were out every night.

The salt mine day work along with night patrols and night watches did nothing for morale. BUT, there would be NO morale problems. . . . And that was an order.

Morale may not have been a problem. Attitude WAS suspect at times.

Quickly, 'No Name' was ready.

CHAPTER 11

Jesus, Doc, that was a fucking minefield! What were you thinking?

From day one in boot camp we were told that our squad was better than the next squad, our platoon was better than the next platoon, our company better, and on and on. From the beginning the Marine Corps worked hard to instill in each recruit the value of individual and unit pride.

The system worked well. Individual and unit performance—a backbone concept of the United States Marine Corps.

Needless to say Marines refuse to give the other branches of the service any standing whatsoever. If you put a Marine in the middle of a group of U.S. Army Medal of Honor winners, that Marine would not hesitate to say that the Army did not know how to fight.

The Navy corpsman attached to a Marine combat unit is the unique exception. Since the Marine Corps has no medical services of its own, the United States Navy has provided each combat platoon with their own Navy corpsman. To the Marines the corpsman was simply 'Doc.'

If first squad went on patrol, Doc went. If second squad had patrol, so did Doc. If the whole platoon went, Doc was right there with them. It would be fair to state that the cry 'Corpsman!' when a man had gone down, had never been refused in Marine history. Doc has complete respect with the down in the dirt Marines. He is one of the boys, but not one of the boys. He is included in all conversations and has to take some of the same shit the rest take from each other, but there is a difference. He is silently awarded protected status.

'Sir' Charles seemed to consider it his duty to give Doc his share of cheap shit. He was always on Doc's back. His favorite was telling Doc that he was like a good waiter. There when you needed him, but otherwise please be quiet and light my cigarette. Doc's usual response to Charles was a shrug and the faintest smile.

Joining our platoon did not give direct title to give Doc crap. It was an earned thing. It didn't take long for the platoon to form a protective perimeter around Doc from outsiders and replacement types. Doc had made plenty of 'house calls' in some pretty ugly places and situations.

Charles was the point man for first platoon and was making his way along on another crappy patrol day somewhere in front of No Name Line. As point man, he was about 30-40 yards ahead of the squad, picking his way along in his usual careful manner when he slipped over a little embankment and down into a rice paddy. A large explosion and Charles went down, hit with something. We all stopped dead in our tracks, spread out, and hit the ground.

Charles was alone in the paddy. He yelled, "Stay out! This is a fucking mine field!"

Doc moved next to Raymond. "Hey, Charles! Are you hurt?"

"Not really, Doc. Only where I am bleeding. Doc—Stay put!"

"Charles—give me an idea where you went into the rice paddy."

"God damn it Doc! Don't come in here!"

Doc determined that Charles was bleeding and went down into the sprinter's crouch.

Raymond spoke up, "Doc, God damn it! You stay put!!!"

"Raymond, you have forgotten that I out rank you. You can't give me orders."

The reality was that Navy corpsmen called their non-commissioned officers 'Petty Officers' and Doc actually did have one more

Chapter 11

stripe than Raymond. In the Marine Corps he would have been a staff sergeant. It didn't matter—Doc was going into the rice paddy after Charles anyway.

"Cover me Raymond!" he yelled over his shoulder, as he was making his way towards Charles. Soon he, too, was out of sight. After a few minutes of silence, Doc's voice rose up. "We are coming out!"

Before long, we saw Doc—all of 5'8" and 160 lbs—with big old long Charles over his shoulder in the fireman's carry, heading back out of the paddy at full speed. Out of breath, Doc dropped his load at Raymond's feet. The release of tension sometimes has a weird effect on the nervous system. Doc and Charles suddenly they thought they were funny. While the rest were still in shock that Doc had even gone into the mine-laden rice paddy, Charles and Doc started into a comic routine. "Hey Doc, is a house call extra? Send me a bill."

"Jesus, Doc, that was a fucking minefield. What were you thinking?"

Doc did not miss a beat. "Charles—I have always been curious if you had blood or a heart to pump it. This was my opportunity to see for myself."

Raymond finally spoke up. "If I hadn't seen that myself, I would not have believed it. Doc—you scared the shit out of me."

Charles got three weeks in the rear to heal and Doc got written up for the Silver Star.

Of the lessons to be learned in life, an essential one is 'DO NOT FUCK with the corpsman in a Marine unit.' They are a protected species. Messing with them would be dangerous to your health.

Chapter 12

Don't try to figure it out—This is the Marine Corps, remember. . . .

After a couple of weeks the pressure from the Chinese on No Name Line let up. No Name was turned over to the Army, and the First Marine Division was headed north. Pack it up and move out.

Baker Company had won the lottery sweepstakes and was selected to man a blocking position. The good news was that the selected position was well situated and looked like it could be defended. The bad news was that our new hill was about three miles out in front of the Division. Wonderful.

We moved on to our new hill and began the routine of setting up, patrols going out, and digging new positions. All with the usual exuberance.

After a long patrol trying to assess the Chinese and what they were up to, the first squad returned to the perimeter for the night. Knowing how worn down we were from wandering all over the Korean landscape looking for our Chinese friends, the skipper excused us from nightly watch.

The rare reprieve meant we could experience that wonderfully secure feeling of being inside of a Marine perimeter, knowing that there were wide awake eyes and alert Marines assuring us of a safe and good night's sleep. The previous two or three days had sapped our physical strength. The nights were still cold and our fart sacks felt good.

Chapter 12

The 'fart sack' was an esoteric and practical name for the standard down sleeping bag. In the field, Marine units ate C-rations. Like all the equipment and supplies the Marines were using in Korea, C-Rations were left over from World War II. That might have been OK for some things such as weapons, ammunition, communication equipment, but the C-Rations most likely had been in some hot warehouse since August of 1945.

Size-wise a can of food in the C-rations was about 2/3 the size of the standard tomato soup can. Each box of C-rations had three cans of tasty, carefully thought out and highly nutritious food. The carefully thought out part was the catch. A least four of the ten menu choices were—in no particular order—pork and beans, beanies and weenies, meat and beans, and ham and lima beans. Hence the OH SO clever name for the sleeping bag.

The sleeping bag was a first class piece of equipment. It kept us warm on the coldest nights and came with an attached pull-over hood. However, the high bean makeup up of the C-Rations created a difficult decision during the really cold nights—whether to keep your head and nose inside the bag or out!

That was not an issue for us on this night. Ours was the deepest of sleep.

That is, until the shout came—"Wake up! Get your shit together! We are moving off this hill in 30 minutes." Comatose to fully awake was a Korea-induced learned response.

As we scrambled for our equipment, we realized there was no noise. No shooting, incoming rounds, bugles, or flares. By Captain's order, we had not been on the perimeter duty and were asleep near the company commander's bunker.

The 'Gunny' had been the one to awaken us. In a line company he was the top enlisted man and worked directly with the commanding officer. Officially, he was in an administrative and coordinating position, but in most cases he functioned as the wise advisor and extension of the head man. Our Gunny had the demeanor and personal characteristics that commanded respect. Another obvious reason to obey was his five or six stripes. Beyond that, his gaze said, "look you stupid shithead—I have spent my life around Marines. Don't try independent thinking."

The 'gunny' of Baker Company had been a Private First Class on the 'canal' and was decorated for his service there. Guadalcanal was the bitter and tenacious action of the 1st Marine Division defending Henderson Field against the Japs. It was commonly believed that the defense of that airfield changed the entire direction of World War II. For us, the simple Marines of Company B, it meant our "gunny" was a step above God.

I grumbled at him, "Jesus, Gunny is there a reason we are moving?"

"Some genius at S-3 ('Marine Intelligence' again) must have figured out that a full company of Marines in a perimeter on top of a single hill three miles in front of the Division was an invitation to be surrounded and creamed."

"For Christ's sake Gunny, why didn't they figure that out before they sent us up here?"

"Smart Mouth, don't try to figure it out. This is the Marine Corps. Remember?"

Down the hill in the dark we went, hiking the three miles to the road block and back into the main line without incident. The move back provoked a lot of bitching and moaning, yes, but no one died from that.

As we passed thru the roadblock, trucks were waiting. Apparently, those in the rear had hatched a new and wonderful plan. These were open trucks that looked like a basic dump truck with hard benches for seating. Most had no cover from the elements.

Chapter 12

Soon we were almost completely loaded in the 6-by trucks, the only exception being—who else?—Charles. He had the truck driver, a young man who looked like he should be going to a junior high social event, aside and was talking to him seriously. Those who knew Charles did not need to get up close and listen to know the essence of the conversation. Almost certainly, Charles was trying to talk the driver into separating our truck from the column and going somewhere other than where the column was going, preferably somewhere where there were creature comforts, a beach, and a nice hotel. Included in the deal for the truck driver would be a massive gratuity. Charles was a born salesman.

Raymond approached. "Charles, get your sorry ass in the truck."

This was a time where it would have been nice to have some meat on your butt. Two hours of bumpy dirt Korean roads in a '6 by' sitting on a wooden bench was ugly. The worst part was knowing that there would be another hiking adventure at the end of the ride. Of course the hike would be uphill every step of the way. And, at the end of the hike, we could expect to be taking over and preparing new positions.

CHAPTER 13

They _are_ coming, and there _will_ be a lot of them.

I was in a grumpy mood thinking that I might as well be in chains with an iron neck collar. My 'slave master,' Boost, had completed my load for the coming climb up the new hill. I had my full load of gear on plus the extra suspender thing of magazines for his fucking BAR. Boost was not a big tipper. His only 'tip' was, "Going up a hill with a load, lean a little forward, it helps."

It did feel good to get off that truck and move around a bit—that is, until I got a look at the hills. They were huge. Going east and north in Korea, the hills got higher and higher. Carrying ten times my body weight in ammo for the BAR did not exactly brighten my prospects for the day ahead.

The only good news was that the climb would not be to the top of the biggest hill but more of a cut out or pass between two high mountains. Our new positions ended on one side at a steep mountain cliff. No way it could be climbed. From our last position it went straight up a shear rock face.

Hole by hole, we relieved the Korean troops who had been holding this line. As each ROK soldier was relieved, he bowed and shuffled off. I was puzzled over why we were replacing these troops. Some ROK troops could be pretty good, but others could not hold their ground. Baker Company was here for a reason, but I couldn't see it. When you are a dirt Marine, you do not have the big maps with arrows and grease pencil markings or anything that

Chapter 13

gives you the grand overview of the plan. All you have is the world that exists within your eyesight. Keeps it simple. Trying to figure out the ifs and whys of what we were doing with little to go on was not improving my outlook.

After having been through the drill of relieving someone else on a front line position a few times, I had some observations. Neither the Koreans, nor, God bless them, the U.S. Army were really good at fields of fire. Most didn't do the best job of preparing a defensive position. Even if you only thought of it from a selfish standpoint—it made sense to set up properly. Dig, build, and insulate yourself as best as you could from those who will appear with the intent to victimize your body.

Outside of their U.S. Army provided military supplies, ROK military units did not leave anything of value behind. This war had taken everything from them and their country. Korea had been flattened by the battles up and down the narrow peninsula.

Depending on the individual army unit and the kind of leadership they had, the U.S. Army would leave a position and everything they owned. This day, Boost was like a kid on Christmas morning. The Korean unit had left on foot and the United States Army had left behind a treasure trove of supplies. Boost was like a bum scavenging at the city dump. We found and brought to our new position about six full boxes of 30-caliber machine gun ammo. All marked U. S. Army. A 'visit' to our company supply produced a collection of empty magazines for his BAR. His good mood inspired me to exert myself and get him help to enhance the supply of my favorite item. Grenades. Our new position now had several comfortable wooden seats—empty grenade boxes.

As I was making trips back and forth to the company command post, I passed Gunny, who for some reason had taken a liking to me—perhaps because he saw a bit of himself. Gunny stopped voluntarily and took a couple minutes to answer my early morning question about what was happening.

"Smart Mouth, about your question this morning. Where we are now is a blocking position—a simple pass in the mountains. Our job is to hold this pass and not let the Chinese through.

The Division needs time to set up and get ready. The entire Chinese army is out there and we expect them to try us out."

"Thanks gunny, you have filled my day with joy."

"Smart Mouth—my sincere hope is that the Marine Corps can survive you.

The Chinese we can handle. I only have five years to retire and then I will leave the Corps to you."

As I walked off, Gunny called out, "Semper Fi, and good luck tonight, Marine."

A God Damn slave should have only one owner. Boost was bad enough, but Raymond decided to get in the act. He was heavily into his fields of fire routine. He had been down the hill in front of our positions and had figured out how they would come at us.

Guess what? Our position was where he said they would approach. This information added some enthusiasm to our digging. Our fighting bunker was brought up the scale of quality with more logs and sand bags. We had an excellent view in every direction—front, side, and back.

Sergeant Perfection surveyed and surveyed until his plan for every position on the platoon front was the best it could be. Squad by squad he went over the briefing he had from the CO.

It was frightening, hearing him talk of the numbers the Chinese had. It was more than scary when he described their views on the value of human life. Army units had been overrun and wiped out. The Chinese were trained to come, and come, and keep coming. Stopping them once would not be enough. "Don't let down if you stop them once. They will try as many times as they have people to send."

Raymond evaluated each position one more time to be sure it

CHAPTER 13

had an OK view. "Can you come into the trench and see if something was moving at the back? Can you control the back? Can you throw grenades back there without them rolling back into your own trench?"

"They may come tonight, tomorrow night, or the next but they are coming and there will be a lot of them. No matter what happens—stay put in your position. Shoot or grenade anything that moves that is not in a position. If anyone moves in front of or behind the position next to you—shoot him. He doesn't belong there."

This night would be 100 % watch.

Chapter 14

Protect the automatic weapons

The absence of roads and the presence of the mountains between this pass and the rest of the Division, left us without the supporting fire of the 11th Marine artillery regiment. They needed direct lines of fire not available here. Not good.

As with each line company of Marines, we had a weapons platoon with machine guns and mortars. Without the artillery regiment, we would need to depend on our own 60m and 80mm mortars.

The mortars were shaped like a stovepipe sitting on a small metal baseplate, and did not need direct lines of fire since they could fire up and over the tops of hills with a trajectory of fire like a pop fly to shortstop. The 80 was bigger—and could reach the equivalent of the outfield bleachers.

The most fascinating thing was the accuracy. Mortar operators re-aimed their weapons on a daily basis and with each new location. They could put one in your back pocket from a long way away. When several mortars were working together they could walk a row of explosions up and down the area in front of our positions. Devastating to an attacking force. Every day and with each new location, the mortars' aims were reset.

The barbed wire in front of these new positions wasn't bad, considering that we had not had much time to prepare. It still required some Raymond and Moose adjustments and their stamp

Chapter 14

of approval on the quality of our work. Barbed wire was a great deterrent that generally discouraged most people. Ours was located about 30 to 40 yards in front of these positions, strung on criss-crossed metal poles buried deep in the ground. We placed extensive booby traps and mines along the possible approach route and on our side of the wire.

One type was a grenade with a tripwire. Grenades came in cylindrical cardboard boxes. We would take the grenade out, pull the pin without letting the spoon fly, and then return the grenade to its box without the pin so it was ready to go. Then we tied a string or wire to the grenade handle and attached it to a tree. When the wire or string was moved, it would pull the grenade from its container, the spoon would fly, and powie!

We also had some other innovations. We attached empty C-Ration cans with pebbles in them to the barbed wire. That way, if they got past the booby traps to the wire, the cans would make a bunch of noise and serve as a decent warning system.

Two new guys arrived the day we were setting up the new positions. Raymond quickly assigned them to experienced men—the Professor and Herman. Possibly the only truly mature people we had, both had brains and cool heads. Raymond ordered them to give the new guys a crash course for what we all knew was going to be a tough night. He gave the two new guys the simple command: "Listen to and absorb every word these two guys tell you."

Knowing the Professor and Herman, the crash course would revolve around the things that would happen tonight or the next night to affect their nervous systems. No basic weapons stuff. The only weapons talk would be to go over fields of fire and the important job of protecting the automatic weapons. The two experienced Marines took the new guys aside and began explaining the sensory experiences.

"There are uses for the senses the human body possesses that will take on a new dimension when things become this personal and close at hand. There will be continuous explosive sounds combined with dramatic physical changes. Dirt, rocks, trees, and debris will fly in all directions with the ground shaking and continuing to shake, seemingly never to stop. An explosion close by will always be followed by a tremendous change in air pressure, so great it could physically move a full sized man. There will be a complete urgency to every second and partial second. Physical movements need to be totally concise with zero wasted effort."

Herman and the Professor continued their patient explanation:

"You will need to be able respond to each situation while controlling a maximum adrenalin level. Though your mind will seem to move in ultra slow motion, you will need to see in all directions and block out unimportant physical happenings and noises. The night will be full of noise, advancing hordes, incoming mortars, and a wide variety of multi-colored flashes of light."

"Each of us will feel alone in the middle of a constantly developing story; one with no written script and no known ending. Many things will not actively register at the time, especially thoughts of personal safety. The mind will kick in later with a variety of weird, delayed responses. It will also replay the total night complete in every detail. Elapsed time estimates from various participants will vary greatly."

Raymond set each position. One 30-caliber machine gun was backed up to the cliff. Anyone attacking would go first after the automatic weapons. Raymond chose Monaghan and his assistant machine gunner to man that 30. Why? Simply because Monaghan had a backbone of steel. A skinny little red headed kid from South Boston with gigantic balls and a great nervous system. Monaghan's position commanded the entire approach.

Our job was to protect the machine gunners.

The trench extended down the side of the hill from Monaghan's gun to the Professor with his BAR and one of the new arrivals as his rifleman. In the next bunker down the trench line Raymond placed Herman with his BAR and another rifleman. The lowest spot in the U-shaped defensive position was assigned to Shapiro and his machine gun. As the trench line moved up the other side of the hill, Boost and I were placed in position to protect Shapiro. Of course, Boost had his BAR.

Chapter 14

Raymond finally finished placing each of us to protect Monaghan, Shapiro, and their weapons. He reviewed our fields of fire, and reminded us of our responsibility to defend our automatic weapons. The placing of our fire power was as good as it could be.

Up the hill to the left, the Chinese approach to our positions was a tougher one with a more dramatic slope. Raymond still set each position carefully, placing another machine gun along with its own group of protectors to cover the sweeping approach.

Raymond had gone down the hill and had seen that there was a ridge on either side and a path up the middle. As you neared the top, it narrowed. This was the only real and logical way for them to come at us.

We had these positions as well prepared as possible with the time available.

Nothing that we had done would come as a surprise to those who planned to take our place on top of this hill.

The only one who was able to nap was Boost. Herman and I had many debates about his nervous system, coming up with a number of theories about his electrical wiring. The favored one was the idea that he had been born with no nervous system. The Professor had discounted that theory as not scientifically possible. His theory was that Boost's heart only beat three times a minute—something like a hibernating bear.

Chapter 15

Tonight's story has no written script, no known ending. . . .

Night came and with it the wait. The wait. The wait.

The Chinese lacked a sophisticated communication system. They substituted flares along with off-key bugles and yelling. The flares—red, white, green, and yellow—served as the only distraction during the wait. They were launched like mortars. White ones illuminated the area. They would have been fun to watch under other circumstances, but the Chinese flares were not for entertainment. When the Chinese started with the color flares, we knew to watch out. A single color was the signal for the entire Chinese army to come looking for you. They knew which color, but we did not. A nasty little trick. Flares with their unique sort of a pop and hissing noise could have a profound effect on the body elimination systems. Each change of color tightened the sphincter.

"Shit."

The off tune bugle. A yellow flare. The bugles and screaming started. They came.

The wire slowed the first ones and intense fire cut them down. Our mortars walked down the hill behind them and cut their ranks. They were fully aware that these first guys had no chance and many more came behind them.

The noise level was brutal. Their mortars were all over us. The automatic weapons and grenade noises blended together. Besides

Chapter 15

the rocks, dirt, and branches, whole trees were flying through the air. Sound was present in huge and varying decibels.

Many Chinese soldiers from the first wave got tangled in the wire and died. The next wave used them for stepping stones. Some of these got to the top of the barbed wire and died. More followed, continuing to climb on top of their own dead. They kept coming.

God bless the gunners, Shapiro and Monaghan. The two machine gunners were constantly at work. Each was totally dependent on his assistant to keep the belts coming out of the metal boxes and into the guns. No tangles, no interruptions. They kept both 30s fully in action. Not a lost beat to overheating, lack of ammo, or stoppages. Each machine gunner needed to raise and lower his gun barrel to accommodate for the attacking Chinese who had made it to the top of the bodies on the wire and those who had made it over.

Our own flares kept coming. The white ones kept the area well lit up. Each flare lasted about 15 to 20 seconds. The eerie light gave us the opportunity to choose where to concentrate our fire.

From our bunker, Boost was pouring it on and I was going from one side of the bunker and into the trench to pop anyone who had made it closer. Boost was protecting the machine guns, so he needed protection. I kept up heavy rifle fire and tossed one grenade after another toward the wire.

Figures kept reaching the top of the wire and heading our way. A couple seemed to get past the trench. Suddenly I saw two of them up and over the trench line to my right. I yelled to the replacement in the next bunker "New guy . . . back . . . back!!" New Guy's rifle cracked several times aimed toward the rear of our bunker.

'Work the rifle and throw grenades' was the order of business. They kept coming over the wire and over their own bodies. They continued to fall.

The M-1 rifle was a great weapon. Accurate—and if you hit someone with it they stayed hit. The M-1 used a clip that held only 8 rounds. Once fired the empty tin clip flew out by itself and the chamber closed. Continuous fire with an M-1 was accomplished by bringing the chamber handle back with the side of the hand while flipping in the new clip in one motion. Under fire it became almost automatic. Done quickly. Again and again.

Without the BARs and the machine guns, there was no way the M-1 would have been enough to stop this attack. There were just too many Chinese at and over the wire. A rifleman's job was to get the strays. Protect the automatic weapons. Keep on humping.

How long before they stopped coming? I don't know. After forever, it stopped. Our mortars stopped and it got quiet. Real quiet. The white flares from our side became less frequent, but were often enough to watch for someone coming.

Boost made one of his lengthy speeches. "It's not over."

This he followed with a command, pointing at the empty BAR magazines. "Fill them up and stack them here."

No time to argue with the master, I quickly refilled the magazines from the boxes of ammo obtained courtesy of the U.S. Army and arranged them. Clips for my M-1 came out of the cloth bandoleers. They were organized and stacked in various critical spots. Pockets were loaded with clips. New supplies of grenades were removed from their cartons and stacked in piles for easy access. Each grenade ready to go.

Chapter 15

OH Fuck! More colored flares. More bugle shit, more screaming.

They come—on red this time.

A repeat of the first attack. Intense and noisy. Lots of metal flying through the air. More noise, trees, dirt, and rocks.

How long did the second wave last? Don't know. Again, they stop coming.

It was quiet looking out toward the wire; literally dead quiet. Bodies were stacked on the wire, in front of the wire, behind the wire along with pairs and singles scattered on our side.

Out of the intense quiet of the night a loud voice comes from the next bunker.

"Nice try, assholes!"

It was 'New Guy.' No one had had the time to learn his name.

We had the 'silence on line at night' thing told to us so many times, it should have been deeply ingrained. But, what difference did it make? Why be quiet when they knew where we were anyway?

New Guy joined 'our club' that night. His cry into the night had made him one of us immediately. An instant legend. Replacements are supposed to be quiet and usually were. New Guy started something with that yell into the night.

A couple positions up the slope. Hack started yelling at the entire Chinese Army. "Take your chicken shit Chinese army and sleeze ball tactics and shove them up your rotten ass, who do you think you are fucking with?"

Up the line another loud voice—"Have you ever played king of the hill?!"

Two or three guys yelled back at the same time "Yeah!!"

"Well this is OUR fucking Hill!!"

The third wave came behind another red flare. It would have been presumptive to think that they did not have a chance. They may have had a chance, but they got stuffed, anyway.

Hack was on a roll. "Come on you weak kneed assholes—this is the fucking Marine Corps not a bunch of pussies!"

"Try again if you have the balls!"

The history books would not note the 'battle cries' that went up that night, but for us hearing a brand new guy and that sawed off little shit from New Jersey challenging the entire Chinese army was truly an experience. Were these battle cries for the centuries? No. Did it turn the tide of battle? Most likely not . . . but who knows?

Even Boost said later that it had given him a jolt and stiffened his back. Hack would not let up. He had that thick New Jersey accent. Even IF the Chinese had understood English it would have been a stretch for them to understand his verbal attack.

When they came the fourth time, it seemed like the same intensity. The results were the same. More of them piled up and it finally stopped.

Boost made another speech. "It's over."

Soon the early morning light began to replace the long night. The beautiful and ironic part was that the 1st platoon had taken only three casualties. New Guy, Moose, and Charles. Each caught pieces of flying metal. None of the wounds were good enough for a trip to the rear.

Men of steel? Not really. Discipline under fire. Yes.

The little gully in front of us had bodies in grotesque piles and positions. As usual Raymond had been correct. Our positions were the exact spot where they had to come. The obvious route of approach. A simple fact. He had thought it out before it happened and we were ready.

Chapter 15

The morning was not easy. Whatever you thought during the night, it changed when you looked out toward the wire. A large work party of Korean laborers took most of the day before they had cleared the area of dead Chinese.

We were told that they also counted about 20 bodies who had overrun our perimeter. Three near and behind our bunker. Five were around the command post. Staying put in your position, of course, had been good advice. I stored in my mind that when I got time, I needed to ask Raymond if he ever got tired of being right.

In the early morning I slipped down the trench to see New Guy. I wasn't totally sure that the three dead Chinese behind our bunker were New Guy's work, but I did make a point of telling him that he had done a good job during the night and also to thank him for his prompt response to the "back, back" call.

Cpl Boost—alias Cpl Fire Power, BAR magazine thief, and slave master—announced that he was tired and went over the slope to our sleeping bunker with no more apparent emotion than a guy from the factory going home with his empty lunch pail.

Over his shoulder he called out, "Smart Mouth—fill and stack all of the BAR magazines, get the grenades in position, and set up your ammo. When you are finished with that, you can have the rest of the day off."

That morning our company commander trooped the lines and let each of us know that he was proud to be in the company of men like us. Before the day was over, Raymond came down the trench line twice. Once with the Battalion Commander in tow and once with the Bird Colonel Regimental commander. Both wanted to examine our 'slot.'

Impressive. Good leaders always looked for things that worked and how to get better. Each Marine that they came into contact with, was given a word or two, a pat on the back and a "Good job Marine."

The Regimental Commander stopped at the bunker where New Guy was cleaning his rifle. Watching a guy who had just seen his first combat and had come out standing tall, only to panic in front of the brass, was great. The expression on his face was the basic "don't know whether to shit or go blind." Each one of the officers did the full clinical look at our positions, the approach, and how we had set up.

Raymond stepped back and pointed to New Guy to take over the briefing.

New Guy did some gesturing and pointing, but mostly looked for one of us to come help him. The social interchanges with a Major and Colonel had him at a loss.

My look back said, "No way. You are on your own, kid." It was too easy to get my foot in my big mouth when talking to people that high up in the command chain.

* * *

A night like that will be recorded in your brain for as long as it functions. The images are stamped into some circuit board. What I saw and did, will just remain. The immediate reaction, the secondary reaction, and the group discussions about that night and those who participated will finally end. Then it leaves each individual to try to figure out what had taken place and the whys, the what ifs, and on and on.

We were certainly tested. We held. That will stay with you.

Marine Pride? Guys with their back to the wall? Guys with aggressive tendencies? Stubbornness? Kiss my ass? Protect Each other? The raw fear of dying? Courage? Survival? Nothing better to do at the time? A challenge? Training? Pure discipline?

Take your pick or add to the list if you have your own reason.

One thing I found out—we all found out. An important lesson. Whatever you are doing, having a Marine at your side makes you stronger.

CHAPTER 16

I am not the same person I was yesterday

As far as the Marine Corps was concerned, each young man arrived at Boot Camp with a clean slate. The drill instructors started with nothing.

An important part of the training process was to get each individual to reach down inside of himself. This did not come easily nor by the recruit's design, but each individual would find strengths within himself that he was unaware of. This introduction to the Marine Corps took each new Marine to a place he would not have reached on his own.

The Marine Corps knew this; the young man did not.

The morning after the massive assault on the 'slot,' I was sitting on one of the grenade boxed in our bunker, looking out over the trench into the valley, lost inside my own mind. Hot coffee from the C-rations steamed from my metal canteen cup. As I sipped and stared into the valley, my mind offered up a vivid message, "I am not the same person that I was yesterday."

I thought about a time only five months earlier in boot camp. Our boot platoon was lined up in its regular formation. A command was given and each man was separated by several extra paces. Still in platoon order, each was ordered to extend his arms straight out, palms down. Our rifles were then placed across our outstretched wrists. Nine and one-half pounds of M-1 rifle.

"You will stand at attention in this position. You will not lower your arms. You will NOT drop your rifle. You will not move."

The punishment for the first of us to fail any of those requirements was promised to be excessive.

A Marine boot platoon was arranged in four columns with the four tallest men at the front of each row. From the front to the back of each line the height diminished until it reached the four shortest Marine recruits.

Soon everything began to hurt. The tendons, ligaments, and the muscles hurt. Up and down the entire body, it hurt. The legs hurt. The back hurt. Still, no one moved. Time moved slowly. My mind produced a thought "you are not the biggest nor the strongest, but you are not the smallest nor the weakest. YOU will not be the first to let the rifle fall."

Hurting turned to pain.

On and on. . . Eternity passed.

Finally.

Way up front one of the big guys dropped his rifle. Immediately, the drill instructors pounced on the poor soul and dragged him away. Massive yelling and berating.

OK. Please and thank you for the wonderful experience. Now my dear drill instructor give us the command to put our rifles down.

Nope.

The mind spoke again, "I absolutely refuse to be next."

It went on and on.

Sooner or later someone else gave it up. Inevitable.

After two more let loose of their rifles, the drill instructor finally gave the command to retrieve our rifles from our wrists.

Each of us was a step closer to being a Marine.

During the long night facing the Chinese Army in full assault I discovered something that the Marine Corps had given me that morning on the parade ground. Something of great value. Discovering it was there was finding a treasure.

Chapter 16

From that time forward, I had that knowledge as personal property.

I had known on top of the hill defending the 'slot' that no one was going to drop their rifle.

Not one Marine would go down because another had dropped his rifle.

CHAPTER 17

The long hours . . .

The tour for a Marine in Korea was one year. A large part of that time was spent doing nothing—nothing, that is, except learning new things.

There were countless 12 or 24 hour periods spent on our stomachs. That time might be looking out over rice paddies or down the slope of a pine covered mountain. There was little to do except talk to the Marine next to you. And listen.

This was a place to learn about the human mind and how it works. People who study the human mind for a living never get such an opportunity. During those lengthy periods together, we found out what drove each individual, what scared them, and all of the weird thoughts that went through their minds. Straight forward and un-edited stuff.

During those long hours each pair of Marines found a connection. We discovered how different we each were and how differently each of us thought. We came to accept each other regardless of background, physical size, or quickness of mind.

This acceptance did not happen simply because that Marine might be at your back or at your side in a sudden moment of need.

We learned that below the surface of everyone, except the truly crazy, there is a good and trustworthy person. To benefit from

Chapter 17

that, you did not have to like everyone, nor did they have to like you.

An uncomplicated human formula existed.

Say you would do it. You did it. Say you would not. You did not.

In one year in Korea, simple straightforward relationships surfaced. For me, the long hours with Herman were the best. A special kind of friend. Even if he was from New Jersey, he knew so much about so many things. Every subject was touched and explored.

CHAPTER 18

The Professor

The Professor. We knew him by no other name. Within the society of misfits in our platoon he was our own misfit. A highly introverted man who said little on his own, he spent huge amounts of time staring into space.

There were two qualities that gave the Professor status with our platoon. His ability as a fighting Marine was unquestioned. Under fire the Professor was solid, always where he was supposed to be, did what needed to be done, and protected your back. In simple terms he just plain got the job done.

The more important quality to the rank and file was the fact that the Professor had a college degree: a Bachelor of Liberal Arts from a small Iowa college. A college degree was impressive to us. We granted him special status. It was not something that he asked for nor something that he expected. A close look at the academic credentials of our platoon would include few who had made it through high school. More common credentials would be a "completed" stamped on their record from reform school.

As the resident academic he was anointed to provide information in a variety of areas. Also, he was the final say on all disputed matters. The Professor certified all factual and philosophical subjects.

The professor usually sat by himself away from the din of the general conversation. He always seemed to be looking off into the distance searching for answers to ponderous questions.

CHAPTER 18

On almost a daily basis you heard, "You think you are so fucking smart, we will ask the Professor and see who is right!"

He quietly seemed to like his position. It was easy to see that the respect of the guys was important to him. He took his role seriously.

Getting him to respond required that the subject be of some importance and have some sort of worldly nature.

Watching this bunch of retards sit and soak up what he had to say was a treat. When a topic was introduced that warranted his involvement, he would go over the subject with carefully chosen words that were concise and easily understood. The guys paid attention, because they knew he would not repeat the whole performance. They tried to capture what he said and would rehash it among themselves. When they got off the mark, he would rephrase and give only the essence again.

"That is what the professor said, so I am right." His spoken word was gospel and final.

Probably the greatest of the discussions was on the side of a lonely Korean hill far from our unit. A pleasant day and a safe place. We were sitting and waiting for orders to secure the mission and return to the company.

This discussion was about the Marine Corps itself.

The professor was drawn into the discussion with the question "Professor, what makes the Marine Corps special?" He returned to our world and thought for a moment or two.

"In some ways it is like a religion. In some ways it is like a fraternity." He then covered the college course of Psychology 1A in simple terms.

"Identity. Each of us needs and wants to be a unique person with a picture of ourselves that we like and one that we want others to see."

"Most likely, that person we <u>want</u> to be is based on our personal and emotional needs. We are no different than other people. The men in this platoon have had different life experiences. For some, the Marine Corps was the only open door when we were looking for a place to run and hide. Before we came to the Ma-

rine Corps, none of us believed in much of anything. The Corps took each of us, took away what we were and started over. In boot camp they cut off all of our hair, put us in baggy fatigues and essentially made us all alike."

"Each of us arrived at boot camp with a bravado of some sort and not much direction. No outlet for the forces within us. We all want people to like us and accept us as we are. The Marine Corps offered that."

"At first in boot camp they gave us the basic concepts of the 'Marine religion.' Next, we were given a roadmap. We were immersed in an environment that had structure. Most of us had lacked a regimented life. They gave us a new set of heroes—the Marines who came before us. Real Marines. We were told to pay attention and if we worked hard, we could be like them."

"It was pointed out early and often in boot camp, that we were there because we asked to be there. No one had been drafted into the Marine Corps. The Corps was totally made up of men who knocked on the door and asked to come in."

"Remember how often you heard your boot camp drill instructor say something like 'Just show me the engraved invitation that the Marine Corps sent you inviting your attendance. Show it to me and you do not have to do what I tell you. You came to us and asked to be part of what we are. Now move it.'"

"Human relationships are all based on the needs of the parties. The Marine Corps needed us and we needed them. Look at the men around you. We come from a wide variety of places in the country. We have totally different backgrounds. Each of us

Chapter 18

is a completely different person yet now we all are part of something."

"The Marine Corps is many things to many people. As a military unit it is a blunt force. For the individual it can be a refuge, a career, a stepping stone, a way of life, a home, a security blanket, an ideal, an emotion, or a father figure. In the end, the Marine Corps is the sum of its parts."

As the Professor spoke, he paused with each important word or concept to let the idea sink in, and did not resume until he felt each idea had been captured.

For awhile it was quiet. Big Ski and Killer Ski were off a ways and talking quietly to each other. After a bit Big Ski asked, "Professor, we were just talking about all of the things you told us that the Marine Corps is and what it can be for different people. Can you tell us what it is that makes the Corps better? Is there some single thing that ties the whole thing together?"

The Professor's face showed a rare smile.

"Ski. Libraries are full of books written by the philosophers over the last thousand years. These are brilliant men with curious minds. Thinking and wondering about the various mysteries of life. You belong with them. You have asked a question that I have turned over in my mind many, many times."

"Ski, my answer is simply that I do not know the answer to your question. A single thing? Perhaps not. We both know that there is something special about us. It is real and we feel it. I will keep searching for it. We both know it is there."

Watching a master teacher was special. No kindergarten teacher reading "The Three Bears" for the first time could have had better attention. This classroom had no ticking clock, no next period, no interruptions. Not a single bored student looking out the window.

Trooping back to the company area, Professor was walking beside me. He was silent and had his usual faraway look. I told him, "Professor you are a natural teacher. If you do anything else with your life it will be a waste."

"Do you really think that, or is that more Smart Mouth speak?"

"Professor, I couldn't be more serious. You have a gift. I have been in school all of my life and only a couple teachers that I have had in that entire time could touch you. You could have told those guys that the moon was made of green cheese and they would have believed you."

"Those guys just have a lack of schooling and come from horrible backgrounds. They are mostly pretty bright guys with intellectual curiosity. They want to know what is going on around them."

"That's my point professor—most likely we are all like that, but there are not many people who can do what you just did. You took the big words you know, and could have used, and converted them into ideas. You led them. That is teaching."

"Actually that is one of the reasons I am here. A time out to figure out what to do next. A life-break. I also think they will give the Korean vets a GI Bill like the WWII guys. I need that to continue to go to school. If I teach, I want to teach at the university level."

"Go for it Professor."

The consummate teacher was not finished teaching. He and I hiked side by side quietly the rest of the afternoon.

The return from the patrol was lengthy and the Professor did not speak again until we neared the company area. "Smart Mouth."

"What?"

"If you ever give your brain time to catch up to your mouth, you can do anything you want in this life."

CHAPTER 19

The fight will always be for the high ground

The Army Second Division had been in trouble. Word was that they had lost most of the 38th Regiment and a Dutch battalion along with it. The Chinese had been slowed but not stopped. The word came down the line that our job at the slot had been pivotal for the 1st Marine Division. Someone appreciated us besides ourselves.

The position we held at the slot had been a temporary one. Holding there had given our Division time to solidify defenses.

Our reward was to continue to move from one place to another. That meant we patrolled during the day and formed a perimeter at night.

Near the end of May the Chinese called off their offensive. They picked up their toys and headed north, choosing new positions near the Imjin River

The brass was never happy. It was our turn to chase the Chinese. Before May was over, we had started our own offensive. The 1st Marine Division role in the northward offensive was to take some high ground near a big Reservoir. High ground. The fight would always be for the high ground.

It was tough going. Hot days sapped our strength. The rice paddies were fertilized with human waste and the horrible odor that was always there got worse with the heat. Because of the

Korean methods used to fertilize the rice paddies, Doc warned us that all water in Korea was unfit for drinking. Dehydration was a potential problem so water conservation was essential.

Though the days were hot, the nights were still cold and very wet. Even the valleys were difficult going with unexpected rain. Another of the 1001 uses for the helmet. Collect rain water for drinking.

Going north, we viewed a reminder of the past month. On patrol 1st platoon passed rotted bodies of the Army 2nd Infantry Division.

As each day and night started, we would have no idea if a patrol or night perimeter was going to be engaged by remnants of the communist forces. They often showed up unannounced and wanted to fight. Some of these skirmishes were minor; some were hard fought.

We could tell in the first five minutes of an engagement who we were fighting. If we bumped into stray units of the North Korean army, they would put up a fierce fight; after all, it was their country.

What was helpful and fully appreciated was that we were again getting the support of our own artillery fire on a routine basis.

Chapter 19

We had missed the 11th Marines. In the field it was comforting to know that you could call on them. Herman and I discussed the giant mystery of the lack of air cover. This caused constant and continued bitching among the men. None of us had an answer, nor did anyone up the line. Something was just not right. So many times in the field a couple of fighters with blazing 50 caliber machine guns or a little napalm would have made the day easier. "Where were they?"

We moved north to the top of the next mountain. From there we had a clear view of a town that had been flattened and a gigantic reservoir. Except for the destroyed town, it was another pretty Korean landscape. The bad news was the view to the north. Every time we would get to the top of one mountain and look north there would be more and higher mountains.

Before June was well underway our Division was sent into those mountains. New high ground. This area appeared to be a grouping of mountains and ridges formed at some point in time by volcanic eruptions. The area came to be called 'The Punchbowl' because of its unique shape.

Our northward offensive had been a tough battle all the way. The 1st and 5th Regiments led the assault, paying the price with high casualties. Seventh Marines were close behind as back up.

Because of extensive casualties in the 5th Marine Regiment our extended two-day 'vacation' as backup ended. Tied into the 1st Marines we continued north, taking one hill after another. Ten straight days. Daily we would take a hill and then settle in for the nightly counterattack.

We continued to secure more high ground. The next project was always to get ready to defend it.

We were a tired bunch, but Herman and I agreed that digging was better than the fighting. Worn down, none of us had the greatest outlook about what we were doing. But we did it.

Chapter 20

Secure the perimeter

We got the command: "Baker Company move out." With the usual commentary on the obvious contradiction of the terms Marine Intelligence, we started hiking north again.

"Where the fuck are we going this time?"

"Well we are not coming back here because we are taking all of our stuff with us."

"Are you sure the Commandant didn't consult with you on this move?"

"I really had something else to do today."

After a while hiking the chatter stopped as we concentrated on putting one foot in front of the other. Our full Marine company made a long line. 300 or 400 Marines. We had three rifle platoons, machine gun sections, mortar sections, and our company headquarters guys. Even with the full company moving out, the spread between each individual was kept to at least about 10 to 15 yards.

Periodic stops were made so the ridges and hills on all sides could be checked for unfriendly people who might have thought an ambush would be a good idea. Each time we started up again, the spread between each man was closely monitored by not so friendly sergeant types who understood the difference between too much space and too little. They repeatedly doled out the

CHAPTER 20

standard Marine advice, "don't bunch up—one grenade will get you all." Solid advice. The other part of the equation was the accordion effect. If the spread got too great, the poor assholes at the end of the company would have to spend their time running to keep up.

Minutes turned into hours. One step, another step, and another. Every so often you needed to shift the weight of the pack.

Our packs contained everything we owned. Anyone who had been in Korea very long, carefully selected essentials only. Generally that meant a couple days of C-Rations, clean socks, good luck charms (including, if possible, a small symbol of every known religion—just in case), and a poncho. When we started out on one of these pleasure hikes, we had no idea how long we would be walking or how far. If we started out with something, we had to carry it all the way because dropping a single item of any sort would leave behind a sign that we had been there. Dropping something would also give you a face to face opportunity to respond to one of those sergeant types.

We made room for extra bandoliers of ammo and grenades by leaving out the luxuries of life like a toothbrush and soap. That was pretty much the pattern unless you were the indentured slave of Cpl Boost. In addition to his extra full load of BAR magazines, I was required to carry about five extra empty BAR magazines inside my shirt. Over our time together the complaints about being his burro had fallen on deaf ears. Only once did he respond to my continuous references to my slave status. After being loaded in the required manner, I opened my fly, exposed myself, and made the statement, "If I am going to be treated like a burro, I am going to look like a burro." Even 'Cpl Composure' had to give a small smile.

The empty magazines did have a purpose. When we reached our destination, Boost and his burro fanned out and methodically raided any source available for 30 caliber ammunition. The BAR, the M-1 rifle, and the 30-caliber machine gun all used the same size cartridge. Finding and stealing a full box of machine gun ammo worked perfectly. We would remove the shells from the belts of machine gun ammo and fill all our empty BAR magazines.

—74—

That task finished, Boost/ Mr. Firepower would be quiet and we would then be ready for whatever happens.

We started to climb out of the valley. We kept climbing. And we continued to climb. This was one tall hill—not really attached to anything else. Upon reaching the top of the hill, we formed a company-sized outpost in the middle of nowhere, at least two or three miles north of the rest of the Division. Discovering that we were basically out there by ourselves in the middle of nowhere, the disparaging references to 'Marine Intelligence' became more than intense. This position had been used before, maybe even by both sides. The 360º view of the surrounding countryside revealed trenches, bunkers, and devastated foliage—all indications that there had been considerable action here before. Hard to tell if it was action going north or south.

"Secure the perimeter." The three magic words meant physical labor. Whoever inhabited this hill, of course, did not know and properly understand the fields of fire concept. "Yes, Raymond, sergeant Sir. I will begin to dig immediately."

Naturally he was right in his assessment of the area and the ability to defend it, but it had already been a long day. Still, the night WOULD come and perhaps bring 'visitors' with it. I, too, wished to be ready, so the digging started.

About 30 minutes into the work Pete summoned 1st squad and assigned our digging to others. This was not good news—definitely not time off for good behavior.

CHAPTER 21

"Snow Fucking White"

Raymond was giving out orders. "Probing Patrol for 1st squad. Saddle up. We go in 10 minutes." Probing patrol was one of those cute Marine terms. A probing patrol meant to go until you saw someone or else someone shot at you . . . then you knew someone was there.

Pete led out, followed by the platoon radio man. We followed him back down the hill and off to wherever he had been instructed to probe. Once we were off the hill and after a long hike through the Korean countryside, we discovered a huge roadblock made up of downed trees, big branches, and boulders. A big sucker, it completely blocked any access to motorized vehicles and was a better than average notice that someone was near. SOP (Standard

Operating Procedure)—keep the hell away from the road block. Whoever built it had surely also zeroed it in with mortars.

We changed direction. Following the stream, we moved down into a gully and up the other side of the hill and above the road, Pete was having some problems with the radio and was unable to make contact with the company. After positioning each of us, he and the radio operator headed around the corner of a rock outcropping, trying to get a better signal.

As soon as they turned the corner Pete walked straight into it. Burp guns—at least two of them. His body flew backward and he went down. Behind him, the radio guy did not seem to be hit and had dropped to the ground behind the rock.

Boost moved right up a draw with me close behind him. Charles, Hack, and Moose went left while Los Hombres spread out up the slope to give a base of fire. Up the draw we got lucky and caught the guys who had ambushed Pete between us. A few guys and not well organized—Boost crucified them.

Jose went quickly to Pete . . . and shook his head. Following my hand and arm signals, Jose and the radio guy dragged Pete back to the stream embankment. Suddenly, the rock outcropping and road block erupted with mortar blasts. The area HAD been zeroed in.

I gave hand and arm signals and we spread out along the embankment, getting ready for them to come at us. We waited . . . waited . . . and waited. They did not come. Soon daylight was almost gone, so I signaled to the guys to move further down the stream away from the roadblock. Goat gave his rifle to the radio guy and put Pete's body over his shoulder as we moved out. Moving slowly and trying to be quiet, the big guys—Rivas, the Professor, Moose, and Herman—took turns carrying Pete.

Well downstream from the road block, we crossed the stream, moved up the side of the hill, and set up a makeshift perimeter. By now it was dark as pitch. Our perimeter circle might not be perfect, but it would work. We became more than quiet.

It was amazing how we could whisper, pass the word, and not make a sound, hoping the noise of the stream would absorb

Chapter 21

whatever noise we created. In the dark, I located the radio guy and gave him instructions. "Try the company one time. Say this and only this. One transmission only. If they get it fine—but no second try."

"Smart Mouth here. Peterson dead. Be back tomorrow night. Leave the porch light on. OUT."

Responding to the radioman's curious look, I said "I just don't want anyone to come out looking for us. We certainly don't want to stir up a hornets nest here. I also don't want to get shot on our way into the company perimeter."

Message sent.

Then I told him, "Pass the word. 50 % watch. Sleep on your stomachs—no snoring. Sleep as close to each other as you can stand. The body heat will help."

The plan for this patrol had been a simple out and back. We were unprepared for a night outing and certainly not ready for the drop in temperature. After a miserable cold night, morning finally came.

With the morning light, perched pretty well up on the side of the hill, we had a good view. We could see the road, down into the valley, and the roadblock. Our positions seemed to be hidden from view.

"Goddamn that sun feels good."

I then told them, "Guys, unless someone has a better idea, we are going to stay here until dark. We are out of sight and maybe by night the Chinese will forget us or think we have gone. I know we are all hungry, but I think waiting is the best idea."

No dissent.

"OK. 25 % watch during the day. Get some sleep. Radio guy, lets see if we can raise the company."

After two tries we were in. The radio guy handed me the phone.

"Skipper. Smart Mouth here. We are in the middle of something here. Can't really tell what. We are going to hole up until dark and then head back. I can't tell you the size of their group. Real big, I think. Huge roadblock zeroed in with mortars. Don't know if it was simple ambush, accidental contact, or the whole Chinese army. The army-sized thing, if I had to guess. Pete's dead. He just walked into it. We are bringing him in. Going to radio silence, unless we get something new to offer. OUT." I disconnected.

Radio guy looked at me. "Smart Mouth! You are supposed to give him a chance to talk."

"I might not have wanted to do what he said."

It was mid-afternoon when Goat shook me. "Smart Mouth there is a jeep coming up the road."

I came out of the dense fog of pleasant sleep. Goat continued. "We put Pete's binoculars on it and it looks like an Army Jeep."

"What the fuck!" Staying under cover and taking turns with the binoculars, we watched the jeep pull all the way up to the roadblock. I gave hand and arm signals to those awake and watching. The main signal was the one finger across the lips. Quiet.

At the roadblock, what looked like an officer and two enlisted men got out to take a leak break. "Shit."

We watched mortar rounds scatter them. The enlisted men dove for the stream bed and the officer flew under the jeep. Goat groaned. "That dumb shit."

Jose was at the foot of our small perimeter and closest to the roadblock . He grabbed his rifle and scurried down the side of the hill to get within shouting distance.

"Get the fuck out from under that jeep and into the stream you dumb shithead! Move your rotten ass, now! You dumb fuck, they have the roadblock zeroed in."

Unlike a line officer, this officer carried some suet, but responded appropriately. He scrambled away from the truck and dove over the side of the embankment. Jose had no more than yelled "stay put asshole," when the jeep disintegrated with pieces flying in all directions. He yelled out again. "Stay put asshole!! If you don't move, they will think they got you. Don't move a muscle until I tell you."

Chapter 21

Two hours later Jose gave the word. "OK butthead. The three of you—one at a time—crawl along the stream bank toward that huge tree by the bend in the road. Stay well below the level of the road. Stay low and move slowly. We have you covered."

Once they got to the tree, Jose collected them and carefully led them back to our spot up on the side of the hill.

The officer had a name tag. Major Samuel Logan. The enlisted men with him had no stripes.

I shook my head. "Jesus, Sam, what the fuck are you doing out here?"

Major Logan replied, "We are a photo unit. I guess we took a wrong turn."

"Sam, you are about three to four miles into enemy territory. The main line is south. That was some wrong turn!"

The Major looked at me with the single stripe on my dungarees. "Marine—what is your rank?"

Charles, close by in a hole where he had been sleeping, chimed in. "Major, his rank is currently leader of this unit and don't give him any shit. The former leader of this unit is that body over there. Him, we are carrying out. You, we might have to think about. Do exactly what the man says and you have a chance of getting back in one piece."

Major Logan responded. "What is your plan, leader?"

I explained the current plan. "Major we could use some help with the carrying from you and your two guys. We are pretty worn down and haven't eaten for two days. It's going to be a long walk and a tough climb. If you help with the carrying we can have all of our guys ready to defend if we need to.

It was a long walk and a tough climb. The two enlisted men and the Major quietly shouldered the load of our dead sergeant. They were not line troops and in less than great condition, but made not one complaint as they took turns and shared the burden of bringing Pete back, as we made our way back through the countryside and up the hill.

About 100 yards below the perimeter wire we stopped. The two army enlisted were behind me and the Major was the last man in the column taking his turn carrying Pete. The voice from the perimeter called out. "Who the fuck is out there?" "What is the password?"

In the lead spot, I answered. "Stick the password up your ass! It is Snow Fucking White and about 10 or 12 fucking tired, hungry, and pissed off dwarves. If you shoot us you had better kill us all or the last one of us left will kick your fucking ass."

The voice answered. "Come in Smart Mouth . . . and bring the dwarves." The two army enlisted got the giggles. They couldn't stop. No doubt it came from the fatigue and huge emotional relief of making it back in one piece. When they finally got it under control, one said "Some password!"

The last guy through the wire was a completely exhausted army major who gently laid Pete down and all but collapsed. The first guy at the wire to bring us in was the Skipper who greeted us with "Welcome home, Snow Fucking White, and please do not kick my ass."

"Sorry Sir, I didn't know it was you. Skipper, this is Major Samuel Logan, United States Army and his staff. Three army guys with brass balls."

Jose stopped long enough to offer his trademark smile and his hand to the Major. "Sorry, Sir about the bad mouthing back there at the river."

The Major took Jose's hand a gave him a firm handshake and a arm around the shoulder. "Thanks, Marine. Without you I'd be melted into that jeep. You call me whatever you want."

The Skipper gave the traditional Marine greeting. "Welcome aboard, 'Major,' come up to my bunker and tell me about it."

Chapter 22

Purple Hearts and PFC Cushing

The Purple Heart is awarded for injuries sustained in combat. We knew there were exact guidelines for this medal, but none of us ever totally understood what those rules were. Just one more thing that didn't matter if we understood or not. One fact did rise to the surface. We knew that the best way to receive one would be to have it awarded in person and not to your mother. If Mom were to be awarded your Purple Heart, she would get it with a flag and then hear taps.

To get a Purple Heart, anything that drew blood met the standard. Blood always counted. One of the classic blood events happened to one of our replacement Marines. He went along on a four-man night patrol with Rivas, Escamilla, and Killer Ski. Object of the patrol—what else? To bring back a prisoner. The format of this patrol was a little different due to another brilliant idea from above: sneak up to the enemy lines in the dark of the night, grab a Chinese soldier out of his fox hole and run for it.

On the surface, the plan was a simple one. Choose a big guy. While the three others covered him, he would sneak up, muscle the Chinese soldier out of his hole, throw him over his shoulder and then they would all run for it.

It worked. They brought back a prisoner and everything was okay, except for the designated big guy. A replacement kid. He successfully dragged the Chinese soldier out of his hole. The

grabbing and pulling went according to plan. But, during that part of the capturing process, he left his thumb exposed and the prisoner damn near bit it off. Blood. Purple Heart. Great story for the grandkids.

Having success with harebrained ideas like this was always bad because the genius who thought it up would just come up with another equally brilliant idea.

Doc's favorite combat blood story was the kid who tripped a mine and had extensive bleeding in the groin area. If you couldn't believe Doc, who could you believe? His version of the incident was interesting. Perhaps the kid was in shock, but he refused to let Doc tend to his injuries until Doc had verified that the fun and family producing parts of his body were intact.

We all thought that our buddy Cushing had a magnet in his body. If any piece of metal was flying about—it ALWAYS found him and it always drew blood. Four times. Never anything very big nor something that seemed to hurt. Each time it was in some part of his body where it didn't seem to matter.

Doc was a constant nag about the country we were in and the diseases that lurked. Places like the rice paddies and its human fertilizer. He had us well-conditioned about the potential for infection. Cushing was like the rest of us when we would get a nick.

Show it to Doc, get it painted with something red, get a small bandage, patch the hole in the dungarees and move on. By the

Chapter 22

book, Doc would write it up as a combat injury and Cushing would get another Purple Heart.

Neither the wounds or the awards seemed to be a big deal to Cushing. He was a completely outgoing guy with movie star looks—a face with a cherub quality, dark wavy hair, and a twinkle in his big blue eyes. It would be easy to be jealous of a guy with his looks, but that was not the case with Cushing. He had such an open personality, you couldn't help but like him.

Besides, each situation where he caught a piece of something was during some sort of fire fight where the shit was hitting the fan and we all felt that he was entitled to his Purple Hearts and told him so. It didn't seem to effect his outlook one way or the other.

The coin flipped.

The squad was in the middle of the valley when we were jumped by a good-sized bunch of Chinese. Kind of routine stuff, except that Cushing was the point man (that lucky guy who was in the lead of the strung out column). Suddenly from nowhere a Chinaman with a burp gun charged. His Burp was pointed right at Cushing's chest from about 8 feet. He pulled the trigger . . . but nothing happened. Charles was second in the line, and before Cushing could react he cut the Chinaman down. The Burp gun had to have jammed. Later both Charles and Hack verified that they had heard it click. 750-rounds-per-minute from that weapon would have cut Cushing in two.

The Chinese, unlike the North Koreans, discouraged easily. When it appeared that things were not going their way, they had the good sense to leave. We extracted ourselves from the valley and got back to the perimeter without any more incidents.

The only difference was that no one said a word to Cushing, that day or after about what had happened. It was like talking to the pitcher in the dugout in the 8th inning of a no-hitter. A luck and jinx thing.

About two weeks later a shell from the standard afternoon artillery barrage landed directly on Cushing's bunker. . . . Being a bunker constructed by the Sgt. Raymond Gotshall Construction Co. with lots and lots of sandbags and logs, the bunker held up.

Cushing came out of the bunker covered with black soot looking like the lead in a Minstrel Show. His hearing was lousy for a couple days but other than that he was untouched, despite the fact that it was a DIRECT hit.

Cushing had brushed off the four Purple Hearts as though they had never happened. However, after the artillery shell direct hit of his bunker, he became quiet. Again, it was some sort of understood thing among us—we did not discuss it with him. It wasn't like we got together and made a grand decision. Hard to tell why, but no one said a word to him. Cushing and the rest of us went about as if nothing had happened or was happening.

Only days later Cushing and the rest of his fire team were headed out for their turn on a nightly listening post in front of the company. The rains had left the slope slippery. Cushing was leading and slipped on the mud and pine needles. As he fell, he began to slide down the trail on his backside. The slide carried him directly through a wire attached to a trip mine—one of the nasty kind that jumps into the air, explodes, and sprays the area with a million pieces of metal.

Strangely, by the time it exploded, Cushing's slide had taken him far enough down the slope that nothing touched him. Had he tripped it with his foot in normal stride, he would have been hamburger.

In a short period of time he had three times looked death straight in the eye, yet each time he had walked away. His body walked away . . . but his nervous system did not. It was damaged beyond what it could handle. The ironic part would be that none of the three incidents qualified him for another Purple Heart. Blood counted—damaged nerves did not.

After this third incident, Doc tagged him and sent him back to Regiment. Doc wasn't a world class nerve or head doctor but he knew from looking into Cushing's vacant eyes that it was time to end this phase of his career in a Marine line company. Doc wrote on the tag "the thousand-yard stare."

Cushing spent the balance of his Korean tour back at the Division level, where it was much quieter. A tough Marine and a good guy.

CHAPTER 23

Dark Korean nights

The going north, then south seemed to be over for a while. Somewhere up in the mountains of North Korea, we were turned from day and night fighters into construction workers.

The United Nations forces had established a main line of resistance, 'The Kansas Line.' A solid defensive line from one side of the Korean peninsula to the sea on the other side. Each fighting unit was assigned a sector to defend. Our 1st Marine Division had positions high in the mountains near the Sea of Japan.

We built trenches, fighting holes, and massive protective bunkers. Live-in bunkers were built on the reverse slope. Hour after hour was spent digging, filling sandbags, and cutting logs. This mountainous area seemed to have been created from volcanic activity with the rocks looking like cooled molten lava. Tough digging.

Then there was that god-awful barbed wire. The farm boys, especially Moose, took great delight from our bitching. They had been building fences with it for years and completely enjoyed our misery. Barbed wire was horrible stuff to work with. First you needed to dig holes in the difficult rocky soil. Each hole needed to be deep enough to secure the long metal poles while still leaving enough above ground to hold the barbed wire. Each pole was notched to secure the nasty pointed wire. Finding a suitable place to dig the holes was bad enough. It took real muscle to unroll and wrap the wire around the pole. Just plain hard work.

The rumors that were flying around were all about the peace negotiations. Someone seemed to be trying to end the war. No one up the line of command appeared to be worried about an imminent attack. You could always tell how worried the Marine decision makers were by two things: the percentage watch at night and the frequency and design of the patrols sent out.

Percentage watch at night was divided by agreement among the men. You could change every hour, every four hours, or any formula you wanted depending on individual preferences. The Marine Corps did not interfere. It was always left to the men on line to determine who made up the awake and watchful quotas. The Marine Corps took a simple position: 'Get the job done or we will stand you against the wall and shoot you.' An effective approach.

Nighttime meant patrols. Sometimes there were attacks on our positions at night as well. Standing your assigned percentage watch, however, was different. Waiting and watching in a stationary position in the quiet of the night was a unique mental experience. The mind could take massive turns from the quiet uneasy anticipation to the fearful readiness that came with night noises.

For the most part darkness was your friend, but it could play horrible tricks on your mind. There was dark, darker, and pitch black. You simply sat or stood alone in the trench or bunker staring into the night. There was no defined outcome for the next minute or hour. The array of uncertainties was immense. Alone in your position in the dark of the night, there was a delicate balance between fatigue, adrenaline, and watchfulness.

We had reason to believe that the Chinese and North Koreans knew who we were—Marines—and we felt they would try someone else. That did not help during the hours spent peering into the Korean night.

Sitting or standing absolutely still allowed a measure of blending into the night. Some chose to cover their watch time in their bunker, some chose their fighting hole, and some chose the trench.

Chapter 23

Boost and I fashioned a cut out at the back of our trench where we could sit with our backs to a tree.

Of course, the patrols in front of the line continued.

The salt mine type work, the night patrols and night watching did little for troop morale.

As expected, in June the rains came. Monsoons, deluges—either would have been an appropriate description. Farmboy Moose was the self-appointed monitor on rainfall amounts. He gave the June and July totals to be over 20 inches each. Everything was affected. Patrols, construction work, and daily living.

On patrols, slipping and sliding up and down the mountainside and into the valley was routine. Getting across a stream in full gear was always iffy. If your fighting hole, protective bunker, or sleeping bunker was not properly trenched, everything you possessed got wet. Once your sleeping bag got wet, it stayed that way. Up in the mountains, the nights were cold, a wet sleeping bag was a disaster.

Morale may have been good, but attitude was suspect.

Sometime in July rumors started that we were going to be relieved and sent into reserve.

Some army unit would be taking over these positions.

"God, I love the United States Army" became the phrase of the day.

CHAPTER 24

He was a hit man for the mob in Brooklyn

The rain that had started in mid-June, kept on and on . . . and on. When July had been under way for a week or so, the rumors had turned into the official word.

"The Division is going into reserve. We are turning Kansas Line over to the U.S. 2nd Division."

We were more than ready to leave. We needed to leave behind the constant rain, living in mud, and just plain general misery we had experienced over the past three months.

The U.S. Army arrived looking fresh and clean.

Of course, nothing ever happened with 1st platoon without an incident.

When a Marine unit was replaced on line by another unit there was a simple straight forward procedure based on professional courtesy. Positions on a defensive line are exchanged one at a time. Whether it is a perimeter, a main line of resistance, or just holes in the ground, it was done the same way. A timely process, but it worked.

Hole by hole; or bunker by bunker we exchanged places with the soldiers. The troops taking over were given an individual briefing about what to expect, shown the fields of fire, told about what to expect at night, the habits of the enemy, along with anything unusual about the area. Not the worst idea in the world.

Chapter 24

There was absolutely no reason not to use the same system with the 2nd Division, U.S. Army. After all, we should be grateful—these were the good guys who were getting us off this mountain. Things were going along in an orderly manner. The Army personnel were stashed behind a hill and sent up one or two at a time. As positions were exchanged, then the next pair would move up.

I was coming back down the trench line after our exchange of positions and was being even more vocal than usual. Totally animated. "God damn stupid fucking doggies !!!!"

Goat was sitting by the road waiting for the rest of the squad to come off the hill and made the mistake of asking, "What's the problem?"

"Those dumb assholes wouldn't listen to me when I was telling them about the fields of fire. All they were concerned with was a single question, "Where is the "bug out hole" in this bunker? Bug out hole my ass—he wanted a rear exit to the fucking bunker. Fucking Army!!!"

The next soldier getting ready to go into the line did not miss my tirade and he took exception to the content of my remarks. He and I started to exchange uncomplimentary words—unfit for the family dinner with Aunt Grace. We appeared to be headed toward a more physical confrontation. Before the guy could get to me, however, Goat was up and in between us.

Still agitated, the young soldier looked upward into Goat's face, and heard, "Hey Soldier Boy, I am going to give you some advice. First of all, if I were you, I would leave him alone. He pissed me off once. I tried him out and he handed me my ass."

As Goat led me away, the second Goliath of 1st platoon was coming up the trench line. Moose. The soft spoken gentleman that he was, Moose spoke quietly to the young soldier. "Sorry about that buddy. I have a deal for you. Find your commanding office and give us some adoption papers to sign and we will give you that sorry little shit for your very own. We have to put up with that big mouth all the time and we would gladly give him away. Of course, there is one other issue to consider—his job before he was in the Marine Corps."

Moose paused a bit for effect. "He was a hit man for the Mob in Brooklyn."

Moose then followed Goat and me around the little hill and down to the road where the truck was waiting to take us to the rear. Out of sight of the Army troops and around the corner of the hill we broke up, laughing and slapping each other on the back as we started to climb into the truck. We thought we were pretty damn funny. The last weeks had been rough, and we were tired clean through. This was a group where laughs had been few and far between for some time.

Raymond wanted to know what was so funny. When Goat and Moose finished the story, Raymond looked at me. "Someday, someone is going to finish you off. I want to be there."

Undaunted, I looked directly up at my beloved platoon sergeant and said "Hey big boy, you want to try me? You don't see any keep off signs on this Marine." Maybe it was just that we were getting off that hill and heading to the rear, but our whole truck thought this was the funniest thing they had ever heard. Even Raymond.

From the next truck, full of equally fatigued Marines, the platoon sergeant yelled over. "Hey Ray, what's going on?"

"Nothing George, I just have the fucking Marx Brothers in my platoon."

Chapter 25

Sgt. Smart Mouth

For once sitting in the back of a 6-by truck with no shock absorbers on a bumpy Korean road seemed like a luxury ride. Each of us felt like we have covered every inch of the Korean peninsula on foot over the last three months. Up and down the mountains and through the valleys.

"Where are we and where are we going?"

"Do I look like your fucking travel agent? If the Marine Corps wanted you to know, they would have told you."

For a miserable day in the rain, we were pretty lighthearted as the vehicles cleared the front lines. The standard Marine poncho was a decent piece of equipment. No more than a slick tablecloth with a hole for your head, but it did the job. Our truck had no canvas cover. The waterproof trusty old steel helmet completed the job of staying dry. Another of its 1001 uses.

Nothing, including the rain, really mattered. We were headed south and away. By late afternoon the convoy of trucks reached a beautiful valley complete with its own brisk river. We were ordered out of the trucks and each unit was assigned an area to erect new homes. Pup tents.

Half of a pup tent was standard equipment for each Marine. At some point in time each of us had been issued tent stakes to go with it. Those had long since been thrown away along with the toothpaste and other non-essential stuff before embarking on one of those long Korean hiking events. We scrounged some new stakes and went to work.

Boost was architect, engineer, and straw boss. Ours went up quickly. His leadership included an awareness of the most important factor of pup tent construction—situate on a slight incline and properly trench to redirect rain water. Our bayonets made up for two of our missing tent stakes. The predominate thought was to build it, get in it, and sleep for a week.

"First platoon fall out and fall in." Now the intense bitching DID start. In place of long overdue sleep we were marched down to the river single-file where there was a huge squad-sized tent. Water from the river was being sucked up and into the tent. Steam billowed out. It was just what it appeared to be—a gigantic shower tent.

"Take off everything you have on and throw it into that pile. Everything!! All the way down to your little pink asses."

Fatigues, socks, underwear, dungarees—everything. The socks and skivvies might have been changed at monthly intervals, but the mud-covered fatigues were so caked with dirt and grime that

Chapter 25

they might have stood up by themselves. Ugly reminders of reality. Our bodies were as bad or worse than our fatigues with almost three months worth of ground-in Korean soil. Not just dirt, but ground-in dirt in every body opening. Places that even your mother had not tried to clean.

This was a genuine lifetime shower event. How could something so simple be so joyful? Tons of hot water and soap on the tired dirt bag body.

Next on the agenda was the ultimate indignity. Before being allowed to leave the tent, we formed a line of naked bodies. At the business end of the line corpsmen were wielding something that looked like a plain black stove pipe. From the end of this device came a large and constant flow of fine white powder. Stand up, bend over, turn and expose every inch of your body. White powder up the kazoo and to other sensitive adjacent areas. A demeaning treatment. Need and logic did not sooth the offensive nature of the act. The individual's sense of dignity was not an issue. We were being deloused with DDT.

At the far opening of the tent were piles of fresh smelling, clean clothing. Find your size and outfit yourself from inside out and top to bottom. Most likely they dug a huge hole and buried everything we had been wearing. It surely had mites, ticks, amoeba, and other moldy things we had never heard of. A three-month accumulation of creepy crawlies.

We even got new boon dockers (boots). In the pile of new and clean dungarees, I spotted a dungaree jacket that had the 5 stripes of a Technical Sergeant. Being a devious soul, I selected it as part of my new wardrobe. An overwhelming compulsion arose to put on the new Sergeant dungaree jacket and visit Raymond. Time to demand some respect with my new 'shower rank.'

Instead of a "yeah, that's funny," I got a single finger pointed toward the shower tent along with a mumbled threat which might have included severe physical violence. He held up the five fingers of his other hand probably indicating the time frame I had to accomplish the change. The man took this Sergeant thing too seriously. He needed sense of humor lessons.

CHAPTER 26

The myth of male bonding

We were brought into reserve to rest our minds and bodies. Sleeping uninterrupted through a full night ranked right up there with the hot shower. This reserve also meant that we received replacement Marines.

A replacement in an established combat unit did not immediately become 'one of the boys.'

An invisible barrier existed. Boost's original advice to me when I arrived, "Be quiet for a few days and it will work out" had been good advice.

Experiences such as a single rifle shot coming in your direction changed all that. Personal differences were forgotten. It happened in one way or another to all of us. Whatever characteristics you found offensive about another Marine simply evaporated.

Adversity provided a framework for new and strong friendships. Holding up under all kinds of conditions earned respect.

The general rotation plan for Marines in Korea had become a simple stay alive for 12 months and then you could go home. These replacements allowed the last of those who had fought at Chosin Reservoir to go home. The Reservoir had been one of the toughest Marine battles in the History of the Corps. They had both the right and need to leave Korea.

Chapter 26

After a few days of rest, we started an intense and steady diet of training. Hills, weapons, tactics, conditioning, information about who we were fighting and why. It was good for the replacement guys to watch those of us who had been in this country for awhile. We paid attention and it rubbed off on them. It seemed to get through to them that what was happening here was important and real.

The prevailing rumor revolved around another amphibious landing like the 1st Division had done the previous fall at Inchon. The training schedule was concentrated and physically hard, but we were given ample time to ourselves and with each other.

Basic Marine rule—do not leave the troops alone for very long. Have some sort of program to keep them busy. A crude movie was set up on the side of a hill with wooden benches. There was time for us to catch up on sleep and lots of recreation type things. Volleyball, softball, and even horse shoes. The strangest was the shot-guns that were made available for the hunter-fisher types. Hard to believe that there was actually game in the woods.

The total bad news for me was the boxing ring. When Escamilla rushed through the flap of the squad tent to inform me of the boxing ring and equipment, terror went through my heart. 'Es' was a big raw serious kid about 6 feet and 175 pounds. One of the Hombres.

During the previous months he and I had been alone on top of a mountain, doing watching and listening. During the course of a full day, "Es" had told me that he had been an amateur boxer and hoped to pursue boxing as career. For lack of something better to talk about, I informed 'Es' of my own eight successful professional fights and perfect record in the ring of eight and zero. During the conversation I even offered to help him when we got back to the states. "I will work with your footwork, punch, and style." Of course, there had not been a shred of truth to the story. All hot air. Anyone else would have said BS and laughed it off. 'Es,' however, took it as gospel. His career as a boxer was very serious to him.

Today was real. 'Es' all but dragged me protesting all the way down to the new boxing ring. No objections, nor explanations worked. 'Es' forced the gloves on and dragged me into the ring.

This was pure joy for 1st platoon. Instant patrols scattered throughout the area to find the rest of the guys. Most were found and gave 'Es' lots of encouragement.

One of the early lessons learned in the sport of boxing is the importance of arm strength. Keeping the arms up for a three minute round is an accomplishment by itself. Arm exhaustion sets in fast.

After about 10 minutes of having my head snapped back with left jabs, 'Es' took pity on me. During the recent months of fighting up north we had been together, side by side, and back to back—far more than a few times. We were close friends. Finally 'Es' relented.

For me, the myth of men bonding was destroyed.

The men of 1st platoon that I had lived with, fought beside, and protected had failed to fully recognize the seriousness of my situation. They were too busy rolling on the ground, pointing, and laughing hilariously.

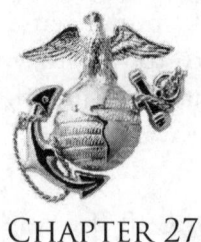

CHAPTER 27

Never leave them alone . . .

It was just Marine talk when we trashed the Army. We knew that there were some good and some bad. Mostly good.

There in that pretty little valley we had decided that the Army was not all bad. They sent their engineer corps and turned this muddy meadow into a passable living area. Squad tents, mess tents, and the shower tents. All with real wooden floors. Sleeping on a standard military cot and off the ground was pure heaven.

After almost three months of living in a totally uncivilized manner, the potty facilities alone were a definite up-grade. To an outside observer the new potty facilities would not be considered something fancy. To us, after an extended period of time of simple squat and dump in the forest, this was a pleasure. A far more suitable situation for contemplating the world around you.

First they dug a huge hole. Next came a wooden support. Finally, the finished product. The creation was topped off with a solid piece of wood about the size of a kitchen table. Holes were cut to accommodate four customers at a time, two facing in each direction.

For those Marines with too much time on their hands and owning a camera, this was one of the more popular picture taking opportunities. We were easy to entertain.

A basic Marine rule remained—don't leave us alone or we will get ideas about entertaining ourselves.

Charles stood alone in the creativity department.

The night he had the rotating watch of the battalion supply tents he observed that the supply tents were full of good stuff. Much was designated for the officers' mess.

Charles came up with a plan. We would rig the rotating watch so that one of us was on guard duty at the same time at each of the four corners of the supply area. (It was ludicrous that the Marine Corps felt the need to guard a supply tent from its own!) Battalion had cleverly set watch duty on the supply tents using one Marine from each of the companies and one from the artillery unit sharing each time period. Every four hours during the night, four new Marines took over. This simple concept encompassed the fact that none of those on guard duty knew each other.

Hack and the Battalion supply clerk were friends from boot camp. Hack generously filled in for him for a couple hours. During his time as supply clerk, Hack re-arranged the guard duty roster. At 0300 hours, the four guard posts were manned by none other than four members of first squad. Rivas, Villareal, Herman and Little Ski. No question, they were definitely watching the supply tents and each other. The canvas side of one of the supply tents went up. One after the other of 1st squad entered and scurried out with a full case of something. A clean and simple heist, the contraband was in our tent quickly and secreted under our cots.

Was the middle of the night raid a success? Kind of a yes and no thing. Evaluating the theft of the century, we found that we had managed to steal 14 cases of the largest size cans of fruit cocktail. When we finally left reserve, there was plenty left for the next

Chapter 27

occupants. Many years would pass before any of our group would consider this item to be a delicacy.

Never leave Marines alone without some sort of organized activity.

The toughest part for the brass in these reserve areas was dealing with the local Koreans. The Japanese had annexed their whole country in about 1910 and the Koreans had suffered under their cruel rule until the end of World War II, so they had not had long to recover before this war began. It did not appear that they had much before, but it had gotten worse. Much worse. Poverty plus. The meager things we had and did not want were precious to them. Whatever was given to them was highly appreciated.

What was hard for the brass was keeping them away from us and us away from them. Though the effort was made to maintain separation with plenty of Army and Marine MPs, it did not work.

The age old needs of fighting men were available with the locals—whiskey and women. Hard to figure which was the lower quality item. It took a real hero to drink the local brand of whiskey. The brand name was "Old Camel." The name alone was reason enough to abstain.

My friend and personal hero—Boost—had three weaknesses. Hoarding BAR magazines, beer, and the treasure the local beauties had to offer.

Boost didn't wait for the girls to come to him—he left the reserve area and foraged into the villages. Every time when he returned he smelled like a garbage pit. The return was always marked by a small smile on his face. No amount of verbal abuse stopped his venturing off into the countryside. I tried every entreaty and threat up to and including resigning from my post as burro. Nothing carried enough weight.

Beer rations for the troops.

Now this made sense. The good news was that the average young Marine did not drink much. The bulk of the enlisted Marines in Korea were in the 18 and 19 year old range and hadn't had time to start drinking. The ration system allowed for the beer to be distributed to the troops at the rate of two cans per man per week. Of course, the system was destined for failure.

Payment was required for the two allotted beers. Not much, but payment. Some didn't want it badly enough to pay. This opened one door. We scooped up personal indebtedness, people who failed to exercise options, intimidation (new guys), and outright bribes. In the end we collected far more of the beer than our allotted share. Good beer—American brands like Bud or Schlitz.

In his travels into the villages, Boost had passed an abandoned well. We rigged a netting and lowered our accumulated beer rations into the cool water of the well. By now it was July and a hot Korean summer. Our stash stayed pleasantly cool. The well was also isolated and away from the main regimental encampment.

After the daily training, our select group would head off to our peaceful spot to hoist a couple. First platoon only or by invitation. It couldn't have been a more beautiful spot. On the side of a hill, quiet, with an outstanding view of the valleys, streams, and mountains.

These gatherings were special. Even the guys who didn't help us consume the beer went along. First platoon was alone in the world with each other. Discussions were relaxed, free flowing, and covered a wide range of subjects. It was sort of a turn thing and the topics were lead by a wide variety of people. During those moments, we had not a care in the world.

It was the Professor's habit to have a couple beers and doze off. On one occasion he surfaced and inquired about the content of the discussion. Moose told him that we were discussing the pros and cons of Homer's *Odysey*. . . . Almost blew the Professor's mind!

The coming times would make the group outings at the well far more special.

The only time we got foxed was when it was announced that the next beer ration was to be "Ashai." A Japanese beer. Some declined to drink beer made in Japan. Many were still mad at the Japs for Pearl Harbor. Ten years had passed, but feelings were still strong.

Chapter 27

Most of us overlooked the boycott philosophy. Beer was far more important at this point in time. We just sucked up more options and were very proud of ourselves with 3 full cases purchased and paid for. What arrived was an unexpected surprise—each wooden case had 60 bottles of full quarts.

Timing is everything. Not long after it arrived we were saddled up and ordered back up north. An great investment gone sour.

CHAPTER 28

Kimchi

Taking an entire division off the front line was a huge organizational task. No problem for those of us with no responsibility for it—they pointed and we got in the truck and left.

Marine units are made up with everything in threes. Division, Regiment, Battalion, Company, Platoon, Squad. Three parts in each. The basic plan when something is going on, is to send two parts to go do something while the third is held back ready to help.

Being in reserve was not as good as being sent home, but being taken away from the front line positions worked for us. In reserve we were not required to defend, attack, or be on alert all night. The guys in the 2nd Army Division were doing that for us somewhere up north. We were situated about 3 or 4 miles behind their lines. Each Regiment was prepared to move up and cover 2nd Army Division if needed.

The whole idea of reserve was for us to get rested and retrained while still being ready to respond if something unusual happened.

Even in a division reserve status no Marine went about his daily activities without some sort of weapon—not even to the mess tents or our new potties. That problem was solved by purchasing or otherwise acquiring some type of side arm to carry such as a hand gun

with a holster. Trying to eat a hot meal on a tray while balancing an M-1 rifle or BAR was a pain in the ass. We wound up wearing the pistol and holster from the day we put them on until the day we left the country. Even back on line with our regular weapons, we kept them as a permanent fixture on our hips.

From the beginning every Marine was made to understand that he was a fighting man first. At the Chosin reservoir, the cooks, typists, headquarters personnel, and everyone else had taken up weapons and joined the fight.

The whole reserve thing was such a great change of pace from the previous three months. Those in charge constantly reminded us that this was not a YMCA summer camp. They could say it, but we went about each day as if it were.

The California guys never wore a shirt unless ordered to. For them, getting their tan back was a requirement. The area around each Regiment was always protected by some form of outposts. In all directions, people were placed strategically to be sure no one snuck up on us.

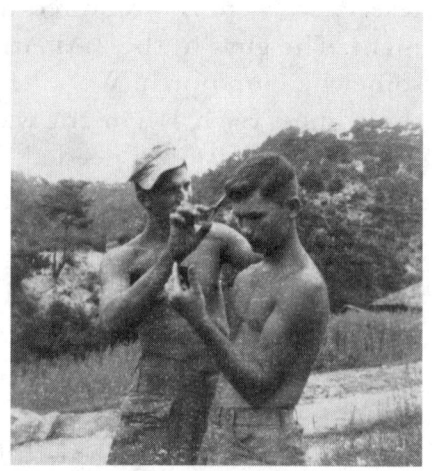

Groups of three or four men were placed where roads crossed, on hills, and other vantage points with radios and then spent what was usually a leisure day just watching. We were not exempt from these assignments. Raymond generally sent two experienced and two replacements on these excursions. The brass required the watching for security purposes and we had no objections, because it meant a no training day. Nothing much seemed to happen on these outings. Rotations were every 12 hours, so we got to sit, watch, and talk by the hour. Relationships that had been formed under fire were now extended to a more personal level. After a couple of these watching trips into the countryside, you knew the names of every one of the relatives of your companions and every life experience from their first memory to the present moment.

The small watching party was sent with food and water. On one such assignment, we were quietly sitting and talking on a small wooden bridge watching a stream and an empty dirt road. A couple hundred yards downstream a couple of Koreans had a small fire and a big pot. They appeared to be cooking something. Periodically they lifted the lid and checked the contents.

Great ideas from great people. 'New Guy' said, "What they are cooking has to be better than those dry peanut butter sandwiches they gave us. Let's see if we can work an exchange."

I answered with a shrug, "I don't know New Guy, but why not?"

The two replacements were not invited into the decision making process. In our platoon, replacements got the same routine as small children, "Speak only when spoken to."

Obviously, we knew best.

Exchanges of ideas between people of different languages, got worked out somehow. The Koreans saw our great looking sandwiches. After a lot of hand action and gestures, an agreement was arranged and all of the sandwiches were handed over.

We gestured toward the pot and held out our canteen cups. 'Papa San' lifted the lid off of the steaming pot. When the lid came off, our response was unanimous and instantaneous. Four Marines reeled backward. The smell was beyond ugly. It bore a strong resemblance to Boost when he returned from his countryside wanderings.

These Marines had met the national dish of Korea. Kimchi.

Chapter 28

God only knows what was in that particular pot. Latter the Professor gave us a run down. He told us that most likely it was a combination of rotted vegetables, rotted fish, and garlic.

A deal was a deal.

The Koreans got to keep our sandwiches and they, with our blessings, kept their kimchi.

CHAPTER 29

The big brawling stud Marine

"Come on Smart Mouth, tell us about the jail in Japan."

"Hey-no big deal"

Rivas prodded, "Some guy in Charlie recognized you and said you cleaned out a bar in Kobe, Japan on the way over here and got into a massive fight with the Army MPs. I know this guy and he is not a bull shitter. He told me that you and two other Marines were delivered to the dock in handcuffs when they were pulling up the anchor of the troop ship in Kobe. The guy said that there were three jeeps full of Army MPs and one of you in the back seat of each jeep. This guy said you were in his training platoon at Pendleton. He is sure it was you."

The squad had been lounging on cots, reading, or dozing, but the tent came to life at the possibility of a good story. So I accommodated them, "OK-which version do you want to hear?"

Moose, "How about trying the truth, Smart Mouth!!"

"OK. Moose only for you. Most of what he said was true, except the cleaning out of the bar and a massive fight with the MPs."

Jail in Japan

Three of us—Montgomery, Locisero, and I—were going down a street in Kobe and went into a Japanese bar. There was a blond lady sitting at the bar and an empty stool next to her, so I ordered a beer and sat down. She was a Russian of some sort and I gave it the full range of my Russian sweet talk. Pany mya Paruski or something like that and she smiled, so I had her drink refilled.

Trying to get across my carnal desires was not working. She had a little English, but the conversation was going nowhere.

Then I noticed a commotion behind me. I turned around and saw Montgomery arguing with a single Army MP. The basic dispute centered around the fact that this particular bar was off-limits. Montgomery was contending that he was a Marine and didn't have to do what the Army said.

The MP left and I continued my drinking and weak attempt to work something up with the nice lady. I was interrupted again by more commotion. Montgomery was a big guy and was getting loud. Now there were three MPs. They seemed to be politely pointing out the fact that there were plenty of bars in the area that were not off limits.

"There are other good bars, just not this one. OK?"

At some point Montgomery crossed their line of patience and started to get pushy. Big Mistake!!! Some scuffling and minor pushing was starting, so I decided to assess the situation. I turned and got off the stool and headed toward the area of the dispute. . . . My mistake!!

My move towards the ruckus was interpreted incorrectly. One of the MPs cold cocked me with his night stick. Ankles and elbows, they hauled me out.

I came to my senses in the Army MP station, a converted old Japanese jail with wooden bars. Montgomery, Locisero, and I were in a single cell in the middle of the room. Montgomery had eventually been subdued by numbers. Even though Locisero did not enter the fray, they took him along apparently deciding he was guilty by association.

Montgomery spent most of the night being a world class asshole, throwing out Army-related insults and whatever else came into his mind.

In the early hours of the morning one of the MPs on duty came to the bars and talked to me. He was an older man with about 5 or 6 stripes and a calm demeanor. "You need to shut that guy up–he is pissing everyone off. Are you aware that if that ship pulls out for Korea in the morning without the three of you, you will be charged as deserters? I think the Marine Corps still shoots deserters. If you can shut him up, I think the Lt. will let you out of here and put you on the troop ship just to get rid of him."

Locisero and I listened as the Sgt. spoke. Being stood against the wall and shot by the Marine Corps was not our idea of a good time. My head hurt and the large lump inflicted by the night stick was throbbing. I was in a definite foul mood.

Montgomery was one of those guys whose mouth was even bigger than his size. In fact, it was easy to figure that he was mostly mouth. He was just showing off. By this time my attitude towards him was not good and I was pissed about getting hit on the head because of his stupidity. Looking up into his face, I announced that his dental work would need replacement and a rectal surgeon would be needed to repair what I was going to rearrange. I put my finger in his face "Not ONE word out of you until we get on that boat. Not one word."

Enough was enough. It seemed as though he got the message. He finally shut up.

I called the MP over. "Sergeant, Can you please ask the lieutenant to come over? I would like to speak to him."

"Lieutenant–This stupid looking loud-mouthed Marine has seen the error of his ways. I promise you he will not utter another single word in your jail."

It had been a long night for the Lieutenant too. He looked at Montgomery searching to see if that single word was forthcoming. It did not.

Soon after daybreak, they brought three jeeps. Each of us was handcuffed with our hands behind our backs. Three

Chapter 29

jeeps, each with two fully armed MPs complete with the formal white helmet and MP arm bands. One of us was placed in the backseat of each jeep flanked with MPs sitting high above us. The jail lieutenant sat in the front seat of the lead jeep.

Because the time schedule was a bit close, the jeeps went quickly through the streets, even giving a few blasts of the horns and sirens to get people out of the way. You can imagine how it looked and sounded as we arrived at the dock where our troop ship was preparing to leave! It could not have been staged any better to get maximum attention.

Naturally the troops were lining the rails and everyone on board had to crowd forward for a better view. In what turned out to be full of drama, they unloaded us, removed the handcuffs, and the MP Lieutenant led us up the gangway and turned us over to the officer of the deck.

The Marines along the railings made a lot of noise and seemed to enjoy the show.

The Lieutenant had made the prisoner exchange and turned to go down the gangway. Big mouth Montgomery called out to the Lieutenant–and, as he turned to look back, Montgomery flipped him off.

End of legend.

Chapter 30

When a Marine gets a medal, it is also for those of us around him

Pass the word. First Battalion 7th Marines were to fall out at 1300 hours for a medal ceremony. Our instructions were to wear clean utilities and look like Marines. The Battalion and Regimental commanders were making the presentations.

Even in the middle of a clearing in the middle of nowhere Korea the medal ceremony was impressive.

First, the regimental colors were presented. The colors and streamers hung proudly from their staffs. Each streamer represented a Presidential Unit Citation earned by the 7th Marines. A well-decorated military unit.

Our Regimental Commander spoke. He told us we were special. He said that we had fought like tigers these last months. The full bird Colonel made it clear that it was an honor for him to be our commanding officer. Not one of us knew his name, but he sure looked and talked like a Marine.

Sanchez, from second platoon, and Doc got their Silver Stars. It was the second one for Sanchez. Our platoon leader got a Bronze Star. Once we were dismissed, Charles invited Doc to our tent for a celebration. First, Doc had to stay for picture taking by the Navy. They were as proud of him as we were.

After the ceremony, we moved back to the comfort of our squad tent.

Charles could always be counted on to come up with the unusual, and this occasion was no exception. After all, it was his sorry ass that Doc had carried out of the mine field. How he did it, no one will never know, but he came up with four bottles of Four Roses American whiskey.

When Doc entered our tent, Charles spoke. "Attention on Deck for the United States Navy. Stand at attention. Present Arms." Each of us stood straight and tall and gave Doc a snappy salute. Doc was a shy man, but there was no question that it got to him.

Charles then gave a toast—whiskey in metal canteen cups with handles. "To the swab jockey with Elephant Balls. Hear! Hear!"

We knew that it was not required that each of us go on every patrol. Every time a patrol went, though, Doc went with them. He was constantly exposed to the dangers on each and every one of the forays into enemy territory. The only weapon he carried was a .45 on his hip for personal protection. Doc was out there far more than any of us, but since he was so quiet, we forgot at times what he did on a routine basis.

Doc didn't hang out long with us. On his way out of our tent he stopped at the opening. He looked back at us and said, "Guys, I would trade that Silver Star for your salute any day of the week."

When Doc left to go back to the Corpsmen's tent, the conversation turned to the Bronze Star the platoon leader, our lieutenant, had received. He was an OK platoon leader, but the wording of the commendation seemed to say that he did a bit more than any one of us remembered.

He had been with us four to five weeks and had gone a couple platoon probing actions. He got his job done like the rest of us, but it was agreed within the group, that no one had seen him do anything special.

The conversation shifted to the particular patrol mentioned in the citation and to Villareal, who had been on that patrol. The way we remembered it, a couple guys had gotten their tits in the ringer and Villareal had been the one to bail them out. He had definitely gone out on a limb and made some pretty ballsy moves to get the job done. No one seemed too upset about the lieutenant getting a medal but mostly they were disturbed that Eduardo had not been recognized.

Since Charles and I had already hashed out this dilemma, I piped up, "Charles, it is your party—explain to them how it works."

"OK. Guys—listen. Look at the ring on the Lieutenant's finger. You will see the same ring on the finger of our Executive Officer. Those are rings from the U. S. Naval Academy."

Goat interrupted, "How did they get in the Marine Corps if they went to a Naval Academy?"

Charles responded, "When you get out of the Naval Academy and graduate near the top of the class, you get a choice of which service you want to be in. The Navy or the Marines. These guys must have chosen the Marines."

Chapter 30

The graduates from the service academies become like a special group—they watch out for each other. Cover each others backs. Promotions, performance reviews, and stuff like that. That Bronze Star is part of that clubby thing."

Moose turned to Hack, "Harold, that isn't right!"

Hack, "You are correct Moose, it is not right but it is just a form of reality. That is all. Just the way it works. No harm done."

The Four Roses ceremonial whiskey was finished and Charles produced a bottle or two of the local stuff. "Old Camel." Needless to say, some declined this kind offer, most turning it down with derogatory remarks about its appearance and tacky label. Some were very rude about the quality of the product, referring to it possibly being some sort of liquid produced by a real camel.

After being invited to speak on medals and stuff, Charles kept the floor. Between the Four Roses and a touch of "Old Camel," he was more than ready to deliver a message or two.

For awhile there was not a sound or comment as Charles held court. "Look—every one of us in 1st platoon has put himself in the line of fire. You candy-assed replacements will soon get your turn. That alone entitles each of us to a medal. Every man who has ever put on the Marine uniform is entitled to a medal. Just putting on that uniform means that when the time comes for you to put it on the line, you will stand tall.

It does not mean that you are superman or impervious to fear. It means that when the shit hits the fan, you will do your job and also know that the Marine on either side of you will be doing the same. Courage is not the absence of fear, but overcoming fear and getting the job done.

If you think that Doc had no fear going into that rice paddy and carrying my worthless ass out, you are dead wrong. Doc had courage because he overcame that fear. In our time here in this country we have all done it and will do it again.

How many guys do you think there were in WWII and here in Korea that did big time hero stuff and got killed on the spot when no one was looking? Mama gets an American flag and a Purple

Heart, in the place of her son. You just can't give medals to everyone. They are a symbol. When a guy gets a medal it is for of each of us around him.

Always give credit to those who receive them, because one way on another, they earned it."

Charles was eloquent . . . and correct. What he had said of others also applied to him. We had seen him go "above and beyond" more than once.

His speech over, Charles took a swig and said "Hey this 'Old Camel' is pretty good whiskey! Maybe I can import it to the U. S." This was typical Charles. Though his reasoning at that point might have been clouded, he was always thinking and always hustling.

Charles could be aggressive and abrasive. Most of the time he acted like he was certain he was smarter than we were, and maybe he was. This day, though, he gave us all a lift with his ceremony and speech.

CHAPTER 31

Pay day stakes

First platoon. Everywhere we went, we went together.

There were various activities for the Marines in reserve, including a makeshift outdoor movie theater and a movie every night. We all went or none went. A small USO show passed through. We all went because they had a couple of real live girls and we wanted to look to be sure we remembered what one looked like.

Among the units, there were some naturally talented people including singers, dancers, and magicians. Someone had the idea to organize a talent show. <u>That</u> we all went to. During the show some guy claimed to be a hypnotist. When he went on the stage, he got cat calls from his fellow Marines who didn't believe in that hocus pocus.

The hypnotist asked for a volunteer so we sent one of our replacements. It was not real 'volunteering,' with Goat pointing to the stage and saying "You. Go."

It was the damndest thing. The kid was hypnotized and told he was in the middle of a mine field with incoming mortars. His reaction was scary—he did the fastest two-step. It was clearly real to him. We left as new believers in the art of hypnotism. Afterwards, our replacement remembered nothing.

The poker game started soon after we arrived in reserve. It started as a game for the big hairy-chested guys—those 'sophisti-

cated' 20-year-olds with all of their worldly experience. Of course, issues had to be resolved! . . . such as, how much to play for, what worked as money, and who could play.

None of us had real money. They had given us some sort of script that was supposed to be money. It looked too much like monopoly money, so it was not acceptable. We came up with a system called "Pay Day Stakes," an arrangement whereby you would eventually draw the money from the paymaster and settle up. You bought into the game with a piece of paper on which you had written your name, serial number, and an amount of money. When you ran out of that money, another piece of paper went into the pot.

Little did we know at the time how some of those scraps of paper would bring tears to these grown young men in the months to come.

It didn't take long before the heavy hitters of the poker world—Hack, Herman, and Boost got bored with level of betting and the quality of the players. They dropped out. Little Ski had dropped out early because of what he called " low standards of poker integrity. " He declared that he could not play for ethical reasons. Funny little guy. To the end of reserve, whenever they were playing he continued

Chapter 31

to try to impose his personal standards for poker on those playing. This was accomplished by yelling and making disparaging remarks about the quality of the players and their heritage.

Rivas dropped out when someone introduced a game called 7 card stud Mexican poker. He didn't drop out because of the name of the game. It was because 2s, 4s, and 6s plus one-eyed jacks were declared wild. He dropped out because "that is not <u>real</u> poker!!" Not to mention the fact that the guy that tried to introduce that version did not even know if six jacks beat seven 10s.

New Guy came into the game after announcing his expertise at poker. His first question was, "Do two pair beat three of a kind?" It went downhill from there.

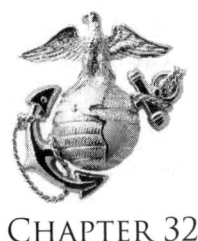

Chapter 32

There is no such thing as an ex-Marine

One replacement made his mark with the group immediately. He ran across a friend from his home town that drove an ambulance for the Regimental sick bay, and came back to the tent with several bottles of 190 proof medical alcohol. This moved him up the acceptance scale dramatically.

Hack immediately covered the hard and fast procedural rules that applied to this type of situation. Villareal, Hack, and Herman took possession of the contraband as fully accredited representatives of the squad.

Absolute alcohol . . . for medical purposes only. Since this powerful stuff was about two to three times as strong as vodka, cutting the stuff for consumption was the biggest problem. Juice from our fruit cocktail stash was not the best choice, but it would have to do.

An unplanned private evening squad party.

Collecting in the squad tent, half the group was almost instantly boiled to the eyeballs—especially the Professor.

As usual we became our own entertainment. Without a formal program and in no particular order the topics up for discussion ran the gamut.

Surprisingly, some of the guys were unaware of how or why this war they were fighting in had started. The Professor told about the

North Koreans and their unexpected invasion of South Korea in 1950. He covered world politics and the threat of Communism. He explained that among others Russia, China, and North Korea were communist countries. He lightly went over how that form of government was different from ours. All to an interested audience.

The Professor then explained how Korea came to be divided into the two countries of North Korea and South Korea after World War II. The occupying Japanese surrendered the territory above the 38th parallel to the Russian troops and below that line to the United States. He informed us that we were quite close to that line of demarcation now. Everyone loved to listen to the Professor. Most likely he would have had the floor all night but he passed out and was put to bed on his cot.

Boost was a study on any day. Each word carefully chosen and meaningful. You would expect alcohol to loosen his tongue. Wrong. He simply enjoyed watching and listening to his friends. As the night wore on the slight smile remained in place. Then, the alcohol hit dead center in his brain. He also required the assistance of two replacements to deposit him, still smiling, on his cot.

The Hombres slurred their way badly through two Mariachi songs. Awful. They were hooted down, midway through the second try.

A popular and frequent topic was Boot Camp Drill Instructors. Every Marine who ever lived truly believes that his DI was the toughest and meanest. It became a turn thing and everyone got to tell one story. There can be no doubt that boot camp and how it works is one of the backbone elements of the Marine Corps. The stories were quite different, but if you listened closely, the thread was always the same and involved firm discipline in one form or another—something almost every one of these young men had managed to resist up until they found the Marine Corps.

Jose told one of the best DI stories. Drill Instructors were still allowed to use a variety of forms of physical violence. He described a fellow boot who continually ruined the platoon marching formation because of a lack of understanding about his right and left foot. The platoon would make a turn and this guy would be thrashing about in the middle of the formed lines. Finally the DI kicked the kid in the left calf and said, "Now, when I say left, turn on the one that hurts."

The expression "there is no such thing as an ex-Marine" is a true statement. It really doesn't matter what era they served in, all Marines share the boot camp experience. That part of our lives gives utter strangers a known common denominator.

All in all, it was a great party.

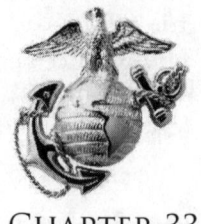

Chapter 33

Yeah, we know . . . start digging

It had been a fun party, and most did not make the mess tent for breakfast.

Raymond entered the tent and quietly observed bodies in deep sleep.

"OK. Ladies. Girl Scout Summer Camp is over. Start packing. We are headed back to the front line tonight."

Unintelligible, muffled responses, and some movement.

Someone managed to ask, "Where?"

"Some place they are calling the Punchbowl. From the maps it looks like it is just east of where we were before. You guys had better get to breakfast, hot meals are coming to an end."

More grunts, groans, and assorted noises.

Once Raymond left you could hear, "Shit!"

"I like it here."

By day's end we were saddled up and ready for the hike north. Our journey needed to begin in the middle of the night because we would need to complete our exchange on line before daylight.

Soon after dark the trek north started. Summer rains had subsided during the day, but not at night. Rain punctuated the night-long hike and we were soon cold, wet, and miserable.

After hours of trooping across the wet Korean landscape and making the final climb up the mountain, the usual hole by hole exchange started. It was literally hole by hole because these positions were nothing but holes with a connecting trench. No bunkers, no barb wire—zilch.

It was our turn to exchange positions, and Boost and I were led down the muddy trench to a simple water filled hole. The two army occupants gave us a grunt type greeting and quickly scurried out of the hole and down the hill. Couldn't really blame them. We were too cold and wet to bitch about the Army.

The order came down that tonight was a 50% watch night.

Boost offered, "I'll take the first one."

"How long for each watch?"

"I'll let you know when it is your turn."

The holes we inherited were a little more than chest deep. Both the hole and the trench were filled above knee level with cold muddy water and there was no sign of the rain letting up.

Out of reserve and back on line. "Who is out there? Would tonight be one of the quiet nights or are they coming?"

The months in Korea had paid off in one respect—most of us, myself included, had acquired a talent for cat napping. Young bodies recover quickly. In a line position, however, this type of rest created other problems. For one, the mind would play tricks. The deepest of sleep could be broken by a huge adrenalin rush. Then there was the recurring dream of falling asleep on watch, which would send four gallons of adrenalin throughout the entire body.

After awhile, I surfaced from sleep, looked up and saw Boost, sitting silently looking north into the night.

Chapter 33

"My turn?"

"No, I've got it."

Two or three times more, I would come to and ask again. Each time the answer had been the same. "No, I've got it." The last time I opened my eyes, it was dawn.

"Jesus, Boost, you are not my baby sitter, why didn't you wake me?"

"I didn't feel like sleeping, and you need the beauty sleep."

How do I love you, let me count the ways. The son of a bitch had been just as tired, just as cold, and just as wet as I.

We had tried to protect our sleeping bags against the elements but they had gotten wet. It would be days before they fully dried.

Raymond appeared. As predictable as the sun.

I looked up at him, "Yeah, we know, start digging."

"There may be hope for you Smart Mouth. You do not learn fast, but you seem to retain some of what you have learned. This hole looks like it is a good place. Build the bunker there, start the barbed wire from that point. I will get some axes or saws, those trees out front have to come down. They obstruct your field of fire. When they are down, cut them in 4 foot pieces for the top of the bunker."

Raymond was then off to the next hole. He assessed the area around the hole where Rivas and Villareal had found their new home and laid out the positioning and architectural designs for the bunker and fields of fire. Off to the next hole.

Our construction work on this line of defense had started. For a week or so we had no nightly interruptions from our friends to the

north, which gave the Raymond Construction Company time to turn a sorry group of holes and trenches into a reasonably acceptable defensive position.

Bunker construction left room for personal architectural ideas. Fundamentals always remained the same—a hole in the ground, sand bags, and logs. The sand bags were rough gunny sacks which we filled with dirt. Once filled, they weighed about 75 pounds each and were ready to be used as the big 'bricks' that formed the bunker walls. The front slit opening of the bunker required careful attention, so that it combined protection and good vision.

After dealing with Raymond over time, we had become fully aware of the balance between personal protection and a full view to the front. After the front opening was properly constructed, a couple of layers of thick pine logs and more sandbags on top completed the structure. We then covered the bunker with branches, leaves, and rocks to provide the appearance of naturalness. Raymond had us well-conditioned—if the bunker failed to meet his standards, we got to start over.

Off to our right about 400 yards the trench line dipped sharply down to a crude dirt road. At that juncture there was a road block with a huge tank as its center piece. From the road, the hill on other side went up sharply. This natural gap was the entrance to

Chapter 33

the whole valley. The shape of the valley in front of us was unique. Without much imagination we could see that it might be the top of an extinct volcano or perhaps a spot where a meteor hit. It was truly shaped like a 'Punch Bowl'.

The valley in front of us was lush with a fast-moving river from the north. This pretty little river made a gentle turn below us and continued directly across our front. Our new line position stood about 800 meters above the valley floor. In the full sun it was a beautiful sight. Across the pretty valley a mountain ridge with several peaks was in full view. The beauty of those mountain peaks would have been marred if we had known we were going to become all too familiar with them. Those were hills 673 and 749.

We were told the hill to our right and on the other side of the road block was defended by the ROKs, Republic of Korea soldiers. No one remembered being tied into one of their units. From rumors the general attitude about them was not a good one because we had heard reports that indicated that they were not always great under fire. If the rumors were true, our real problem was that if anyone were to get past them they would be at our backs. The ROKs might or might not have been good under fire, but they were trigger happy. Every night sounded like the 4th of July.

Patrols went down into the valley on a daily basis. We were well acquainted with the river as we needed to cross it on a regular basis. Generally our patrols were not bothered. Rumors were that units of the North Korean Army were defending hills 673 and 749. That was anything but good news. For the moment, the North Koreans appeared to be content to wait on their high ground.

One patrol from these positions was different from all of the others. Quite possibly this event ended the warm and fuzzy relationship between Raymond and me.

CHAPTER 34

The worst sniper in Marine history

One warm sunny Korean afternoon, Sgt. Raymond came down the trench in his usual business-like manner. "I am looking for three men who qualified as expert with the M-1." Rivas, Escamilla, and I were supposed to be doing construction work with entrenching tools. More bunker building and trench digging. We had been having a less than happy discussion about the nature of our work and bitching about the rate of pay. We had calculated that our $90.00 monthly pay rate worked out to about 15 cents an hour. We had also decided that our delicate hands were not meant for shovel work.

I responded to Raymond immediately, "For Christ's sake, Raymond, I set the record with the M-1 at Camp Matthews. That record goes all the way back to World War II. What do you mean by expert?"

Camp Matthews was the rifle range where all San Diego Marine recruits went during boot camp to learn all about the M-1 rifle. They gave us extensive demonstrations of the weapon and lectures about safety. After more instructions each recruit was given a turn using the rifle with real bullets. We practiced by shooting at paper targets with the circles and bulls eyes.

At the end of the week at Camp Matthews we had a qualifying test. Pretty important stuff. We each got a turn all by ourselves and they kept score. A score of 180 was needed to qualify as a

Marine rifleman. Another 20 points or so made you a Sharp Shooter and those who seemed to know what they were doing and got a bunch more points and became Expert Riflemen. Each category earned you a special badge that you would eventually wear on your uniform.

Of course, I was lying to Raymond. I had barely squeaked past the 180 qualifying mark. Raymond being the straight forward person that he was, accepted my original answer as fact.

"OK Smart Mouth. You go."

Now, there in the trench with my entrenching tool, it dawned on me that this line of inquiry was actually leading to something. "Go? Go where?"

"Sniper patrol. We leave just after midnight. We are going up to that peak you see across the valley. The map shows a number on it, hill 673."

"Shit Raymond, 673 is meters. In feet that is multiplied by three. Almost 2000 feet high. . . . I have changed my mind about going. Give someone else the benefit of the experience. I have something else to do. Besides I really like digging and being here with my two best friends in the world. Going down from our hill alone is about 1500 feet and up that hill another 2000—way too much climbing for me. Besides, there is not time on my busy construction schedule for that kind of an outing."

Raymond always kept his communications to only necessary words. With a simple nod, he affirmed that I was a member of the sniper patrol. He completed his select traveling party with Villareal and Moose and instructed us, "Be at the CP ready to go at 23:30." In a few words, Raymond explained to us that the basic plan was to get down off our hill and up their hill before the sun comes up and be ready to "snipe."

The hour came and we were off. We made our way through the wire and down into the valley using a supposedly 'safe' route.

"Safe, Right!!" I thought to myself. "The whole fucking valley could be full of very unfriendly people." The only good part was that we did not have to wear our helmets. On this type of patrol we had the option of wearing our soft cover fatigue hat instead. Moving at any time with the helmet was a task. It did protect, but it was cumbersome. Going down a hill in the dark of the night was difficult enough. The valley also smelled like shit with its human-waste fertilized rice paddies.

We were under strict orders to be quiet. With Raymond along, we were going by the U. S. Marine Corps BOOK. Not a mumble, grumble, bitch, or derogatory comment. We were told that there would not be a single spoken word on this patrol.

Not having read the BOOK, I was not so sure what was covered there, but since Raymond was the leader of the group. I told myself to pretend I had. Our platoon sergeant obviously had a badly warped mind. He actually believed that the Marine Corps knew what it was doing.

After making it down the mountain, we had to deal with the river, which was swollen, big time, from the rains. I broke the imposed silence to point out the obvious to Raymond. "We can't get across. We had better go back"

"One more spoken word from you before we finish this patrol, Smart Mouth, and I will deal with you personally."

"I was really quite warm, and I wanted to cool off, Sergeant, Sir. Let's find a way to cross this river."

Up was next. Ascending the 2000 foot slope in the dark, and doing so quietly was neither easy nor fun. When the group neared the summit of the hill, Raymond used hand and arm signals to position each of us.

First light found four Marines prone, well spread out, and hidden under low hanging pine trees, apparently undetected. We could clearly see the valley, the river, and our own beloved hill where I would have been sleeping except for a major impediment. A very large and overactive big mouth.

Taking in the view did not last long. Out of the corner of my eye, I spotted Raymond gesturing. I was not caught up with, or

Chapter 34

into all of the hand and arm signals, though they did seem reasonably uncomplicated. The day the Marine Corps tried to teach this particular skill I must have taken a mental day off. What I did gather from Raymond's form of non verbal communication was that I had been elected to take the first "snipe."

There had been movement on the ridge opposite our positions. One of the North Koreans had come out of his bunker to take a morning leak. Another gesture and a formidable look from Raymond. Not much doubt about what he wanted. The look said "YOU, stupid. Take the shot!"

This was one of those things called 'a moment of truth.' The 'truth' was that having barely qualified at Camp Matthews with the M-1 rifle, someone else should have had the honor of going first. I had always considered my performance at the rifle range to be a shortcoming of the Marine Corps rather than my own. Reason being that I naturally fired a rifle left handed, but the Marine Corps would not let anyone shoot their rifle left handed because in their infinite wisdom the shell of an M-1 ejected to the right and would obscure your vision. So the message had been, "You will fire right handed and you WILL qualify." The lefty-righty debate could be argued from either side. I thought about waving Raymond off and considered crawling over to his spot and giving him my insights on the issue. We could then discuss it rationally.

But Raymond's eyes spoke—"Shoot. NOW!!!"

A quick pull on the trigger of my M-1, and a rifle shot echoed over the forest area. "They did teach on the rifle range that squeezing the trigger rather than pulling it helped with steadiness and accuracy.

The bullet did not even come close to the North Korean soldier. He gave no indication that anything had happened anywhere near him. The guy pulled up his pants, stretched and returned to his bunker. At least he could have had the decency to jump, scream, or exhibit some form of professional courtesy. If that North Korean had any sensitivity, and knew what my sergeant's response would be, he would have surely done something more dramatic.

After my errant shot, we went down off the hill and into the valley to find a spot where we could quietly remain hidden for the rest of the day to avoid detection. Once darkness arrived, we made our way back through the river, up the hill, and through the perimeter.

Once safely within the perimeter, a 'Sgt. Raymond shit storm' hit.

Sergeant 'Got Balls' was my friend. He had previously spoken highly of me. He had spoken well of me in general and also about my fighting ability. At times he had even put me in charge of others. Personal relationships have highs and lows.

First came the loud and animated speech about the missed shot. Next about the phoney record setting at Camp Matthews. Raymond was usually a man of few words. I thought he was being too wordy and overreacting, but "Why hurt his feelings?" I thought to myself. "Don't tell him. Let him get it out of his system, he will then feel better about the whole thing."

Then—If I were to live to be a hundred, I would never make a dumber remark. "Raymond, you didn't ask me if my record with the rifle at Camp Matthews was high or low!"

How I came away from that encounter without physical damage became one of our platoon's legends and remained a mystery. The most likely reason was the Marine Corps had hard and fast rules about a non-commissioned officer beating the living shit out of a stupid big mouth PFC.

CHAPTER 35

673—The ultimate moment of truth

September 11, 1951

We had taken hills, attacked, been attacked, been surprised, patrolled, ambushed, and survived the action at the 'slot.' The whole works.

This was different.

In a way, the first time guys were lucky. They simply didn't know what they were seeing. Look up and down the line and into the eyes of those who had been there for awhile—we knew.

This WAS different. Way different.

None of us were antsy to get started and get it over with.

Raymond had passed the word before we started the long climb up this mountain. In the dark of the night in the valley below, he told us our objective—a direct frontal assault to take Hill 673. Two of 1st platoon's squads would make the initial attack and the third squad would back up.

We were to have begun the assault prior to daylight, but day broke and no signal came. Even without a watch, we knew it was at least two hours *after* daybreak. All advantage of surprise was gone.

God Bless the United States Marine Corps for what it is. From the lowest private to the highest rank, there is no back off when there was a job to be done. Though it was now daylight, withdrawing our two-squad attack force of twenty-six Marines was not going to happen. Not an option. The order was to take the hill. We waited.

Hopefully, somewhere behind us someone was trying to point out that it was time for some kind of alternate plan. Pull back, get a superior force, and start over. Looking at the entrenchments at the top of the hill it was obvious that a force of twenty-six men was not going to take this hill, today, or any other day.

For the experienced Marines amongst the twenty-six laying in the dirt and waiting, it was agony. Having the turmoil of a fire fight, or a nasty patrol was one thing. The mind was busy with moving, acting, and responding. Not so here.

Periodically, shell fire to soften up the bunkers and the warriors at the top of Hill 673 started, let up, was quiet, and started again. Each time it stopped, we expected to see the puff of white phosphorus, which was our signal to begin the assault.

Among the experienced, not a word was spoken, not a move was made. Those men waiting for their first action looked over at us 'old' guys. Their eyes looked for a sign, a reassuring nod. Something. Anything to help them understand what was happening around them.

Time stood absolutely still. Flat on the ground, we were each behind any protection available. The body was still, but the mind was working. "Do I have what it takes to stand up and start up this hill? Am I a real Marine, or have I just been pretending that I am?" Or, the scariest thought of all, "My God, what if I am unable to stand up and do it?"

"Today is tomorrow's history."

"God, give me the courage to be a real Marine."

Crouched behind the embankment, looking right and left, I could see most of the twenty-six who were set to begin the assault of hill 673. First and second squads of 1st platoon, Baker Company 7th Marines. I could see most of those who had been with me the last several months. On the far left were Hack and Moose. They

Chapter 35

were hunkered down near a couple of recent replacements. Farthest on the right were Los Hombres. Two brand new squad leaders were waiting quietly, centered and ready in the middle of their squads.

I spotted the Professor, Goat, and Charles waiting motionless in the dirt.

New Guy was in plain sight in a hole behind the only tree stump. Boost and I flanked our new fire team leader with little Ski off to the side. Herman and his new fire team leader were behind another small rise.

Our two new fire team leaders had just re-joined the company. Both had been in Korea before. When it was discovered that they were only seventeen they had been sent to Japan to wait for their 18th birthday and had returned less than a week ago.

Looking up Hill 673, there were two distinct small parallel ridges with gullies between. The slope itself was uphill every step of the way, a 30 to 45 degree angle. At the top it was easy to see the openings of well spaced bunkers. Each was attached by a trench line and each had protective mounds of dirt and rocks. It was hard to tell the full distance to the top of the hill—maybe 200, maybe 300 yards to the crest. What we *could* tell was that there was not a shred of cover with the exception of a couple of natural dips in the ground and lots of shell holes. Pine trees, once plentiful, had been completely leveled, leaving no natural protection. The rocks that had been there and even the volcanic soil had been pulverized by repeated shelling. The ground was nothing but fine dust, the consistency of flour.

Someone ordered this assault. Someone planned this assault. Hill 673 is well north of the 38th parallel and definitely in North Korea. We knew that the people defending at the top of this hill were North Korean troops. This was their country and they were not ready to give it up to us. From where we were, looking up the slope, this assault was an idea that had not been well thought out. Whoever did the planning and ordering the assault had not been with us at the 'slot.' More likely, those who had participated in this planning had never tried a frontal assault. Much less in full daylight.

The positions we had hastily built in two or three days at the 'slot' had been adequate. Nothing like we were seeing at the top of this hill. These bunkers were solidly constructed and most likely went well under ground to provide protection from the artillery. They had been placed well below the crest of the hill and appeared to have excellent fields of fire. The last 25 or 30 yards to the top were wide open and the ground was cut away to provide dropping areas for grenades.

All approaches to the top were well-zeroed in with mortars. A given.

When we had defended the 'slot' there had been plenty of natural cover for the enemy troops until the last 40 or 50 yards. Here we were looking at about 200 to 300 hundred yards of wide open area with no protection. The ridges close to the top were similar to the slot. The two ridges also funneled to the center of a small draw near the summit. Anyone getting near the top of this hill would be forced to center.

For those of us who had been at the 'slot,' it was not time to replay that movie in our minds. Four or five hundred Chinese who tried *us* out using a frontal assault in the dead of the night. We didn't even want to think about what happened to them.

The white phosphorus shell exploded. The wait was over. The signal for the assault had been given.

Twenty-six men went to the crouch, rose to their feet and took the first step.

That first step was the last for both squad leaders. They were cut down by small arms or machine gun fire. The rest of our skirmish line moved forward, well strung out along the two ridges, 15 to 20 yards between each man. Peripheral vision showed progress.

The shit had hit the fan in the ultimate sense of the word. Shells, fragments, dirt, rocks filled the air. The far right of our line was moving forward. The same on the left.

After a dozen steps, the whole world shrank into 30 or 40 yards of focus. Multiple explosions, fine dust everywhere, machine gun fire ripping the ground. The entire area was nothing but flying dirt, rocks, and fine dust. The noises and smells of war

Chapter 35

filled the air.

The whole world was now nothing but our single fire team. Boost was giving everything he had with the BAR, moving forward and pumping fire toward the bunkers at the top. I fired my M-1 from the shoulder and kept moving up the hill—reloading, moving, and firing. The fine dust made traction difficult. Every step was a struggle. Our fire team was in the middle and slightly ahead of the rest of the assault line. Noise, noise, noise. Mortars, mines, machine guns, and grenades. Huge volumes of combined dirt and dust fly. The air was filled with the stink of the explosives.

My throat was dry, layered with fine dust. Difficult to get a full clear breath. This was ugly.

We kept moving forward. Preford, our fire team leader, was moving and firing, headed upward toward the crest of the hill. He was positioned between Boost and me and a step or two ahead of us. Little Ski was no longer with us.

Looking right and left, we saw no one.

About 20 yards in front of our fire team a single big Marine was attacking. He was alone going full speed toward the top of the hill, firing his BAR as he went.

Preford, Boost, and I were still moving up the hill. Preford looked right and left and gave the signal to hit the deck.

As Preford touched the ground, he was thrown into the air, spinning and cart-wheeling, like a rag doll. A huge explosion.

His body remained suspended in the air forever.

Boost and I moved sideways towards Preford and met at the lifeless form that had just hit the ground. Life on this earth for the 18-year-old was over.

A helpless horrible feeling.

At the top of the hill, the single Marine was perched, still firing his BAR and throwing grenades into the open slits of the bunkers.

Boost and I were alone with our fallen fire team leader on the slope of the hill. We had stopped attacking. This attack was over.

We were motionless, one on either side of his lifeless body.

Time had stopped. Preford may have been dead for a minute, five, or ten minutes before either of us would admit it.

It had become eerily quiet. The noises of war had stopped.

Quietly Boost asked "Is that your blood or his?"

Looking down for the first time, I found the entire right side of my hip and leg covered in blood. I tried to move it for a better look, but the leg would not move. "Mostly mine."

Boost told me, "We need to get back down this hill—for sure we are not going up."

"Boost, I can't move the leg. You go."

"Smart Mouth, Preford is dead—you are not. We were not going to leave him and I am not going to leave you. There are mines on this slope, you try to crawl and you will find one for sure."

Whatever separates one person's luck from another will never be known. Boost had been my luck from the moment I got off the truck on my first day in this country.

This day, this place. No one had ever had better luck with partner picking than I.

Boost was quiet for a moment, then spoke.

"Here is what we are going to do."

On his command, I held Boost's BAR and my own rifle. Boosted picked me up along with the entire load. He cradled me in his arms. Fully loaded he took off at full speed toward the bottom of the hill. In a small protected culvert in front of the machine gun positions, he laid me down. The spot was a shell hole and a measure of cover. Boost shouted to those behind the embankment. "We are coming in, no firing!"

Boost told me "You first." The machine guns were silent and I popped my head over the small rise and started to crawl over the hump.

At that precise moment, Monaghan the trusty "Boston Southie" machine gunner chose to open up with covering fire toward

Chapter 35

the top of the hill. The machine gun spit out fire from a barrel six inches from my head. Luck—how does that figure? In the noise and confusion he hadn't heard the "no firing" cry from Boost. Once over the rise I quieted Monaghan and his machine gun with a massive collection of well chosen words. Then I pulled Boost over.

Enfilade or is it defilade? How many times did we hear that during training? Whatever it was, I remembered it was a protected area safe from direct fire. Whatever the term was, we were in it.

Boost and I were in sort of a pile or heap. No words. Nothing. Two physically and completely emotionally spent Marines. Our brains had stopped functioning and the raw nervous system was getting ready to kick in.

The absence of not having every weapon and explosive device of the North Korean Army trying to dismember us was such a simple pleasure.

CHAPTER 36

Herman Sobel and Raymond Gotshall—my heroes

We lay there for some time when, looking over the embankment and up the slope, we noticed movement. Boost and I moved over into holes on the right and left of Monaghan's machine gun.

A single figure was moving on the slope. Up, down, right and left. He would stop, drop to the ground next to what appeared to a body, fire towards the top of the hill, and then move again.

It was Raymond.

Boost commanded Monaghan to resume fire into the bunkers at the top. "Cover him."

Boost and I joined Monaghan, firing into the bunkers at the top of the hill. Boost's next command was to two Marines who had not taken part in the assault and were laying in the dirt behind us. "Fill the BAR magazines." As he emptied each one, he threw it over his shoulder back to the two Marines behind him.

They did as ordered. Filled and returned.

He then pointed to me. Another order.

"Keep him in ammo." The response of the two Marines was immediate and efficient. The orders could not have been more promptly followed had Boost been the Commandant of the Marine Corps. The machine gun, BAR, and my M-1 put out every round of cover possible as Raymond scoured the ridge.

Raymond. He was moving sideways along the slope checking on each of the men in his platoon. He would retrieve one, carry him down the slope, then surrender him to a corpsman. Then he would grab another weapon and more ammo . . . then go back up the hill. Again and again, looking, firing, and moving. Sergeant Raymond Gotshall covered the side of that hill until there was no one left out there with a chance to live.

The best Monaghan, Boost, and I could do was give him as much covering fire as possible.

With the intensity of covering Raymond, I had not even noticed that a corpsman I had never seen before was hunched down and was cutting the pants leg off of my dungarees.

"Got some ugly ones here buddy—but you will live. The good news is that I will clean you up, give you a little blood and you will get a free ride out of here."

The Corpsman started a transfusion of blood, cleaned, bandaged, and tagged me and was off.

In that shell hole, my mind was working and not working at the same time. "How am I supposed to feel? Is it wrong to have a good feeling hearing that I am going to leave?"

By now my nervous system had begun to function normally. Adrenalin was no longer pumping a gallon a second.

Looking up, I saw a familiar face. Herman's hulk had appeared over the edge of my hole. Immediately he piled into the hole on top of me. His eyes were fully dilated—not a speck of white. The huge Marine who had attacked Hill 673 and gotten all the way to the top by himself had been Herman.

Hard to tell about stuff like adrenalin and shock phases. My good friend was somewhere in a combination of one or the other. He was the last one in.

Herman replayed what had happened at the top of the hill and on his return trip down the hill in bursts of words. The tall Corporal had not realized that he was alone and ahead of everyone in the assault. He had seen his fire team leader, the other 17-year-old just turned 18, take a bullet to the head. Herman had no idea that the two other Marines in his fire team had not made it even 15 yards up the hill. He had continued his one man assault to the top, completely focused. Near the crest of the hill he secured a position just under the openings of the enemy bunkers. This single Marine had thrown all of his grenades into the bunker openings and continued firing his BAR into the slits. Only as he had stopped to reload his BAR with the last of his magazines, had he realized that it was completely quiet. He looked around and realized that he alone was at the top of hill 673.

"The most alone, alone feeling in the world."

Herman had always been one of the brighter guys. After realizing he was truly alone, he made the correct assessment of the situation. The bunkers were pinned down and no longer firing. He stood up with the BAR at port arms and sprinted down the two or three hundred yards back to our positions.

He had not a scratch. The big body was untouched.

Not so with his brain. It was permanently etched with each moment.

He had come down the hill and into my hole, landing on top of my bloody leg. All 6 feet plus and 180 pounds.

Herman had just been to the top of hill 673. All by himself. Assaults on 673 were tried daily on each of the following five days. Each attempt was made after increased shell fire and with greater numbers of Marines in each assault. The repeated attempts on 673 and its sister hill, 749, had taken the middle out of the 7th Marine Regiment. There were not enough able men left to finish the job. On day five, two battalions from the 5th Marine Regiment in full assault made it to the top and secured hill 673.

The complete irony was that during the following five days, two valiant Marines earned the Congressional Medal of Honor on hill 673. Both medals were awarded to their parents because each gave up their lives attempting to take that damn hill. Later both Herman and Raymond were written up for that medal, but it was not awarded. Apparently our platoon leader had not seen what they had done. Strange.

Chapter 36

Herman's dilated eyes began to return to normal.

"Hey Herm, would you mind getting your fat ass off my leg?"

"Shit—what happened to you?"

* * *

Twenty-six men entered the history of the United State Marine Corps that morning.

Were we men before? Are we better men now? Who knows? Each man that took the first step on the cue from the white phosphorus would never be the same.

If there is any beauty to be found here, so be it. There IS beauty. Its essence lies in a simple fact. As a Marine, you knew when you took that first step, you did not need to look right or left. You knew that there would be another Marine doing the same thing.

The roll of the dice determines many things.

Many Marines have never been where they needed to take that first step. Those Marines seem to look up to those of us who have. In their minds, they may wonder how they would do.

If they wonder. Just ask me. I know.

On that day or any other day. I know that I would not have to look right or left for them. They too would be there.

Chapter 37

673 in the rearview mirror

Hill 673 was still firmly in the hands of the North Koreans. Raymond had made his last sweep on the slope.

As Doc worked his way along the embankment, he stopped by and checked me over. The plastic bag was done emptying all of its blood red fluid.

"You are out of here, Smart Mouth."

Next he wrote something on the post office-like shipping tag the other corpsman had filled out. He then tied the tag to one of my button holes and started to move off.

"Hey doc, I'm OK."

"If you are OK, get up and walk for me."

"Fuck you Doc, you have a bad attitude. What's this tag say?"

"I want them to check the nerve stuff in your leg, I am concerned because you can't move it."

"Hey Doc, get someone to take me back up by Monaghan. I was doing OK with the covering fire until you guys came up and started the medical shit." They need my expert rifle work."

"Smart Mouth, everything is over on that hill for now and besides, everyone knows about you and the expert rifleman stuff—you ARE out of here. Good luck friend."

Doc cornered Lieutenant LeBaron from 2nd platoon. " Hey Lieutenant—can you get a couple guys to take Smart Mouth to the helio pad, he won't go otherwise." Lieutenant LeBaron came over and announced to me that I was headed to the helio pad for evacuation.

"Sorry I can't leave just now. They need me for covering fire. I am not sure that everyone is back down off the hill."

"Do you see these gold Bars?"

"Sorry Sir, I must have some of that damn volcanic dust in my eyes."

"Damn, I can sure see where your name came from," he said, as he took my rifle. He handed my rifle to his runner.

The lieutenant spoke to his runner. "Tell the Skipper that I am going to the helio pad with a wounded guy and I will be back in five." With that he cradled me in his arms and gave me my second baby style ride of the day. We headed down the backside of the hill.

"You know Lieutenant LeBaron, the guys in your platoon think you are a helluva leader."

"It appears that your eyes have cleared."

"I just feel like a dog leaving. Sure, I am happy as hell to get out of here, but it just doesn't feel right."

The protected helio pad was a good distance away—two or three hundred yards down hill and around a couple turns—the lieutenant carried me with ease.

He had been a celebrity before he came to the Marines and Korea—an All-American quarterback at some small California college. I couldn't remember which school, but his was a name all college football fans knew. At about 5'8" and weighing about 175, he was not a big man, but he was all arms, shoulders, and strong legs. The men in his platoon really did like him and they looked up to him as a real Marine. When we had been in reserve, every brass type officer who had visited Baker Company had to get the handshake thing done with Lieutenant LeBaron.

At the pad the lieutenant called out to two large wounded Marines. These guys were out of action but were waiting for a group to walk to the rear and get their injuries attended to.

"Men—put this man in the line for the evacuation helicopter. When his turn comes make sure he is on it."

"Yes, Sir."

The lieutenant then trotted off back up the trail.

When the little domed contraption made from an erector set with propellers in the wrong place came and landed, it was panic time. The helicopter had dropped straight down from what appeared to be 50,000 feet. It loaded a couple guys and went straight back up

The two gorillas that had been designated as my keepers were also fascinated by the machine and said several things to each other in 'gorilla speak.' They methodically moved me forward in the line.

It was an awesome machine. Nothing to it, but a small round glass box with a seat for the pilot and a windmill on top. It was the scariest thing I had ever seen. In place of wheels, it had two bent pipes for landing. Attached outward from each pipe was a 6 or 7 foot cradle-shaped basket made of metal strips. Each basket had curved sides and the spacing was like prison bars. The basket itself looked as though it had been attached to the pipes with glue.

For the first time that day, I panicked.

"Jesus Christ, guys—I am not going on one of those things. I am afraid of swings and merry-go-rounds. I get dizzy just looking out of a third story window!" No response from my body guards. The copter took two more wounded and I was automatically moved forward.

A bribe was out of the question. Our packs had been taken and stacked somewhere before we made the assault. Nothing to bribe with.

"Hey guys, call me a cab. You aren't really going to put me on one of those things?"

Chapter 37

My turn came and without a word Gargantua and his brother strapped me into the thin metal basket. The most petrified man on the hill, I went straight up, hanging in thin air and looking down through the holes of the basket. Not a muscle moved in my rigid body. Raw fear. I was sure those pipes were not going to hold my 130 pound load.

Chapter 38

Mangled bodies . . . and worse

After what seemed like a 17-hour ride, the flying machine dropped straight down into the middle of a city of squad-sized tents. Quickly the straps were off and I was staring into the face of a well-seasoned navy Chief Corpsman type.

"God, Chief you are the most beautiful human being I ever saw."

"Marine, is the pain really THAT bad? We will get you something, fast!"

"Shit no, Chief. I have used a lifetime of fear on that flying machine. However, I would accept some medical whiskey or about six beers."

In the midst of a tough day, the Chief smiled. "Fucking pussy Marine!"

673 had created a massive work load for this tent hospital. The 7th Marines would have over 70% casualties on 673. The Navy medical units our Marines relied on were working like Trojans with all this damaged meat coming in.

There were holding tents that held the stretchers. Others waiting simply sat on the ground. Some sort of priority system was in place, but not obvious to us casual observers.

A familiar face. Old Tom Moldorn. Tom also had a post office tag but was walking around and did not appear to be injured. Tom was from Charlie Company. Charlie had been given the job to take the next hill over from 673, Hill 749. They had walked into the same type of situation and into the same fan.

Tom was an interesting guy. We had gone through Camp Pendleton combat training together and had come over on the same ship. Tom was one of those guys who verbalized what he was going to do to the Commies and was afraid that the war would be over before he got to see action. Always sharpening knives and bayonets during his discourse on killing Commies.

Nobody paid too much attention to those guys on the ship over. We just kind of scratched our heads and wondered. Of course, anyone going into combat wonders how they will react. Deep in the heart and soul of every sane Marine that ever entered combat is a wish to do no less than hold up his end.

Tom's eyes were wide, empty, and without expression. He spotted me on the stretcher and sat down on the ground next to me, talking a mile a minute. "Hey Mac, what happened?" He pointed to the tag attached to his own dungarees. "Hey, Mac what does this tag mean?—I don't understand it."

Tom was another one of those "Southies," straight out of the tough section of South Boston. Good kid, but school and reading comprehension were not his strong points. The sum total of the hanging tag was that Tom was not psychologically suited for further combat. Most likely, the sword rattling and verbiage during training and on the ship coming over had been to convince himself.

Regardless, his exposure was bloody and a total disaster. He related how he was the only one from his squad that came off Hill 749. Three of those that were killed in Tom's squad were within close eyesight. Bullets had passed through their heads. Nothing had or could have prepared his nervous system for that.

"Hey Tom—good news—this tag says that you get to go to Japan. Somewhere during your time in the Corps, they must have done some testing on you. They are sending you for some advanced training of some sort."

Lying is not always a bad thing.

The hospital operating rooms in tents were later made famous in the Korean War movie and TV series *MASH*. Perfect depiction. Blood and guts and a genuine order-of-need surgery. These tent operations were truly meat markets, set up to keep their customers alive and stable. When this was accomplished the wounded were moved to more elaborate places farther in the rear for more advanced medical care.

I was not really a critical case—especially since the corpsman had given me blood on the hill. Waiting was OK, but watching was not. It was no fun to watch one after another of the young Marines with their bodies mangled and worse. Nor was looking at the back of a large flat bed truck with stiff dead Marine bodies stacked like cord wood. One layer going in one direction and each layer above going the opposite. Stacked six deep. That mental image will not go away in this lifetime.

Finally my turn came and my stretcher was taken into a tent.

Again, *MASH* got it right when they showed just such an operating room with the surgeons scurrying about trying to get the more desperate wounded taken care of. In the movie they used the line "He's an enlisted man—take big stitches." Been there, done that. The Miss America contest for me was forever ruled out.

When the magic surgeon hands were finished, I was loaded into the back of a panel truck. You might have called it an ambulance, but the only real similarity was the red cross emblem on the side. The contract for this and perhaps all military vehicles must always be given to the low bidder. No money was spent on shock absorbers.

The bumpy dirt Korean roads and the pain stuff wearing off produced some creative Marine talk, much of it directed at the underappreciated chauffeur and his ancestors. The 'ambulance' trip was followed by a train ride

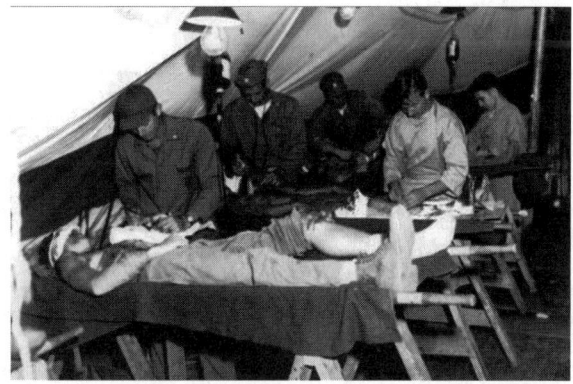

Chapter 38

to the southernmost point in Korea, the city of Pusan. My stretcher and many others were mounted on hooks along side panels of each railroad car. Stacked. There were a lot of customers—plenty of serious cases, but there were others like myself who were not so badly wounded. Navy Corpsmen hustled to take care of immediate needs and seemed to have no shortage of staffing. A train load of damaged goods.

For some of those with a knowledge of pain medicine, this became an opportunity. Of course, there were plenty of Marines in serious pain, but there were also many others wounded but without pain. Nonetheless, the pleas for pain medication picked up.

"Morphine!!" All you had to do was ask and you got an injection.

For those without a true need for pain medication, it was party and giggling time.

Considering the past hours, giggling was an OK thing.

CHAPTER 39

The U.S.S. Hope

We were taken off the train in Pusan, the southernmost tip of the Korean peninsula and put into another 'fancy' ambulance. The roads in Pusan were somewhat better, but not enough better to make the ride pleasant.

One of our four passengers could see out the small back window of the vehicle and gave periodic reports as best he could. He spotted Pusan Harbor and a huge white ship with a Red Cross on its side. It was the USS *Hope*, a giant floating United States Navy hospital.

We were brought aboard in true Navy fashion, with a snappy salute from the officer of the deck. Pretty formal for four PFC dirt Marines. We were not able to return the salute because a Marine never salutes when uncovered (no hat).

After months in the dirt, this ship was beautiful and spotlessly clean. White, white, white. Like guests at a fancy hotel, we were welcomed aboard and shuffled off to the part of the ship where each of us would get individualized treatment.

First things first—we needed to be cleaned up. It would have been preferable to get the first bath from one of the nurses. A Navy corpsman came to clean me up. Every body cavity and crevice had its own personal muck. Cleaning some parts seemed like I was losing a good friend. After awhile that grime had started to feel like a part of me. The damaged leg area, laced with a million heavy metal stitches, had been scrubbed down up north, so it was a bit cleaner than the rest of me.

"Marine—you stink!" My assigned corpsman, Goldie, was a good-natured guy and he would have been happier doing something else, but you would never know it. He acted as if he had looked forward to cleaning up this Marine all his life. His enthusiasm and concern for the individual's welfare was a sign of a true professional. Goldie pointed out that he had applied for duty as Corpsman with the Marines, but couldn't handle the heavy physical part of the training.

"We are getting a lot of business from your regiment and we were told that a bunch more are on the way. You guys must really have stepped in it. Not to worry. We have a great bunch of talented doctors and they are working like crazy."

As Goldie worked me over, he explained how the place worked. "Everything on the ship is done on a priority basis. Your turn for attention is based on the severity of your condition."

The sharp young corpsman asked a bunch of questions when he finished the scrub job, writing down the answers to each on his clipboard. Mostly he wanted to know about various parts of the injured leg, asking "Can you feel this? this? that?"

Goldie was not impressed with the large cuts on my leg that had been done at the tent field hospital. "Christ, Mac , the leg is clean, stitched, and should heal. What the fuck did they take out of your leg? It looks as if they removed a couple shovel blades! The slices are huge! Our Docs will improve on the beauty."

I explained to Goldie a little bit of what I had seen at the tent hospital—that those guys were sewing up chests, stomachs and heads as fast as they could and that the work they had done on my leg was pretty good under the circumstances. Goldie was a purist, and I wanted to let him know that his Navy did the best job they could be doing considering the conditions and demands. It wasn't his job, but every day afterwards Goldie found time to stop by and see how things were going.

I was assigned to a ward—another spotless white walled area where everyone had or would have some sort of surgical procedure.

It was spacious with clean white sheets and a pillow. My bunk was up against the bulkhead (metal wall—more Navy talk).

When Goldie tucked me in, there was one bed between mine and the duty nurse's desk in the middle of the ward. The single bunk between me and the nurse was reserved for the most critical case. She could see the entire area, work on the paperwork, and continuously monitor the badly messed up guy at the same time.

The Marine in that bed took some getting used to. Watching some guy out cold and pale as a ghost was a new experience. Tubes went in and out of every orifice of his body. Extra holes for drain tubes. Glass jars on the floor collecting fluids of rainbow colors and colors not in the rainbow. Blood, plasma, and IV drips pouring into a Marine so colorless that his skin color matched the sheets. Watching the next bunk on a daily basis was tough. No way to know how or if the guy would make it. Finally the color started to come back and he seemed to rise from the near dead to someone that was able to talk and move a little. When that happened they moved him elsewhere and brought in another chewed up guy and it started over. Over the next weeks, I learned to appreciate the professionals who handled difficult case after difficult case. "God bless those people who are able and like to do this kind of work."

Goldie kept me up with what would happen next. I got moved back in line a turn or two when another wave of really tough wounded cases came aboard. "Here's the deal Mac. They are concerned with the nerve stuff in your leg and the fact that you can't move it. Your x-rays show that you still have some more good sized pieces of shrapnel. Those need to come out. There are some flakes and small pieces, those you get to keep. There will be some more cutting, but the doctors promise that they will do a better job with the sewing work. Your eventual scars will be bad but not as dramatic. As soon as that starts to heal, we are sending in a therapist to get you up and walking. That last doctor that was in here feels that you had some severely damaged nerves but that they will respond."

Things progressed just as Goldie had said. At first my leg still did not want to move by itself. The therapist would tell me,

Chapter 39

"Tighten the quadriceps. Don't try to move it. Just tighten the muscle." In the beginning the muscles would not move the leg. A little scary. After more time, the leg moved by itself. This progress got me thinking along a new line of thought. "Next it will be possible for me to walk. Then I will be sent back up to the northern part of Korea."

The next time Goldie came by, I told him about my progress and my thinking.

"Sorry about that stuff Mac, but we did our job. I, for one, am pleased."

The time from when I first knew I would progress to walking again to actually doing it, did take time. Most of it was spent on crutches and exploring the ship—including getting into and tossed out of some places where I didn't belong. Kids that grow up in the desert find boats and ships fascinating.

Goldie also got me a list of guys from the 7th Marines who were on the USS Hope. I toured the ship looking for guys I might know.

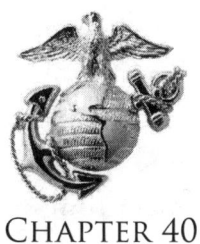

CHAPTER 40

Gabe Sanchez

One name on the list didn't strike home at first. Gabriel Martinez Sanchez, Sgt. USMC, 7th Marines. Those of Mexican heritage used both mother's and father's family names, so it was hard to figure out which was the 'real' last name. When I realized that I might know him, I went to check it out.

The ward where he was located was one of those serious ones; a definite KEEP OUT place. I needed to know if it was the guy from Baker Company and my hometown of Tucson. I decided that sign must be for someone else.

Entering the area, I said to a very serious looking Navy Chief Corpsman, "The chaplain sent me to check on Sgt. Sanchez and report back to him."

"Marine, I imagine that the chaplain can read. If you are unable to read that sign I will spell it out for you. Tell him that Sgt. Sanchez is not ready to be checked on."

I didn't give up easily. "Hey Chief how about if I just look and be sure we have the right Marine, I won't speak or touch anything. That will keep the chaplain happy. He is a full commander and has a bad attitude. I am just doing what I was told."

He bought it. Putting his finger over his mouth to remind me to be quiet, he pointed to the room and the "KEEP QUIET" sign.

In the bed out cold was the palest Mexican I had ever seen. It was our Sgt. Sanchez.

I went back out of the room, "Thanks, Chief. Is he going to make it? He looks like shit."

"Yeah. You should have seen him when they brought him in. Now get the fuck out of here."

The next day, I decided a return trip to the special ward was in order.

I tried a new ruse. "The sergeant and I are closely related by marriage."

"Look shit for brains, you didn't fool me with that chaplain crap, yesterday, either."

"Hey Chief, I like a man who is straight forward and says what he thinks. Can I just sit out here in the hall for a bit and come back tomorrow and see if he is doing OK?"

"Marine, first of all that is a passageway, not a hall." (More of that Navy talk—Navy talk gets boring after awhile. I really don't see why they keep it up.) "Yes, you can sit there if you can keep that big mouth of yours shut until I tell you it is time to open it."

"Hey Chief—I have never really tried that, but you have a deal."

Goldie got me some information on Sanchez and the corpsman was correct. He had turned the corner, but was not ready for company yet.

I continued my daily trips to his room. By now, the corpsman had loosened up and was getting used to me. One day he said, "I think today is the day, Marine. I'll give you five minutes. If the Marine Corps was able to teach you to count, count the fingers on one of your hands and watch that machine on the wall. It is called a clock. The space between the two numbers is five minutes."

Not knowing what to expect, I entered the room. Sanchez had certainly not greeted me like a lost brother when I had joined Baker Company. Strange, considering that we were from the same town. In fact, Sanchez had been pretty cold. Maybe it was the sergeant thing. I hadn't really figured that part out, considering we were both were from the same one-high-school town.

Sanchez's eyes were open and quiet.

I decided to give it a try, "Pendejo! Que tal?" Again with my high school Spanish slang swear words.

His eyes flashed and locked. Sanchez had a reputation in Baker Company as a man with a vicious temper. He not only had two Purple Hearts, but to go with them he had two Silver Stars with citations that had some pretty fancy words about gallantry. No doubt true. It was also said that both times he got knocked down by concussion grenades. That had pissed him off. His response each time was to go after the dummies who threw them. Successfully.

After a moment, his eyes softened and he gave a weak smile. Softly out from the bed came "Cabrón."

As he grew stronger, every day that was nice enough, we went out on the deck—Sanchez in his wheelchair and me on my crutches. It was a beautiful time of year and the sun felt good. We talked by the hour and yearned for the Tucson sun and just a single El Charro Mexican food lunch. One of everything on the menu.

It turned out that Gabe was a couple years older and had not finished high school. We discovered that we had tons of mutual friends. The Mexican community in Tucson was a tight one. Everyone knows everyone.

It took awhile, but finally I asked why he had not been friendly while we were in Baker Co. It had seemed strange to me since Mexican people I had met from both sides of the border all had a beautiful characteristic. If you were not pompous and did not try to act superior or overbearing, the ones I had met would befriend you and open up like they had known you forever. I had come to Tucson as a freshman in high school. I didn't have any friends and it was the Mexican kids who had taken me in. It was a great feeling, never forgotten.

Gabe looked at me and smiled. "You know, Smart Mouth, I just thought you were another one of those fancy east side assholes

Chapter 40

in Tucson, that look down on us Mexicans. Sorry, compadre, I just didn't know."

Each day we got more time on the Chief's clock and the stud of Baker Co. got stronger. I was there for the Gabe Sanchez 'hat trick' when he received his third Silver Star and third Purple Heart. It was very emotional. The bedside presentation was made by a full bird colonel. Uncovered, I didn't even have to salute the colonel. Nice. My limp had almost disappeared, but I faked it a bit for the benefit of the brass. Not long after that ceremony, Gabe Sanchez was headed to Hawaii to a fancy Navy hospital for rehabilitation.

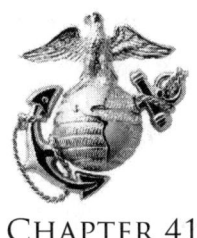

Chapter 41

Back to Baker

My turn to leave the hospital ship and return to my company came soon after Gabe left. Strangely, I felt like I was getting to go home and be with family. Hard to believe I could miss that sorry bunch.

Two other Marines who had been put back together on the *Hope* shared the Jeep ride to the Pusan airstrip. They were also headed back to the 1st Marine Division. Jeep rides were definitely more comfortable without handcuffs.

The three of us began to discuss what would happen to us at Division, something I hadn't given much thought. The other two Marines were quite certain that they wanted to be assigned to some cushy rear echelon spot. OK for them. I didn't know there was a choice. If I was part of 1st platoon Baker Company, why would I want to go anywhere else? I was looking forward to catching up on what had been happening since I left.

We caught a ride north in a huge C-47. I tried to be suave and not let anyone know that it was my first airplane ride. I sat back and quietly enjoyed a new experience.

The three of us arrived at 1st Division Headquarters and were sent to a tent marked Division Sergeant Major. Big stuff. Important man. I carefully managed things so I would be at the end of the line to capture and interrogate the other two as they came out of the tent. Both got jobs at Division. Supply and truck driver jobs. Yuck.

My turn came. There was a captain at a small desk in the corner doing paperwork. I went before the Sgt. Major, who was sitting behind a makeshift desk looking bored with his job. "What kind of skills do you have? Mechanical, typing, truck driving, or what? What would you like to do here at Division?"

"Gunny," I said, addressing him informally so it wouldn't seem that I was sucking up. "I have no skills and I am going back to Baker Co."

"You don't have to go back—you were wounded and out of action for more than 45 days. That means you can have a spot here at Division."

"Gunny, I could hand you a bunch of conversation and I have thought about running my mouth, but I know that I do not get up early enough to snow you. I really just want to go back to Baker."

"Why"?

"I guess you want the simple short version."

"Please."

"Well, Gunny, I have been bounced around a lot in my life. With the guys in 1st platoon, I feel like I am accepted for what I am. I feel at home. Besides, we have been through a lot together with 673 and the 'Slot.' You get pretty close. Aside from that, those guys aren't too bright, and most likely they can't get along without me."

At that point, the sergeant seemed to get interested in the conversation. The captain also put aside his paperwork and came over. "Sgt. Major, I heard him say he was at the 'Slot.' Are the stories about the 'Slot' true, or are they exaggerated?"

I was surprised. "I didn't know anyone except for us called it the Slot."

The sergeant filled me in. "Back here at Division it took the name you guys gave it. It was a gigantic event in terms of the Division. If the Chinese had not been stopped there, they would have spilled all over the landscape and been all over our butts here. The Division would have been in big trouble. You guys did a hell of a job that night."

The captain added, "The outcome of the Slot is well known back here and that action is well documented. What we heard back here, was that there were verbal challenges to the Chinese by some Marines up there. Is that true? Why did you guys call it the Slot?"

I took a piece of paper from the sergeant's desk and sat down to draw a sketch of the layout of our positions. "It could have been more properly called a pass. It was situated between the two really high spots, but as we got ready that day everyone called it the Slot and the name stuck. You know just like 'Ape Shit Ridge.'" Comfortable by now with the sergeant and captain, I continued. "Funny how places get names. Captain, as for the other verbal challenges to the Chinese, I am with you. If I had not had a ring side seat. . ." I pointed to my position on the paper map of the Slot I had drawn ". . . I would not have believed it either."

At that point, I launched into a blow by blow description of that night, including New Guy's famous yell to the Chinese, "Nice try assholes!"

The captain and sergeant major listened attentively to my every word, following along as I talked and pointed at the rough drawing. At the end of my account, I added "The toughest part is about our instant legend kid who started the verbal assault on the Chinese. The night of the Slot, he had not been in our unit long enough for us to know his name, so we all kept referring to him as 'New Guy.' He kept the tag New Guy from that night on. The sad part is that New Guy bought it on 673."

The sergeant major said, "What do you think Captain? Should we let him go back to Baker Co.?"

"Sergeant Major—I think you should send him where ever he wants to go."

Back to Baker.

CHAPTER 42

The Professor makes Sergeant

I returned to Baker Company near the beginning of November. It was not until I got back and talked to Herman that I learned how badly 673 had devastated our ranks. It had gutted us. Of the 26 of us who started up the slope that morning 13 had been confirmed killed in action. Among others, we lost Little Ski, New Guy, 2 squad leaders, 2 fire team leaders, and 4 replacements. They had all paid the price that morning. Dead and gone.

We also knew that at least three of the Hombres were dead and most likely all four. The last anyone had seen of Jose was not pretty. His skinny little brown body was wrecked. At first they thought he was dead but on the last sweep of the slope Raymond had seen a flicker of life and carried him down. They loaded him on the helicopter with blood bags and other paraphernalia, but not much hope.

The make up of our platoon was so different from before. We were, in effect, a new group. In the couple months that I had been gone, another couple of guys who had made it through the debacle on 673, had been rotated home. Another pair found jobs in the rear. We had the core group, but it just wasn't the same.

There was also a noticeable change in the progress of the war. Our company was firmly entrenched on a main line of resistance. The battle for 673, 749, and the rest of Kanmunbong ridge was over. That fight for the hills, ridges, and all of the connected territory had

ended. The move north had stopped the Chinese cold and they had, at least temporarily, given up their idea of attacking. Each side was deeply entrenched on top of their respective mountains. Waiting.

The view from Baker's position was spectacular. High—two or three thousand feet above another beautiful valley with a river flowing through it. The forested mountain area was so pretty that Charles was talking about coming back after the war and putting a hunting resort here.

Fortunately for me, the bunker and trench construction work was finished. The prolonged time there had allowed for the effort needed to make these positions solid. They appeared to be ready for anything. We assumed that the same had been done by our Chinese friends atop the mountain across the valley. Not a scene for total contentment, but certainly better than hiking up and down the peninsula of Korea.

The fighting holes and bunkers were well placed. Each bunker had several layers of logs and sand bags for a roof. Each was given an appearance of naturalness. On hills, trenches and bunkers were always placed well below the forward slope, allowing some outside movement without showing a human silhouette against the top of the ridge. The trench line was then extended up and over the crest of the hill to the rear slope, where we had our living bunkers. Living being a generous word.

Chapter 42

The living bunkers were wide enough to accommodate two people in their sleeping bags at the same time. Inside the bunker a shelf about halfway up on each side of the dirt wall served as a holding place for important stuff. Being on the reverse slope of the hill we could use a candle for light without giving away our position. We simply put a canvas tarp over the opening and no light was visible. The dirt shelf was a place for a small makeshift stove to heat C-rations and hot drinks.

Our cooking stove was a simple thing. Its heat was generated by a small but intense flame from a small can of sterno. When the C-ration can or canteen cup was being heated, it rested on a small tin frame. It was functional and felt very domestic.

The company had been on this line for a while before I returned from the hospital ship and 1st platoon had used their free time well, building a communal bunker—definitely to be distinguished from the company command bunker—on the reverse slope. This was to be social.

The 1st platoon had somehow decided on this community effort. It must have been a major event in planning and construction. I could only imagine this group trying to divide the architectural and construction duties. Counting the number of people from 1st platoon and matching that number with each decision to be made and who gets to make it, painted an ugly picture. Even with its newcomers, 1st platoon had no shortage of self-proclaimed experts.

Nonetheless, the end product turned out to be functional, well-structured, and tucked cleverly out of range of artillery and mortar fire. Size-wise, it held all of us if we squeezed a little. Furnishings were of a variety of available things. The usual grenade and equipment boxes, gas cans, a stolen canvas chair or two, logs, and rocks.

When the geniuses of the Marine Corps did not have us watching down into the valley or thinking up some stupid reason for us to go into that valley or up the side of the other guy's hill, we could usually be found gathered in our new bunker.

Though our ranks had been filled out with replacement Marines, there were enough of us guys who had been in the move north, the slot, and 673 and who had vast stores of knowledge to share such as how to do the things that helped you make it through the days and nights. In that bunker, a replacement Marine could receive a doctoral dissertation on any aspect of being a Marine in combat. There were no lectures but there were plenty of discussions about a variety of kinds of situations. When three or four guys would get together and describe a specific fire fight or patrol action there not a shred of bull shit. More often than not, each saw the event from a different angle or perspective. This was not intended to be a school situation, but the learning value was there for the taking.

The replacements listened. That was the important part. When they asked good questions, they got good answers. It was a two-way street. Learning something here in place of making a stupid mistake under fire, benefitted us all.

There was one area that was never discussed except by those that had been there. Then, only briefly and privately. 673. It was simply too painful. It hurt. Questions in the bunker on that subject were met with silence. The quiet was not meant to be rude, but it was simply a situation where none of us wished to share the intense personal feeling.

As the fall started to turn into winter, the bunker was a warmer place than the individual living bunkers. Temperatures at night were headed south of zero. There were some serious philosophical

Chapter 42

discussions. The Professor was still invited to handle the truthfulness and accuracy of the subject matter, though he still refused to enter many discussions because the subject matter was, as could be expected, not of an intellectual nature.

The Professor still maintained his personal style, quietly contemplating the matters of the world. Pretty much sat in the corner by himself. Goat was always close by. At times you could hear them talk about Jose. Private stuff. Jose, Goat, and the Professor had always been a special group within the group. The Goat never said, but it would be a guess that he did not even make it to high school, much less finish. Jose was probably the least worldly person in the world.

The Professor on many occasions had made it clear to everyone that Goat and Jose were two men with excellent minds. He also made it clear to both of them. He would tell them that the opportunity to use their minds was ahead of them and not behind. Both always had received complete and thoughtful answers from the Professor on any subject. The rest of us, on the other hand, were at times guilty of gigging the professor about his professorial ways and did not always receive the same courtesy.

It was around this time that the Professor's promotion to sergeant came through. Raymond came to the platoon bunker to tell him. Raymond announced that the Professor had made SERGEANT and was going to take over as the squad leader of 1st squad.

The Professor was, by any evaluation, different from the rest of us. If Raymond had said we were to run the 100-yard dash in 9 flat, we would mutter and mumble, then go do it. None of us had the balls to directly challenge one of his orders. Not so with the Professor. It wasn't balls, really, just the Professor.

"Raymond—I told you once before—I am not a leader of men. I will not accept the position of squad leader." The Professor had been a corporal all the time he had been in Korea, but had remained a rifleman. He would not even become a fire team leader.

There was no oxygen left in the bunker. It had been sucked up by every man in the bunker simultaneously inhaling. The Professor had crossed a line that no one crossed—and he was not finished.

He continued. "Raymond, am I not a good rifleman?"

"Of course, Professor, but the Marine Corps says that each squad will be headed by a sergeant and I have no others who are ready."

"Raymond, I have the greatest respect for you and your ability as a platoon sergeant. The way you manage this group of semi-retarded human beings is a work of art. I do not possess similar talent. You must use your ability to manage and find a way to solve this problem. I choose not to rise to a level of incompetence."

We waited. . . . "OK. Professor, the paperwork will say one thing and we will do another."

In the bunker we could breathe again.

They have scales and charts to measure everything in this world except courage. In our minds, having served with and under Sgt. Gotshall, the statements by the Professor would have been off the edge of any of those charts. For the Professor, it was a simple decision.

The Professor remained a rifleman to his last day in Korea—and a damn good one!!

CHAPTER 43

10% never get the word

Marine Axiom. 10 % never get the word. There were a multitude of possible excuses. "Didn't hear it." "Wasn't listening." On and on.

Things would go wrong. That was when the issue of the 10% would come up. We would then debate what went wrong and institute corrections for the future. Sure! 10% will never get the word!!

This was not supposed to apply to officers. With us junkyard dogs and alley cats it was an expected event and hopefully accounted for.

Even if the brass believed that the Chinese had given up their idea of coming south in force, we kept up the watching. Day and night in some form of percentage watch, depending on what 'intelligence' expected to happen on that particular night.

To supplement the percentage watch, there were listening posts. These were made up of a small group—usually three or four men—who went out beyond the barbed wire in front of the main line. How far out in front the listening post was established depended on the situation and the terrain. The object was to find a spot that had a good field of vision and could be defended in some manner. Once the post was set up, the night was spent watching and listening.

The obvious purpose was to detect movement by the enemy and get adequate early warning to the main line. Each night a different spot was chosen. The mountains provided plenty of good places to watch and listen. Before the group left each night, it was carefully noted where they planned to set up. Once chosen, the spot was confirmed and coordinated with the company headquarters. Then the position would be reported up the line to all levels of command. Theoretically they were concerned about the welfare and safety of those going out to protect and warn them.

Because we were currently in stable line positions, we were able to connect the listening post to the company headquarters with hard phone lines. The lucky people going out for the night would have to muscle along a huge roll of real phone wire. They would hook up an old-fashioned 'Ma Bell' black phone once the listening post was ready for the night. The line then would be added to a network—an open line with all units connected from platoon all the way up to Battalion. An old-fashioned party line. Regular nightly communications between platoons, companies, and Battalion went out over the line throughout the night. Strictly limited to important stuff.

A listening post could be anywhere from two or three hundred yards to half a mile in front of the line. As the night went on, each Marine took his turn listening on the phone to the conversations between the company, platoon, and battalion while the other three took care of the attentiveness to the surroundings.

A signal to those in front of the line was given about every 15 minutes from company headquarters. Something bland would be said like "The temperature tonight is 47 degrees." Or something similarly inane. Generally, the message would change each time. When they heard their signal, if all was quiet and there was nothing to report, the man on the listening post phone would tap the plastic mouth piece of the instrument one time with a shell casing. If something <u>was</u> unusual, he tapped twice. After two taps, the person at the company would start asking questions that could be answered with a simple yes or no. Yes was one tap. Two taps meant no. Simple, but quiet and effective.

Chapter 43

One night the group that was gathered to go out was Hack, Herman, and two replacements. Herman gathered the replacements for listening post school. The teacher was both an experienced Marine and a big fucker, so he had their attention. "No noise, no talking, no rustling of equipment. In essence we are not even out there. No one hears us breathe. We are more silent than the wind. We will come back up this hill before light in one piece. OK?"

Hack had chosen a spot he had seen on a recent patrol. He communicated his choice to the Gunny, who, in turn, had the responsibility to inform all levels of command and instruct those at the company who will man the phones and do the periodic communicating during the night.

The crappiest job was the one who had to carry the roll of phone wire out through the barbed wire and out to the listening post. Good job for a replacement. Managing weapons, ammo, plus the damn wire was not easy. Doing it quietly enough under the threat of Herman kicking your ass was even more of a challenge.

One privilege usually afforded to those who went out in front of the lines for a listening post, patrol, or other 'adventure' was the personal option of weapons. It was a fair enough rule. You would be the one going out there and you would be the one who might have to defend yourself. There was no manual or suggested list for this activity. For a listening post, the M-1 and the BAR were too bulky and generally not suitable.

Herman's replacements, however, were not given the option. First, he evaluated how familiar each was with automatic weapons, making it clear that any misrepresentation of their level of familiarity with the weapons would result in bodily harm up to and including demonstrations of the same weapon probing up into sensitive body areas. Herman and Hack would each take 'grease guns,' a weapon that looked like it belonged in an auto shop. A vicious automatic weapon, it weighed about 10 pounds when fully loaded with its magazine. Its ammunition was the monster 45-caliber slug. At close range it was a devastating device.

Without anyone saying it, it was well known that Hack would have his ever-present switchblade. Though every attempt was made to keep the locations of listening posts hidden, on occasion, enemy soldiers had tried to sneak up on one of the outposts and fierce firefights had followed.

The Dean of the listening post school elected for the two replacements to carry the M-2 Carbine which weighed about 6 or 7 pounds with their magazines. Each claimed to have used it and seemed to be aware of how it worked. The M-2 could fire either single shot or full automatic. On full automatic, it could deliver 700 rounds per minute of 30 caliber ammo. It could do plenty of damage, especially in close quarters, but even up to 100 yards away it was deadly. Each magazine carried 30 rounds. Two magazines could be taped together—one in the weapon ready to go and one pointed down ready to be quickly flipped and inserted.

Besides weapons, each man had two pairs of socks and extra clothing to guard against the cold of the night. There would be no teeth chattering, shaking, or noise. Once set up in position on a listening post you were allowed the same movement as a 2-ton rock.

It was time to head out. The "Gunny" was at the wire as the group left shortly after dark and verified that everyone had been made aware of the location of the listening post and expected return time.

Hack's chosen spot was textbook. Under a half moon, two large draws coming out of the valley provided clear sight as far as eyes could see, while the small ridge between them had plenty of craggy good-sized rocks for cover. No one would be able to sneak up on them.

Once at the listening post, they hooked up the phone. By prearranged agreement, Herman and Hack would be manning the phone all night. Neither was ready to assign the task to a replacement. Looking around, obviously the spot had come under artillery fire at some point in time. There were plenty of holes in the ground to hunker down into. A single huge pine stump about 12-feet tall, sat on the nose of the ridge where they had set up.

Hack leaned against the big tree stump and took the first turn on the phones. The others picked spots so they could see in all directions, and all settled in for the first watch.

Chapter 43

Quiet, quiet, quiet. The valley, the two draws, and the night were dead silent.

Hack tapped on the phone, verifying the connection. Another tap about 15 minutes later. Suddenly there was the quietest eruption. Hack, totally animated, was whispering into the phone a mile a minute, breaking rule number one for a listening post. NO talking OR whispering into the phone. There was no mistaking the language. It was totally laced with words he did not learn from his Rabbi.

Herman slid over to assess the situation.

Hack had overheard a conversation between the platoon and the company and discovered that the lieutenant in charge of the mortars was informing company that he was getting ready to zero the mortars in for the night. He announced that his aiming stake would be that 15 to 20 foot tree stump on the end of a ridge about half-mile out . . . exactly our coordinates!!

Hack yell-whispered into the phone. "That's us you dumb mother-fucker—you fire one mortar within a mile of us and I am going to shove that mortar tube so far up your ass, your eyes will pop!!"

Gunny's voice, clear and authoritative, came on the line.

"Mortar section secure the zeroing-in process, NOW! Do not fire a single round. Respond if you understand, lieutenant."

The response came quickly.

"Mortar section secured, Sir."

Gunny re-addressed Hack. " LP [night code for listening post], Gunny here. I will be at the mortar section in 15 seconds. Hang tight."

15 seconds passed.

"LP, Gunny here. I am at mortar section. They are informed and we will not use you as aiming stake tonight—maybe tomorrow night, but not tonight. Hang until I talk to the Skipper about you guys staying out or coming in. Are you ok for a couple minutes?"

One tap.

A short time passed. "Skipper here. Hack, it is your call. If you feel you should come in, it is OK. No heroes. Are you going to be OK out there?"

One tap.

"Skipper here. OK then back to normal procedure. Hack, I request your presence at an educational meeting with our new Mortar Lieutenant when you come through the wire in morning. OK?"

One tap.

"Hack—I took the liberty of telling the young man how you got your name. He will be attentive to your usual candid opinion."

One tap.

10 % never get the word.

CHAPTER 44

Lt. Magoo

The Marine Corps seemed to be using the Korean War as a post graduate course for Ivy Leaguer ROTC types who mistakenly wound up with our Globe and Anchor on their collar. They would come and go. A new lieutenant either got exposed like the rest of us to the tough parts of the war or ended up on three-week assignment in Baker Company after which they moved on. The Marine Corps was field testing their new lieutenants. The boys with gold Bars.

On paper they were the leaders of our platoon. But, neither a gold bar, a silver leaf, or even a star on the collar created a leader. Neither did hearing the word leadership repeated one-hundred-thousand times impart that unique ability. Leadership could be a God given talent—no question, a few individuals were born with it. Leadership could also be a developed skill. Leading began with knowing what was going on in the heads of those you were trying to lead. Understanding people. For some, being a leader could sometimes be accomplished by simply being the best person at a given task.

It was more than fair to say that training camps for Marines and their leaders could not possibly cover the real thing. When people were shooting at you and trying to hurt you, it was a wholly different situation than reading a book or hearing someone talk about it.

The Professor was adamant on the issue of raw intelligence with regard to officers and enlisted men. He told us more than once that there was no real difference in raw brain power. He would explain that environment, cultures, and opportunity were all that separated the two groups.

The trouble with some 2nd Lieutenants was starting with the false assumption that there was a complete and total difference in the IQs of officers and enlisted men, then acting accordingly. Bad idea.

Who knew what they taught in officer school. It didn't take Albert Einstein to know that the backbone of the military will always be the non-commissioned officers. The sergeants. In 1st platoon we had our leader. If you asked us, we would vote unanimously that Sergeant Gotshall was one of those born to lead.

Raymond understood the situation with the rotating lieutenants. He was fully aware that a goofed up 2nd Lieutenant under fire was dangerous to himself and to us. Wisely, Raymond did not leave the evaluation of these new officers to us.

Raymond had rules and Raymond's rules were not to be broken. His set of rules for us concerning those fancy college kids covered all editorial comments and verbal abuse directed at any officer. If we felt that the new officer was deficient in any area, we were to tell him and he would assess our view. The reason for his rule was simple—these new fresh-faced officers arrived completely untested, some with zero awareness that lack of experience might be a problem.

Anyone who displayed unnecessary poor conduct toward a platoon leader would deal with Sgt. Got Balls directly. Not a pleasant thought.

Raymond made HIS evaluation of each new platoon leader.

The good ones were happy to have his help with the job. Some were not interested in his help. Go figure. If you were new and did not know what you were doing and had someone around who did know—duh—ask questions of the person who knew.

For example, 2nd Lieutenant Ivy League rotated in to take over our platoon with its proletariat Marine lowlifes. His priority

Chapter 44

was to let us know who was boss. Raymond was not from Yale or Dartmouth. In fact, he did not have the first day in college—what could he possibly know?

Sgt. Gotshall was a natural at managing people. It did not matter if a man had the eagles of the regimental commander or eight stars on his collar. Raymond could also manage the strong willed, dim-witted uneducated trash he had been given in the ranks of 1st platoon.

Second Lt. Ivy League was in deep shit from day one. In his first couple weeks with the platoon, he ignored Sgt. Gotshall except to give him orders. Surprisingly, there was more than one wise ass in 1st platoon. Borderline insubordination started quickly.

Lt. Ivy League was trooping the line about 3 am. Standard procedure to see if everyone was awake and alert. As he came down the trench line he dropped into my hole, sounding like he wanted to play word games.

"Well Marine, what are you going to do if you hear a noise out there?"

"Throw a grenade and see what happens next, Sir. What's my prize for the correct answer?"

"Son, that's not the correct answer and don't be a smart aleck with me. The correct response is to fire your rifle in the direction of the noise."

"First of all 'Lootenent,' Sir. You are dead wrong and if you don't mind, I don't like you talking in my fox hole. I do not want to attract attention to my position. I do not know what they taught you in Lieutenant School but the flash of a rifle will pinpoint your position and draw fire. A grenade will not. Sir, a few days on line have not made you an authority. Sir."

"Harrumph." And off he went down the trench line.

First thing the next morning Raymond came to see me. "Good morning Raymond, did you come by to fix my breakfast like a good sergeant?"

"Smart Mouth, what did you say to Lieutenant Ivy League last night?"

"I did call him 'Sir.' Did the dumb shit report me? Maybe you can put me in the brig and I can get out of Korea alive."

"Seriously, what do you think of this guy, Smart Mouth?"

"The term incompetent pompous asshole comes to mind."

"I need to go to the Skipper and talk about it. You are coming with me."

"Let me check my appointment book. Let's see. I can re-schedule my hair stylist and my lawyer will just have to wait. OK. Sgt. Sir."

With me in tow, Raymond gathered the arrogant asshole Lieutenant, and we headed to the reverse slope and the command bunker. This was going to be fun, because by now I knew Raymond was not going to let anything happen to me.

As we entered the command bunker, Raymond greeted the First Sergeant.

"Good morning First Sergeant. Sergeant Gotshall wishes to speak to the company commander."

"Aren't we being a bit formal this morning, Raymond? Hey Smart Mouth, I haven't seen you since you came back from the hospital ship. How's the leg? I actually hadn't expected you back! Good to have you."

"Shit Gunny—how the hell could an old fart like you run the war and handle this company without me? You shouldn't be here anyway, with a face like yours, you should be on the recruiting posters."

The company commander had come through the entrance and heard my comments. He chuckled and enjoyed a laugh at the Gunny's expense.

The skipper also greeted me. "Smart Mouth! It hasn't been the same without you. We have definitely struggled running the company in your absence. Did you romance any of the nurses on the hospital ship with your quick wit?"

The skipper turned and asked the platoon leader. "Lieutenant, why are we all here?"

Chapter 44

The stupid shit did not know that the dogpile was going to be on him. He walked straight into it and began to retell the incident with me from the trench during the night.

First, the captain settled the issue of 'fire the rifle or throw the grenade?' "Lieutenant—the flash of a rifle is a dead give away on your position."

Secondly, he recounted my exploits as a Marine under his command. Well, he laid it on a little thick, but it sounded OK to me. I was thinking about chiming in with a self-endorsement for a promotion, but this was too much fun.

"Smart Mouth, would you please wait outside while your platoon leader, platoon sergeant, and I attend to some business?"

"Yes, sir."

Outside was not out of earshot. I made sure of that. If there was a sound made by a rectal surgeon cutting a new asshole, it must have sounded like the lecture the Skipper delivered to poor old 2nd Lieutenant Ivy League.

"Lieutenant I am going to be concise in what I have to say or we would be here a month. It starts with the misconstrued idea of a raw 2nd Lieutenant correcting or advising a seasoned combat veteran on how to conduct himself on line."

Next he covered the subject of listening to his platoon sergeant. He advised 2nd Lieutenant Ivy League that Sgt. Gotshall was known and respected all the way up to the regimental commander. His nickname—Sgt. Got Balls—signified that respect. He was dealing with a decorated Marine who had an excellent record of handling himself and his men under a variety of combat situations. "You should have been smart enough to recognize that and ask him questions so you could learn."

At the company commander's request, 2nd Lieutenant Ivy League packed and left 1st platoon later that day. He would assume a position in supply at the Division level. Hopefully he would get advanced training in counting skivvies.

Then there was the other extreme.

One of the platoon leaders we inherited was a genuine midget, ugly as sin with glasses that had lenses an inch thick. This guy would have been the last guy to replace Clark Gable on the movie screen and must have stood on the same box as Hack to pass the minimum height requirement. Marines liked to laugh and poke fun at others for entertainment. We were cranked up to have fun with this one.

What us dummies in 1st platoon did not know was that upon arrival, the new lieutenant had immediately sat down with Sgt. Gotshall and pointed out the obvious.

"Sergeant, I don't know shit, but I can learn. You run the platoon until I figure out how to find my ass with both hands. I will support your decisions 100%."

Another leadership quality. Knowing the difference between what you know and do not know.

Raymond was a savvy guy, college or not. He knew the hoodlum masses he commanded and was fully aware of the simplicity of our minds. He gathered us quickly when the new 2nd lieutenant was not present. The message was a straight forward one, even for Raymond.

"Fuck with the new platoon leader in any way and you fuck with me."

Pretty simple and easy to understand. None of us had ever met the man who would choose the short side of that offer.

It worked out that the new lieutenant was one of the good ones and we liked him. He held his own every step of the way and didn't take long to earn the respect of our band of village idiots.

The funniest thing of all happened a month or so later. The platoon had been out on patrol and had stepped in shit. As he had before, the lieutenant took part and led the way as it was supposed to be done. He had become one of us. We kicked some Chinese ass and everyone made it back without a scratch.

After coming back up the hill, the whole platoon was crapped out on a grassy area inside the company lines. We were a little giddy because we were returning without damage to anyone.

Chapter 44

The lieutenant was shooting the breeze and enjoying the moment with us for awhile. Then he got up to leave. He stopped and turned to us and in all seriousness said,

"Hey guys, I have been with you for a month and a half. I have busted my ass to do a good job. I consider you guys to be my friends, but not one of you has ever called me Lieutenant Magoo. How come? My friends at home all call me Magoo."

Moose saved the day.

"Lieutenant. We have too much respect for you to do that."

We all knew that the Lieutenant would never know the full truth. It was true that we respected the lieutenant, but this time the respect issue and the fear issue came out the same.

A more truthful answer to his question would have been "Abject Fear."

The name attached to that fear was Sgt. Raymond Gotshall, USMC.

CHAPTER 45

Winter in North Korea

The first flakes of snow were always an event. This year they came shortly after the Marine Corps Birthday. November 10, 1951. It took the United States Navy to remind us of that most important holiday. The Navy had not forgotten.

That afternoon we had just finished with our daily Chinese 'Hello, we are still here' shell fire. About 3 or 4 each afternoon old Charley would fire about 50 rounds of 76 artillery shells into our lines. Just like clockwork. We knew it was coming and always elected to be in our bunkers and well under cover.

Today was different. Someone spotted one of the one engine Navy forward observer airplanes, the kind used to spot for artillery. It came chugging along in front of our lines with a banner strung behind it which read "Happy Birthday Marines."

It was followed by other airplanes, the slick fast ones. They dropped napalm on our friends on the slopes across the valley. One after another they came. We stayed out and watched as they dropped the big containers on the Chinese positions. When napalm was released, it fell

–181–

awkwardly end over end on the way to the ground. When it hit the ground, the jelly that was mixed with the gasoline exploded and lit up. Fire spread across a large area creating a spectacular overall effect. When they finished dropping the napalm, they circled, got in line, and took turns emptying all of their machine guns and cannons on the enemy bunkers. A great show!

At the end of the performance the little Piper Cub airplane came putt-putting across our front again, with the banner streaming behind—much to the delight of the watching Marines. There were a lot of Marines waving and yelling.

Thanks, guys!

The snow indicated that winter had come. Not December yet, but winter.

This year the Marine Corps was better prepared for the intensely cold Korean winter. The winter before, 1950 at the Chosin reservoir, had caught the Marines well short on winter gear. Those guys in the 1st Marine Division had nothing with them but the plain high top shoes and light jackets for the bitter below zero weather. Those that made it through that operation had plenty of frozen and frostbitten feet.

We were issued warm fur lined pants and jackets with hoods in addition to down sleeping bags with hoods. The novel thing was the thermal boots. Toasty. Wear them and walk around for a short while. Take them off and the feet give off steam. Word came down when they were issued—"Get frostbite and you get a court martial to go with it!" Equipment-wise, we were ready for winter.

Once it started to snow, it never stopped. Since our

positions on this hill were high with open and steep slopes, we believed that the weather conditions would keep us from being attacked. Our fighting bunkers looked like igloos. The sand bags and the log tops were covered with ice and snow. Each bunker was dug well back into the mountain side. Because the back part of the bunker was well below ground level the dirt was not frozen. Boost and I acted like two prisoners trying to tunnel out of jail.

We kept digging further back into the mountain, dumping the dirt on the reverse slope and fashioning a private living room to go with our personal armory. It was not tall enough to stand in, but we could sit at the small table made from grenade boxes and play gin rummy by candle light.

There was one other caution from above. Do not stand your watch in the trench at night with your sleeping bag wrapped around you for warmth. While a temptation, it was a bad idea. If you got too comfortable and warm, you would fall asleep. The Marine Corps would still shoot you if you fell asleep on watch.

Body functions were much harder to deal with during these twenty to thirty below zero days and nights. Getting all of the layers off and squatting in the snow would never be a joyous experience. After dealing with the layers of clothes, there was the issue of the weapon. The hard and fast rule from day one in Korea—do nothing without your weapon. It was OK to lean it against the tree within reach. But, if it slipped during this delicate process, do NOT grab it by the metal part! Naturally to be doing a good job on the function part, the hands would be out of the gloves and bare. If you grabbed the metal part of the rifle, the hand would immediately freeze to it. Separating the frozen skin from the weapon was a painful process. You would not make that mistake twice.

CHAPTER 46

A hot meal, Charles, and a lesson . . .

It was near Thanksgiving, maybe even Thanksgiving Day. The word came down to 1st squad that Division was sending up a hot meal. Every day Korean laborers, 'chiggy bearers,' made the long climb up the reverse slope to the top of our mountain using back trails from the valley floor to deliver supplies to us. Today they had brought us hot 'real' food.

Those poor bastards. A tough war had destroyed their country yet they were working like dogs. Most likely their pay scale was next to nothing. These short and squat laborers—most of them older men—carried huge loads on their backs using a wooden A-frame, or *chige*. The pointed end of the A extended about two feet above their heads. The bottom stems of the 'A' almost reached the ground. Somehow on that skimpy frame they carried monster loads up the narrow winding trail to our hill about 1800 to 2000 feet above the valley.

You had to respect them—they were hard workers and brave. Those of us who went on trips back to Battalion knew that there were spots on the trail that were exposed to direct artillery fire. We knew when you got to those spots, you had to run like hell. Yet the chiggy bearers walked that route on a daily basis.

A fully loaded Marine carried about 70 to 80 pounds of gear. Their load usually looked to be about 200 lbs. They delivered our ammo, mortar rounds, water, and our beloved C-rations. They were also always loaded with something for the return trip. Sometimes they carried wounded Marines, but even when there were no wounded they had something to carry down.

We had been on C-Rations for an extended period of time and were pretty excited about getting a hot meal. A real Thanksgiving turkey and dressing feast. Special. We inhaled the dinner. While we ate, the bearers were grouped and waiting for their next load and the return trip to the valley. Once our meal was over, Charles spoke to their English speaking guide and told him to have the bearers wait in place for a couple minutes. They stay seated quietly in the typical Korean squat.

Charles, our resident California expert, might have been the biggest mouth in Marine Corps history. He was one of those high energy types that appeared to be moving and talking even if he were asleep. Always ahead of the game and figuring things out, Charles did also consider himself to be above us all in social grace, knowledge, and worldly things. Still, Charles was in every respect a solid combat Marine. Totally dependable under fire, he always held up his end and usually part of someone else's. Because of that, we wrote off the mouth as a California thing.

Charles moved in among us and began a speech. "Look you slovenly low life assholes, we have just been served a fine hot meal. If you dumb uncultured fools do not know better, I do. The waiters will be tipped. Everyone of you stupid shits get off your ass and search your gear for something you have that would be of value to them. Think about what you possess and part with something that means something. There are 12 of them and 12 of us."

Each of us went to find something worthwhile. Among the items that came forth were a couple of watches, a fancy Swiss Army knife, one purple heart, one bronze star, a St. Christopher medal, and other assorted valuables. Reassembled, Charles explained the Korean culture and issued instructions. The exchange would be made individually to each bearer by one of us. He directed us to include a slight bow after a presentation was made. Our bows were returned. A unique and touching human experience. This presentation ceremony might have been a high point in the entire Korean War.

Chapter 46

If we didn't learn something on the reverse slope of that hill on that Thanksgiving day, we were incapable of learning.

Thanks Charles.

The only bad news from the meal was the ice cream, carefully carried up under frozen conditions. We had been on a steady diet of C-Rations for a couple months. Naturally, we pigged into the ice cream. For some it was too rich for the system which resulted in some gastric problems and some throwing up, but it was generally agreed that it was worth it.

CHAPTER 47

Smart Mouth, you are not smart enough to be a Sergeant

Raymond approached. "Smart Mouth I need to talk to you in my bunker."

"I will try to work you into my busy schedule. Is a week from Monday all right with you?"

"NOW!!"

"What's up Raymond?"

"Try listening to me, it will be a new experience."

This came with another of the devastating looks like the ones that my mother gave me. I kept that thought to myself, wasting another opportunity to suck up to him and let him know my true and warm feelings about the similarity between him and my mother.

"Look Smart Mouth We are getting filled back up with replacements for the guys we lost. There will be six added to first squad and I am making you acting squad leader. You are good at what you do and I need you to take over the squad. The rest of the riff-raff will follow you. They trust you. There will be 2 three-stripe sergeants among the replacements. I want you to get them snapped in, seasoned, and ready for squad leader spots. Both have been in the Corps for four or five years, but have never been shot at. Stateside all the way. They volunteered to come here."

I remembered how the Professor had handled it when Raymond had tried to make him a squad leader, so I decided to give the Professor method a try.

"Jesus, Raymond! I am serious! I am a follower, not a leader."

The ever-so-stern look again.

That approach having failed, I tried a different one. "Raymond, how the hell am I going to boss around two Marine Corps sergeants? They won't do what I tell them. I haven't even been in the Corps for a full year."

Another silent look.

"OK. Sergeant Sir. Like always, I will do anything you ask me to do, but if it doesn't work out you will hear about it."

"Two things Smart Mouth. One—I hear from you on a daily and constant basis anyway, what do I have to lose? Two—yes, they will respond to your suggestions, commands, and orders. They are Marines."

"OK, Raymond, you talked me into it. You are such a smooth talker. By the way, Raymond, will I be promoted from PFC to sergeant?"

"Smart Mouth—you are not smart enough to be a sergeant."

Later the same day the order came down the line. "First squad. Report to the company command post, NOW."

Trouping to the reverse slope the conversation among the Marines sounded like the 'old' days. "Harry Truman wants our collective opinion on how to clean this mess up."

"Nah, the Commandant wants us to look at some proposed uniform changes and give our approval."

Entering the command bunker with full equipment was a task unto itself. It was made of sand bags, with a canvas door flap and an opening that was too narrow. With BARs, extra ammo, and other equipment, it was a chore just getting into the small area.

The replacements Raymond had mentioned had arrived and were sitting quietly. There were six of them fresh from the states.

Two of them did wear the three stripes of a buck Sergeant. This was going to be their first patrol action. The chatter stopped when we noticed an unfamiliar lieutenant looking over the table and a map.

"Greetings gentleman. I am Lieutenant Armstrong, your new platoon leader. I will get around and meet you all personally but we have been assigned to send a squad recon patrol to observe enemy activity down in the valley, near the ford of the river."

Goat spoke up. "Lieutenant, I can save a lot of government money and ammo and tell you what we will find. We have done this before and it is always the same. There is nothing there. They see us and then they come down off of their hill and try to kick the shit out of us. If we leave them alone they will stay up on their own goddamn hill."

Hack chimed in. "You know Lieutenant, PFC Goat is not too bright, but for once he is right."

With that, the balance of the board of 'experts' began adding their comments. This was one of those situations that they did not teach in Lieutenant School. They tried to teach how to get control and keep it. The new lieutenant tried. He cleared his throat. "OK guys, they gave me this platoon and these orders, here is what we have been told to do."

Charles spoke up, "That is great, Lieutenant. Does that WE mean you are going? That would be good because then we will have competent leadership. They just put Smart Mouth in as squad leader, and quite frankly he is sub-standard, using any known leadership standard. Actually, having Smart Mouth as squad leader sucks. He can't find his ass with a mirror."

"No, I will not be going. A lieutenant only goes on full platoon patrols." He then made the mistake of saying that he had learned that just a couple months ago in Lieutenant School. Comments followed, including those about using us as training dummies for post-graduate Lieutenant School. Finally, he regained control.

Lt. Armstrong described the route and asked for the squad leader. "I am told that PFC Mackinaw is squad leader." This announcement was followed by new noise—a generous series of boos

Chapter 47

from the older guys. The lieutenant then handed me the binocs, map, and compass.

Control was completely lost. The bunker was in an uproar.

Goat declared. "That's it! I am quitting the Marine Corps. I am going to my bunker and writing a letter of resignation."

Hack added, "Me too. Over the hill."

Even old quiet Moose joined the fun. "Well Harold, if you are going over the hill, so am I."

Hack offered, "Hey Goat! I'll write your letter and you can add your 'x' for a signature, since you rebels never learned to read and write."

Lt. Armstrong again had lost control and the Lieutenant School had definitely not addressed the subject of outright mutiny. The command bunker flap opened and in walked Sgt. Gotshall, a man of presence. Control instantly returned and it quieted.

"Lt. Armstrong, is there a problem?"

"I was preparing them for patrol."

Raymond turned to me. "Smart Mouth, this is your squad, what gives?"

"Raymond, these ingrate assholes are not appreciative of the caliber of leadership the squad now has. Actually, Sgt. Gotshall—it is my belief that the problem really started when the lieutenant gave me the compass and the map."

That comment was met with renewed loud noise and affirmative support from the ranks.

"OK Smart Mouth. Give the compass and map to Hack. The rest of you, listen up, NOW!!!"

The revolt had ended. Raymond turned to the new officer. "Lieutenant. The real issue here is that you would have had the same response if Smart Mouth had led you on a patrol that was supposed to go down into the valley and back and you wound up 2 miles behind the enemy lines. Smart Mouth can fight and lead but not with a compass and or a map in his hands. He has an unmatched level of incompetence in those areas."

"Sgt. Sir—I remember how pleased you were when I delivered a prisoner to you from that patrol."

Raymond ignored me. "OK ladies, enough BS. Listen and do. This is the Marine Corps, not your knitting group. There will be no vote taken at the end of the session."

"Lieutenant, you are free to finish the briefing. You have my personal guarantee that you will have their undivided attention."

The silence from the previously noisy peanut gallery indicated they had captured the idea.

Off into the valley.

CHAPTER 48

Operation Roy Rogers

Somehow Division had managed to get four or five tanks up a narrow dirt road and into the middle of our defensive positions. The reason for the tanks was a mystery to us. The tanks were placed along the main line of resistance between our bunkers.

The men who had positions near the tanks bitched constantly for a very simple reason—tanks drew fire. Who needed that? Why and what purpose did they serve? 'Marine Intelligence' was at work again.

For Boost, however, it was a Godsend. Maybe it was his sweet innocent smile or because he hung around and asked tank questions. The tankers thought he was an aficionado of tanks. They were wrong. He stole them blind. Our bunker/armory was over flowing with good tanker stuff.

Farm boy Moose had been a fisher-hunter person in Minnesota and he loved guns and enjoyed playing with any kind of weapon. He came up with an innovative new game—sniping contests with the company 50-caliber machine gun.

Boost stole several belts of 50-caliber machine gun ammo. A belt of this type of ammo had a tracer bullet every 10 rounds. When the 50 was fired using the belt of ammo, the tracers produced a red streak and the gunner could see where his stream of fire was going.

We took turns with one shot each with one of the tracer bullets. The game was to see who could put a round into the opening of one of the bunkers on the opposite hill. Good entertainment.

The call came for everyone to come to the command bunker. The first order of business was that regiment was in need of a man with experience fixing radios. Herman, who was sitting next to me, immediately put his hand up. "That is my hobby and I am licensed."

Herman was selected to leave the platoon and take the job repairing radios at Division. I was in shock. We had been close for all of these months, having shared a million long talks and having been together in plenty of tight spots. We were the closest of friends.

Herman looked over and, sensing my shock, put his arm around my shoulder. "Look little guy—be happy for me. I have only two months left here and I want to go home in one piece. You know the song. I'm tired and I want to go home."

"You never told me that you knew anything about radios."

"I don't. They have an off and on button, right? I will fake it. Can't be that hard to fix some of them and the others I will drop from 8 feet and call them broken beyond repair."

"Herman, do me a favor. When you go, do it when I am not looking."

Our attention was then back on Raymond, who had taken on a serious look. "Guys, the Marine Corps has just made its biggest mistake ever."

Chapter 48

The bunker got very quiet. Raymond was slow getting out what he had to say. Then, with a smile he said, "The Marine Corps has promoted Smart Mouth to Corporal."

This announcement was greeted with a standing ovation with plenty of whooping and hollering from my peers. When it quieted down, Raymond continued.

"This just came down from Regiment. A patrol. It has been given the name 'Operation Roy Rogers.' Six men from First Squad will go down into the valley where we have spotted enemy activity. Of course, they want a prisoner. You are to take this length of rope and put it across the trail like a cowboy lariat. When one of the enemy steps in it, you pull him in and tie him up."

As could be expected, the bunker went nuts.

Raymond let it go on a minute and then took control, apologizing and acknowledging that he voiced the same opinion when they told him. "OK Corporal Smart Mouth—pick 5 guys and form a plan."

One of the new sergeants, Sgt. Murphy, raised his hand. "I'll go. Raymond told me that if I stayed close to Smart Mouth, I would learn. I am truly curious about what I will learn tonight."

I did not have the heart to make the 'old' guys go on this patrol. It was past stupid. I selected all new guys for the patrol. I told my newly formed patrol, "The really bad part is if we get someone in the rope. If he happens to have a burp it could go in any direction."

Regardless, we were no better off than Raymond. He had no choice and we had no choice.

"Any ideas?" I asked the group.

Sgt. Murphy loosened up the group with "May I?"

"Help yourself Murph."

Murph laid out a fairly simple plan. "We should go right after dark, wear lots of extra clothes, and expect to spend the night. We have to be careful of the weapon the guy is carrying. If he does have a Burp we need to be well covered behind big rocks." The guy sounded like a leader. He then told Raymond that we needed more rope so we could be far enough away if we were unlucky enough to have someone walk into our great trap.

The patrol plan was set in motion. It was a beautiful clear full moon night and getting in place early had been a good idea. We positioned ourselves so that we could see anyone coming a mile off. We formed two semi-circles, each positioned on opposite sides of the trail and situated so that we would not wind up shooting each other. We were well back and protected by trees and rocks. Even if the over-all idea was lousy, Murph had come up with the best possible way to approach it.

We waited quietly.

As dawn approached, we figured that the Chinese were much smarter. They stayed home and just before light we trekked up the hill and into the lines empty handed.

Arriving, we had another of the classic password experiences. Passwords were, for the most part, pretty dumb, though they did serve a purpose. These replacement types had heard the whole range of stories about passwords. Kind of a tradition sort of thing. In reality a password was a necessity. Naturally, if you heard Shirley followed by Temple, it would not be a Chinese soldier. The creativeness of the Marine mind made the innovations much more fun and worked just as well. Most revolved around some form of obscenity combined with one or more body openings.

Of course, the password for this night was to be 'Roy Rogers.' When challenged coming in, the guys behind the wire were supposed to yell out 'Roy!' Our response would be 'Rogers.'

"Roy" came from behind the wire. The long night laying in the snow and cold having done nothing for outlook and attitude, the replacement guy on point of our returning group yelled up toward the wire "Hey, do you have a brother?"

"Yeah."

"Well, fuck him too."

It had been a very long and cold night. We had laid in the snow all night freezing our asses off under low hanging pine trees

Chapter 48

waiting for our prey. Now was not the time to test us. You had to be proud of Murph and the other guys for their attitude in doing something that had no merit.

CHAPTER 49

A mutual admiration society

North Korea was a seriously cold place during the winter months. The Professor had done some map work and plotted our positions. We were in a mountainous area far north of the 38th parallel. Our weather expert, Moose, reported that the night temperatures were dropping into the range of 30 below zero. It was near the end of February or the beginning of March.

Raymond had left us. The Regimental commander had requested him for an open position—something to do with operational planning or something.

Murph had moved into the platoon sergeant spot. That was an easy change for us because we all liked Murph and it was obvious that he knew what he was doing. His style was more laid back than Raymond's, but just as effective.

Then the word came down that the Skipper, our company commander that had led us all these months, was also leaving to go to Regiment. Promoted to Major, he would be the S-3, or Operations Officer. He had been only the second company commander during our time in Korea. Soon after I came, the first CO had jumped into a hole at the same time as some kind of explosive and had lost both legs.

From our vantage point, it was a lousy idea and a great one at the same time. No question, he deserved the promotion, but it meant we were going to get someone else. It was a strange feeling. The Skipper was part of us. He had all the tools to be a leader. Never a doubt that he was one of the boys, but there had also never been any question about who the lead dog was. He asked us questions and requested our opinions. These were not just lip service questions. When he asked you for your opinion, it meant that he wanted it.

Murph came down the company line and had taken each man, one at a time, to the command bunker for a personal meeting with the new company commander. From what we had heard from others as they came back, was that the Skipper had used the occasion to thank each man for the help they had given him. Pure class.

When it came time for my turn, Murph said "He wants you and Boost at the same time. Come on, the war will hold until you get back."

At the command bunker, Boost and I passed through the canvas flap and stood at attention. The Skipper said, "At ease. Take a seat and make yourselves at home."

Turning to the new company commander, he said "Captain Nelson, the big good looking one is Corporal Bustamate. We call him Boost. The ugly midget Marine is Smart Mouth."

He then took us both by surprise.

"Captain Nelson I had these two come at the same time for more than one reason. One reason is because you will never see one without the other. The more important reason is to tell you that you will never meet two better Marines."

An emotional moment.

He continued. "Captain Nelson. Like many of the good things in life, these two come with some warts."

"I'll start with Boost. Before you are here very long, someone will accuse Boost of equipment theft. When that person comes with the accusation, you might as well assume it to be correct. Boost does steal things and he also gets the other one to steal for him. What they steal are things like empty magazines for Boost's BAR, boxes of machine gun ammo to fill those magazines, grenades, and anything else they can find that goes bang. If you stay on line for any length of time their bunker will look like the Division armory. The boxes of grenades will be stacked in position ready for use. The empty BAR magazines will be filled with the stolen machine gun ammo—also stacked and ready for use. Boost is the only Marine in history to fire 5000 rounds of ammo during a fire fight when he only carries about 500. He is a one man base of fire."

"When they do come for them, do yourself a favor, lie and cover their sorry asses. It will pay off when the shit hits the fan."

"Now the other one. If he asks you for permission to speak, give it some thought. If you are not in the mood for a lot of conversation or don't have the time, just say, 'not granted.' This one has a lot to say. Let me give you an example."

"His previous platoon sergeant came to me and requested that I recommend Smart Mouth for officer candidate school. He has the necessary two years of college. The sergeant and I agreed that he had leadership qualities and that the idea had merit. We brought him up to the command bunker to share our brilliant thoughts with him."

"He asked for permission to speak, which was granted. Then for permission to speak freely—also granted. 'Fuck both of you, Sir.' was the free speak."

Chapter 49

"Platoon Sgt. Gotshall almost had a heart attack. I gathered myself and asked for the reason for his response. Smart Mouth offered this 'Sir, I appreciate the thought, especially from two men that I have great respect for. My response is in no way was disrespectful. It merely is an expression of my personal feelings. I have been here in Korea for 8 or 9 long months. If you send me to Lieutenant School, when I finished, they would send me right back here. Under no circumstances, do I wish to return to this country. My total goal, at this point in my life, is to get out of Korea alive, return to the sunny University of Arizona campus to drink beer, and chase girls. There is a second reason. The Marine Corps has taught me many lessons. Perhaps, the most valuable lesson is that I am not good at taking orders. I will always be a Marine but there is no place for anyone in this Corps with that personality trait.'"

Boost quietly asked, "Skipper, may I speak freely?"

The Skipper answered, "Boost, I always listen to you."

Boost pointed to the Skipper's feet and addressed his new commanding officer, "Captain Nelson, those are big boots to fill."

The whole thing sounded like one of those mutual admiration societies.

It was.

There is nothing wrong with admiration societies if they are based on sincerity.

It was.

CHAPTER 50

St. Patrick's Day, 1952

March rolled around. Those of us of Irish descent were looking forward to St. Patrick's Day. "It's been a long fucking winter." Not only was St. Paddy's day coming, two days before word that we were leaving these positions had come down the line.

As usual, the word that we were moving had inspired floods of rumors. For a change, the most common one was the correct one. The entire Division was going somewhere.

For the experienced, this was not good news. Good news would have been something like getting to go back into a nice safe reserve area far behind this line. Our general opinion was that we had a turn coming for a well-deserved rest with warm tents and hot food.

Daylight came on St. Patrick's Day. It was nasty, cold, overcast, and ugly. The outlook and demeanor of the troops seemed to match the day. The exchange on line with the Army troops replacing us had taken place in the standard manner. Hole by hole. The consensus was that we were going to have a long day on St. Patrick's Day. No pleasure hike.

We had held these same positions for at least three months and they had become almost homey. During that time we had accumulated equipment and things to make life more bearable. But, our instructions for this day were to pack everything up and be prepared to hike out. Where? How far? Who knew?

Boost, Charles, and I were huddled assessing the situation. We were distilling the rumors and mixing in previous experience and trying to figure out what was happening. Charles looked over at the Professor and realized he had offered no opinion, so he asked the Professor directly what he thought. There was still not much of an answer, so Charles got up, went over and sat down next to the Professor and this time asked him directly what was the matter.

What we should have remembered was that the Professor was due for rotation. After a bit of prodding by Charles, he reminded us. "I was just sitting in that bunker waiting to be called and sent to Division for rotation and now this. Something is going to happen and it is not good."

Combat gets to different people in different ways. There can be no question that the young make the best fighters. They just do not get into heavy thinking and merely allow the situation at hand to dictate. The exuberant but mostly blank mind of youth becomes an asset.

There was no question that the Professor was more mature than the rest of us. It was not only the fact that he had the college degree, but he thought things through many times and was always aware of what was going on around him. The rest of us were still in that phase of life where we were drifting along, promising ourselves that we would think about it later.

Too much thinking can weigh a man down. In the end, especially in the type of situation we were in, it would get to you if you thought about it too much. The Professor wasn't ready for the 1000-yard stare, and most likely would never get there, but some of the preliminary symptoms were showing.

Charles was speaking to the Professor in low and soft tones—unusual for Charles. "Sorry, Professor we just forgot. We are selfish bastards and we were thinking too much about ourselves and our getting to go home in a month. We forgot that you went first."

With that, Charles put his arm around the Professor's shoulder and gave him a small hug. Charles assured him, "Look Professor I know what you are thinking. Here's the deal. I give you my personal guarantee that I will get you out of here safely and in one piece."

Boost and I exchanged looks. We were young men who rarely touched in any way, much less to show affection or warmth. Here was Charles, who had always demonstrated the emotions of a salamander, being a comforter.

For the past months that had stretched almost into a year, we had all walked the same troubled path. Individually we had some special relationships. Each man had found a buddy for life on a single patrol or some other tight spot that they alone had experienced. That wasn't really the essence of it. We had watched out for each other, protected each other, grieved together, and laughed together. We had watched each other mature and grow into men.

Charles had just provided us with another lesson. What we shared in individual relationships went very deep. Surface appearances and general conversation rarely reflected the feelings that were underneath. Emotions went far deeper than we knew. We couldn't have expressed those feelings in words if we tried. The closeness. It was in there and would stay there.

The Professor brightened and admitted that he was mired in wanting to go home and the change in scheduling had bothered him. "Enough is enough. I am ready to leave. I want to go home in one piece."

Murph came by and filled us in. We had liked Murph from the first day. He was a good one. Murph knew he was never going to be Raymond to us older guys and didn't try to be, but he possessed all of the characteristics of a true leader. You felt like an equal when he was telling you exactly what you were going to do. It was almost like he was asking for help at the same time. Leading for him, was not confined to merely giving orders.

He asked for our assessment of instructions for the platoon on how to prepare for moving day. Boost said "Murph, tell them to pack as light as possible as it will be a long day. Don't take anything that is not essential." Boost could not have been more correct.

That St. Patrick's Day, well into darkness, we plodded along on muddy trails and roads, suffering a miserable cold rainy Korean

Chapter 50

day. We walked hour after hour with our weapons, ammo and full packs. Late that night, the column entered a collection area.

The Professor announced to our group, "This is the whole Division. Look at the equipment. Everything we have. This has to be all the regiments, even the Artillery. We are up to something big."

Mess trucks were feeding huge lines of Marines a hot meal. Our mess gear was filled with real food and canteen cups with hot coffee. No one even knew or cared what we ate. We were hungry and tired Marines. Back in the boot camp days there had been some picky eaters who complained about the menu and methods of serving and often left the mess hall without eating. Not today. Eat the food, drink the coffee, and get in one of the waiting 6 by trucks. Each truck had almost enough room for a full squad . Even the bench seats felt good after the long day and we had a canvas cover to shelter us from the rain.

The full stomachs felt good. Before many miles down the bumpy Korean dirt road we somehow found a way to arrange our equipment, use the truck floor, benches, and each other and sleep. In appearance, it could have been a pile of puppies, kittens, or earthworms.

St. Patrick's Day March 17, 1952. . . . Some holiday!!

CHAPTER 51

Good news, bad news

The truck ride across the peninsula of Korea took forever. Unknown to those of us bumping along the horrible Korean road system, we were headed for something called the Jamestown Line. No official word had filtered down. The only scuttlebutt that seemed to have substance was that the Jamestown Line was somewhere north of Seoul itself.

Rumors fed on one another. The Jamestown Line rumor was backed with an additional rumor that the Chinese had boasted that they would celebrate the big Communist holiday, May Day, May 1st, in the streets of Seoul.

The crow might have been able to easily cross Korea from the mountains near the east coast to the Jamestown Line and cover the 150 miles quickly. Not so for this gigantic column of the 1st Division. We were not traveling in a straight line.

From mountain positions near the east coast all the way across Korea was a long way. The Professor was put to work to figure out what was going on. It was good for him to get his mind working and off the fact that he should be on his way stateside. Back in 'Professor' form, he gave us a lesson:

"Korea is a peninsula approximately 700 miles long with the Sea of Japan on one side and the Yellow Sea on the other. Straight across the peninsula from east to west, Korea varies between one hundred to almost two hundred miles wide."

"This country has been overrun and conquered a number of times over the centuries by various people. Each time it has been invaded from the north, they came the same way. The terrain invites the use of the same route, a traditional invasion route. The capitol of Seoul is dead center in that path from North to South Korea."

"If the rumors are true, it is most likely that the 1st Division is going to be placed in the middle of the invasion route to discourage the Chinese from keeping their threat. Every other unit that the Chinese fear will be on either side of us. The most likely would be the British Division and people like those vicious Turks."

"There are a couple huge rivers that will complicate things for both sides. At this time of the year they are going to be flooding with melting snow. Any way you look at it, it is not a pretty picture."

Had the Professor known that after we reached the Jamestown Line he was being pulled and headed home, the lecture might have gone on. As it was, he fell silent while each of us tried to sort out our fate.

Somewhere after a million hours of discomfort we sighted one of the Professor's rivers. Huge and raging. A long pontoon wooden bridge across the river appeared. This stirred up the troops.

"That sucker is a one-way bridge. Wooden, one foot above the level of the river, and actually floating on pontoons!"

"A floating bridge! I am not going over that son-of-a-bitch on this stupid truck."

"No way would we make it across—that water has to be freezing."

That bridge was not in use and we kept going. Our Division column seemed to string out forever. The next bridge was the same type and again passed by, much to our relief.

Not so with the next one. As we approached we could see the trucks, one after the other going across the low, swaying bridge. Each moved on the wiggly bridge slowly and the column was backed up for miles. Tanks, jeeps, artillery, and trucks of every description crossed as we watched.

When we were within 50 yards of our turn, one of the replacements did the Catholic Sign of the Cross. Only the last remaining smidgen of Marine pride kept the remaining truck passengers from doing the same in unison. It would also be very un-Marine like to jump off the truck and run for it, though each of us gave it some thought.

The bridge moved gently back and forth and gave every feel that we would be dumped into the frigid water. We agonized but finally made it across the raging wide Han river. Bravado began to creep back in.

Once we were over the river, some master plan kicked in. Of course, the brass had not come by and briefed us on it. The column split a couple times and each split headed in different directions. The 1st and 5th Marines headed off to move into front line positions.

Off the trucks, stretching and lounging felt good. It had been a long ride capped by the scary bridge. Murph came to first platoon with the 'word.' "Guys, at first I thought we had drawn a good straw. It shakes out this way. Because everyone thinks so much of 1st platoon Baker Company we are getting a special assignment. The 1st and 5th Regiments have been give an area too large for them to cover. First platoon has been assigned to the 5th Marines."

"We will man outposts in front of the main line of the 5th Marines. I don't know how far in front that will be. Listening posts. This is supposed to improve the odds. Not sure whose odds. Sorry."

Turning to the Professor, he added, "Professor, I just got the word, you are not going with us. You are going home. You report to Division. Take you gear and move out."

Charles, Boost, and I were standing together as the Professor got his stuff together and started to leave. There was a collective happiness among the three of us. There was a time to go. A time when you just don't have it anymore. That time had come for the Professor.

The Professor started off and had gone about twenty yards when he stopped and turned back toward us, raised his hand to

Chapter 51

about belt level, and gave a gesture that could have been interpreted as a wave or a salute. He quietly looked each of us in the eye. We each returned the simple motion in the same manner. Then he trudged off.

We got back in the trucks and were off to be with the 5th Marines.

Another new experience. Separated from our own 7th Marines and alone in the world.

We felt fortunate to be assigned to a company commander who seemed happy to have us. He praised us individually and the 7th Marines collectively for helping him out.

The positions his company had inherited from the ROK Army were pathetic. He put his Marines to work immediately to get this area ready for the coming attacks. There was monstrous work to do. This place looked more like a military rest area than defense positions. The positions had been covered to protect from the rain, but certainly were not ready for an attack.

The other two squad leaders and I were assigned outpost positions, jointly picked out at a meeting with our new commanding officer and Murph. The company commander asked for our help in choosing the appropriate hills where we could be the safest while at the same time providing him with protection and a warning system.

"You guys are going to be out there. I want your ideas."

Considering everything, each hill chosen had the necessary elements we looked for. We felt like we could make them work. First squad had the middle of the three positions. Our outpost was on a hill about 500 feet high and approximately 1500 yards in front of the main line. We were separated from the other two outposts by about 500 yards. We were situated where we could have supporting fire from company mortars and 11th Marines' artillery.

The session with the new CO, Murph, and the squad leaders was all business. Everyone's input was taken into account and decisions were reached. Murph would stay at the company command post to coordinate.

During the discussions each of the squad leaders and Murph routinely referred to and addressed me as Smart Mouth, but our new company commander stayed with the formal Corporal Mackinaw through the entire briefing.

How strange to be slow in responding to your given name.

CHAPTER 52

Passing the torch

Charles, Boost, and I gathered the squad and laid down the law. The three of us had come a long way and had transformed from students to teachers during our time in Korea. Somehow in the evolution of the Marine Corps this happens. Each generation does its job, teaches the next, and moves on. The torch gets passed. So much of it happens without ceremony or ritual.

I addressed the squad. "Here is what is going to happen on this outpost."

We were next in line to go home and fully intended to be on the boat headed to San Diego. Charles made it clear that anyone who stood in the way of that objective would not be alive to see us leave–this by his hand, not that of the Chinese Army.

Quietly, but firmly, Boost supported Charles.

We took turns doing a 'Raymond' on the men going out in front of the company lines. Every facet of defending a position was covered and attentively listened to. It wasn't because we were the brightest in the world, but we had listened to Raymond enough times. Being ready WAS important and real.

Privilege of rank. Squad leader.

I made a quiet observation.

"God, it is great to move up in the world! Boost had to find a new burro." He appeared to have checked out the replacements using muscle mass as the qualifier. The kid he had chosen was huge.

I told the oversized Marine what a privilege it had been to serve in a similar capacity. Plain and simple–under fire, Boost was a force. Out of habit or respect, on the first trip out to the outpost I also carried an extra load of magazines for Boost's BAR.

The CO gave us his best wishes at the wire as we moved out to the new positions which were to be our 'home' for the next six weeks. The spot was perfect for an outpost with high, steep inclines approaching from all directions and great vision of the surrounding area.

We dug deep and set great fields of fire. The terrain was a bit different from the mountains on the east coast. There were plenty of good sized rocks which we bullied into and around our positions.

As we had come to expect, these kids were a good bunch of Marines. They would do well when we left them. That, however, did not excuse them from preparing. The outpost was brought up to 'Raymond' standards–which were now our own.

The communication with company was put in place and functioning. A hard phone line. More of the old World War II equipment, but it worked.

We made regular daily daytime trips back to company to enhance our fire power. These were done in full daylight at varying times–full speed on the trip in and almost as fast, even though fully loaded, when returning.

Boost's reputation in Baker Company had made an impression on the Marines who also carried the BAR. They had heard the stories about Boost and his exploits under fire. He almost had a fan club. Boost WAS one of a kind. Copying him was a good thing.

Each day we were more ready and armed to the teeth. The extra grenades we brought on each trip back to company were a real

CHAPTER 52

asset for these positions. The steep slopes surrounding our hill allowed them to be rolled down the sides. Very discouraging for anyone trying to come up.

The Chinese were exceptional at reconnoitering. Determined, quiet, and patient. They had started probing so all three of the outposts were on full alert every night.

The Chinese were going to test us. Every night at least one of the three outposts had someone bothering them. Twice our phone lines to the company were cut. Each time the phones went out, we also received visitors at the rear of the position. Both times we used our massive fire power along with plenty of grenades and they went away. Each time we put the phone line back in action the following morning.

It came to pass that the mid-April date for our rotation home had come and gone. Days passed quickly on our little outpost. Daily routine was interrupted only when our individual turns came for the dash back to company for resupply of ammunition and food. There is always huge competition between units in the Marine Corps. It even reaches the issue of which boot camp you went to. San Diego recruits were called Hollywood Marines and Paris Island guys took heat about not being real Marines. But at this time and in this place it was not true. We got plenty of positive attention and were treated like heroes by the 5th Marines. They heard the action we were getting every night out on our hill and knew we were handing out more than we got. While the Chinese stayed busy poking at our outposts, the 5th Marines were being allowed time to build an adequate line of defense.

When we took our turns making the 1500 yard ammo and food sprint to company we would hear "Hey, you guys from 7th Marines have king sized balls." Respect from peers was the best and it always felt good–especially coming from a real fighting outfit like the 5th Marines.

One day, Boost reminded us "Tomorrow is May Day."

Charles and I said it simultaneously, "Oh shit."

Mid-day the call came from the CO. "No one really knows what is going to happen tonight. Tomorrow is May Day. They may come in force or they may not come at all. I am not leaving the three outposts out tonight. Just after full dark, I am pulling you back. Bring everyone in. Get them packed and ready before dark. Don't overload. I want you in quickly and cleanly. All three outposts will come in at the same time."

To me he said, "Corporal, I ran into your old gunny and he filled me in on your name. By the way–Smart Mouth, you, Boost, and Charles leave us after sun up tomorrow. Time for you to go home. It has been an honor to serve with you. Good luck Marines."

That night the command came and we were quickly off the outpost and back inside the main line.

A long night. April 30, 1952. May Day Eve. The fireworks were awesome. All night the line in front of the 1st Marine Division was a nonstop gigantic display of light and explosions. From dark to dawn, artillery and mortars walked all over the area in front of the positions.

As we waited, we talked about New Guy. No doubt, if he had been there he would have yelled "Come and get us if you have the balls."

It was a long night without sleep.

The good news was that they didn't come. The Chinese boast to be in Seoul on May Day had not materialized.

Soon after sunrise the three tired Marines from Baker Company, 7th Marines, with full gear, walked south together. From all directions others came and moved out with them. They were all Marines who had finished their part of the job here and were going home.

There was no need to look back because there were Marines holding these positions. When there are Marines to do the job, never look back. The job will get done.

* * *

There is a unique simpleness in what we possess as Marines. Perhaps not as much simple as uncomplicated. Each of us had found something, in a variety of ways, as we passed through the

Chapter 52

ranks. Something strong. We had learned from our predecessors in Marine history. Those who made that history. We started out trying to emulate them and ended up being them. It was time to pass it on.

Without knowing it, the three of us had handed the torch to the next group of Marines, just as it had been handed to us. The Marine Corps is resilient because each generation of Marines does its job and makes sure that the next knows how to do the same. We want the torch passed because what it represents is real, strong, and part of us.

We had passed it.

There was still a lot to happen the next 14 months in Korea. Bitter fighting continued in Korea until July of 1953. Especially bitter in these positions.

CHAPTER 53

Only a friend would sit and listen

The lunch at El Salto was a beginning. Once Alma opened the gates, the story of the year in Korea came forth—the good, the bad, and the ugly.

After a long lunch, we had agreed to continue at lunch the next Friday. There were more stories than even I realized. The Friday lunches became regular. At times it was more like a therapy session. More than once a story uncovered reflections on painful subjects that caused too much emotion and required a change of topic. Alma especially enjoyed the stories where I was the butt of the joke.

Alma loved the stories —only a friend would sit and listen and ask for more. Though she had worked with me so long, she said she came to understand me more fully and saw sensitivities and emotions that had seemed non-existent to her. She also said she now understood my determination level and why I did not let others intimidate me.

The Marine Corps and the year in Korea had totally changed the young man that I had been. Its impact created lifelong changes.

Telling the stories also added to my sense of urgency to act on meeting Herman and renewing our friendship. Over 50 years had passed. Time could be running out. With Alma's help and full encouragement, I made arrangements to attend the reunion of the 1st Battalion, 7th Marines in South Carolina.

CHAPTER 54

First Platoon Baker Company together again

When I arrived at the reunion, I found Hilton Head to be a great destination with a large luxurious hotel on a beautiful beach. The main lobby was covered with Marine memorabilia, banners, and a variety of pictures of the Korean countryside—including plenty of snow pictures. The entire hotel was decorated for the Marine reunion. There was an exhibit of the full history of the 1st Battalion 7th Marines: Guadalcanal; Henderson field, where 1/7 held against wave after wave of Japanese; World War II South Pacific islands where 1st Battalion stood tall; and a whole wall of pictures of the Chosin Reservoir showing the 1st Division Marines who fought their way to The Sea of Japan after being surrounded by the entire Chinese army.

I found a spot on the spacious veranda of the hotel where I could see the entire parking lot, and watched . . . and waited. Herman had told me that he would not be recognizable after all of these years. "There is a lot more of me, than when you saw me last."

He was wrong. As far away as the far end of the parking lot, it was easy for me to pick him out, even with a full head of white hair and a few added pounds.

Even as we embraced, we started to talk. Nothing had changed. It was as if the years since I had last seen him were gone. We picked up where we left off as if it had only been a month ago. Just as we had done in Korea, we talked as if we were all alone in the world. All morning, through lunch, and into the afternoon the gaps in time were filled. We also found that neither of us had made contact with any of the other guys from 1st platoon.

Late into the afternoon, we settled into chairs near the tennis courts which allowed us access to an outdoor bar. The tables were filled with people chatting. A beautiful, pleasant day. As a couple of beers touched together in salute, my eyes caught something. "Herman—Look!"

"What?"

"Look at those four guys playing doubles with matching shirts and hats."

"Yeah...."

"Look at the old guy with all that white hair—take a good look."

"Shit—is that Charles?!" Herman started to get up, but I grabbed his arm.

"Wait. It is Charles ... but let's get him good. I have a plan."

As we watched, one of Charles' backhands hit the tape and fell back on his side of the court. A loud voice from our table called out "what a terrible backhand that guy has!"

Some people looked up, but then went back to their own conversations.

About five minutes later, an errant overhead went way beyond the back line. Again from the tables at the end of the court: "If I had a lousy overhead like that, I would give up the game!"

Charles was obviously annoyed, but he couldn't spot the source.

Herman and I waited until the match resumed and came onto the court from opposite ends.

Our old friend's eyes flashed. He was massively pissed by the invasion into his space.

Herman called out, "Charles—you dumb asshole—it's Herman and Smart Mouth! We would appreciate a more positive response after all we did for you!"

Chapter 54

"Jesus Christ!!!"

"No, just us."

After long embraces, Charles turned to his tennis partners. "Gentleman—these two misfits with a total lack of manners, were my subordinates in another life. They were such wimpy assholes, that I had to hold their hands, think for them and watch their sorry asses every step of the way."

"The big fucker is Herman and that little shit is Smart Mouth."

The tennis partners turned out to be the pilots for his business jet and his general manager. After introductions all around, Herman and I issued the proper condolences to the three men playing with Charles and made it quite clear that working for Charles must be a complete shit job.

The tennis game ended and the three old friends sat at a courtside table. No one else existed.

Herman dove in first. "Hey Charles, we always knew that you would own the world. Catch us up."

"When I got out, I went to school and studied hotel management. I have made it and lost it several times trying to learn how to do it right. Finally hooked up with some good people and the cards fell right. This hotel is part of a chain we bought out of bankruptcy."

"That may be the only good part of my life story. Along the way I have destroyed every personal relationship that I had. For example, I have four ex-wives; five ex-children. I was so damn busy and driven, I overlooked the good stuff."

Charles' cell phone rang and he wandered off where he had privacy and his conversation would not bother others. While he was off, Jim, his tennis partner and number one man came to the table and ordered beers.

I took advantage of the moment. "Jim, tell us about Charles."

"The man has the Midas touch. Most of it is that he knows how to treat people. His integrity is unquestioned in the industry we work in. Says he will do it and he does. Says he is not going to do it and he doesn't. But, he has left a swath of personal relationships behind. Seeing the two of you, put the biggest smile on his face I have seen in months. I see something very special about the relationship he has with you."

"Personally, I am not 40 years old yet and he has made me wealthy beyond anything I might need. I could quit tomorrow or right now, but I would not want to miss a day around him. I learn something new every day."

"He owns this hotel and about a third of the hotels in the chain outright. The rest we do a management thing where we get our return off the top."

"Somewhere when we were working, he saw that this hotel was hosting a reunion for 1st Battalion 7th Marines. He said something about it being his old outfit and had me look into it and be sure that everything was done as it was supposed to be. He found out that the Marines called the 'Chosen Few' would be here. Charles said that they were a very special group of people. He wanted to meet some of them."

Charles returned to the table and asked Jim, "Is it OK with you if we leave early tomorrow and not today? Can we get where we are going in time tomorrow?"

"Sure boss, it will work. I will go and get the pilots to file a new flight plan."

As Jim got up to leave, Charles said "Wait a minute, Jim. I want you to take a good look at these two because tomorrow between here and St. Louis, I am going to tell you about them. When I told you that they were subordinate to me, I lied."

"The big one has the balls of an elephant. He took one hill in Korea all by himself. My sorry ass was beaten up and I had to be dragged down, but I saw him and can't believe to this day what I saw him do."

"The ugly little dwarf with the snow white hair is the meanest man you will ever meet. Don't cross him. I did outrank Smart Mouth by one stripe, but he led and I followed. If he covered my

Chapter 54

butt once, he did it 6 or 8 times. Somehow he always made sure I made it back in one piece."

The rest of the day and into the night we talked. At first, most of our conversation covered how the time and experiences of the year in Korea affected our thinking and shaped our lives. Except for Doc, Charles also had not had any contact with the others from first platoon. Doc had finished his Navy time, gone to college and Medical School, and was a heart specialist in Iowa. As a tradition, Charles and Doc had spoken every New Years Day since Korea.

After awhile, the other guys from our platoon became the main topic. We all wondered about where life had taken each of them. Inevitably, 673 came up. What we did and saw that day was totally etched in our minds, down to the smallest detail. Amazingly, after 50 years, each of us had a clear memory of that horrible day.

We talked about how special those in 1st platoon were and we made a vow to search for those who had made it off that hill. More of a blood oath than a vow.

During the long time we spent talking there was something that did not need to be said. First platoon was together again, here this day. Now, the same as in the hills of Korea, we were going to stay together.

Where had the years gone?

Charles "Shit guys, you two may be that last pure human relationship I have had. Isn't that sad?"

I responded, "Kiss me Charles."

Chapter 55

All present and accounted for

During the months that followed, the three of us stayed in close contact, calling on the phone at all times of day and night. Great fun. When one of us found another member of the platoon, we called instantly to report.

The most incredible find in our search for first platoon members was our very own Jose. Alive and well in Texas. That word passed through the group like lightning. His telephone did not stop ringing. Pure joy for each of us. Hard to believe that he had survived.

Some were harder to find than others, but one by one those from 1st Platoon Baker Company were accounted for with two exceptions—Sgt. Raymond Gotshall and the Professor. None of us could remember the Professor's real name. None of us was really sure where we were headed once we found everyone, but we continued the search.

Finally, we got lucky. Herman found some Marine archives with a roster of Baker Company from September 1951 that gave full names, ranks, and serial numbers and found the Professor.

All the three of us could dredge up from our memories of Raymond was that he had come from Denton or Denison, Texas. I searched the archives of both local papers and produced a hit. . . . It was the toughest of blows. Raymond Gotshall had died many years

Chapter 55

ago, but his widow was still alive. Before I called Herman or Charles, I decided to call Mrs. Gotshall.

. . . This would be a tough phone call. Raymond had been such a force in our lives.

"Hello?" came the voice on the other end.

"Mrs. Gotshall. My name is Don Mackinaw from Arizona. I served under Raymond in Korea and was trying to find him. I just found out that he has passed. I did not know."

"Mr. Mackinaw, Raymond died almost 25 years ago. He served in the Marine Corps for 25 years and died of cancer six months after he retired. He was Sergeant Major of the 1st Marine Division in his last post."

"Mrs. Gotshall, I cannot tell you how important he was to those of us who served with and under him. It makes me very sad to know he is no longer with us. No finer man ever wore the uniform of the United States Marine Corps than your husband. Those of us who served together in Korea have been reaching out to find members of our old platoon the last several months. I do not look forward to passing this message to them."

"Mr. Mackinaw, please call me Mary. Raymond always talked about one of his men in Korea who was from Arizona. Do you know who that was?"

"It could have been me. I have always lived in Tucson, Arizona."

"Tucson? Really?!? I could use a favor in Tucson."

"Tell me who you want me to kill and I will call back when it is done."

Suddenly there was a gigantic pause in the conversation.

"Are you, by any chance, Smart Mouth?"

"Guilty."

"Over the years, I heard Raymond tell a variety of 'Smart Mouth' stories. Some were told a million times. I feel like I know you. When he told a couple of the stories, he always got quite animated . . . or maybe the word is agitated."

"I think I know which ones those were!"

"Seriously, Mary, tell me what I can do."

"My grandson Raymond, named after his grandfather, is a student at the University of Arizona in Tucson. Raymond is dating a girl from one of his classes. They went to a family party at her grandparents' home in South Tucson. While they were at that party, there was a drive-by shooting.

I want him to come home and finish his education in Texas, but he has refused. He is stubborn like his grandpa. Will you talk to him?"

"Sure. Give me his address and phone number. I will talk to him and call you back."

Chapter 56

A lifetime ago

It was truly a lifetime ago. My mind went back to those Korean Hills. Raymond.

I had been a wet behind the ears, snot-nosed, smart aleck kid. Raymond had kept me alive and started me on the road to becoming a man. Every thought, move, or action in that year of life was based on the influence of Raymond Gotshall.

Not a father figure. More of a god figure.

He knew how things were supposed to be done. More importantly he had known how to communicate with each of us. Maturity was not our strong point. Raymond simply accepted us as we were and made us better. He was one of those rare people that told you something and you automatically knew it was the correct thing to do. Fifty years ago he had taken a kid and turned him into a Marine.

It was difficult to believe that any malady, disease, or infirmity could have claimed him. Raymond had been bigger than life.

"Alma. I am going to lunch with Raymond's grandson. Try to make me feel important and tell me that the business will not run without me."

"OK, Smart Mouth."

"I am pretty sure I am going to fire you when I get back."

CHAPTER 57

Raymond Gotshall III

As I headed to meet Raymond for lunch near the campus, I was hit with a sudden avalanche of emotions. Weird. Thoughts, images, and faces from another life and another time. Korea. So much that had been long buried hit the surface all at once.

"Get it under control, you have a job to do here."

Picking out the kid from the crowd at the entrance of the restaurant was easy. He was a big, rangy, raw kid with Raymond's sandy mop of unruly hair.

Once we were inside with our food, the initial awkwardness wore off quickly and we started to get acquainted, covering the small talk of school and future plans.

"Raymond, I talked to your grandmother on the phone and she wanted me to convince you to come back to Texas to finish school. She is frightened about what happened at that party. Personally, I wanted to meet Raymond's grandson. Your grandfather was a very important person in my life."

"If anyone needed help growing up, I did. I tested Raymond's patience on far more than one occasion. He had a variety of names for our relationship. He characterized me as the most insubordinate Marine he ever met. There were a variety of adjectives that he added to that word insubordination. Each one of those words

Chapter 57

let me know how close I was to the edge of his patience. Borderline, overt, calculated, and on and on. Bottom line, in the end we trusted each other under fire and we had a genuine friendship. . . . I don't mean to go on too much about this and take up all your time."

"No, please Mr. Mackinaw. I only know my grandfather through pictures. I appreciate anything you have to tell me."

"Did you know that he was written up for the Congressional Medal of Honor? A hill in Korea with only a number for a name. 673. I saw what he did that day and there is no question that he earned that medal. On that particular hill there were five days of the most vicious fighting you could imagine. In the deluge of awards earned and given, his efforts were overlooked and his medal was reduced to 'A Letter of Commendation with a Combat V.' He was disappointed when he showed it to me, but he understood. Two Congressionals were awarded for that action—both earned. Your grandfather deserved the third."

I could tell you all the stories, but we would be here for weeks. Tell me about this South Tucson thing."

"I am not ashamed to admit that what happened scared the hell out of me. It is hard to believe that someone would open up on a family party with automatic rifles. I will never understand the mentality of someone who totally disregards what can happen when you fire high powered weapons into a family gathering full of children and old people."

"What were you doing in that part of town?"

"Stella and I go to the U of A together. We have been dating and she invited me to go to her grandparents' house for a family party. It was just a normal family party—Mexican food, hot dogs, aunts, and uncles. The whole works. All of a sudden a car pulls up in the alley and starts shooting. All hell broke loose. People were grabbing and covering the children. How no one was hurt is a mystery."

"Any idea why they were shooting at that party?"

"Stella recognized one of them from high school. He dated her back in high school and somehow thinks that she shouldn't date anyone. Stella can't stand the guy. It would just be normal ex-boyfriend stuff if it were someone else. She is afraid of him—with reason. In South Tucson he is called 'The Enforcer.'"

Raymond III studied me. With those eyes on me, again there was that feeling of familiarity. He must have decided I was safe, because he continued. "The part that I didn't want my grandmother to know is that he learned that Stella brought her college boyfriend to his 'hood.' He has put out the word that the drive-by was a warning and he has threatened to kill me if I don't stay away from South Tucson. According to Stella, he is capable of it. My grandma doesn't know the whole story—and she wants me to leave. You can imagine how she would feel if she knew. I do plan to return to Texas for graduate school, but not until I finish my bachelor's degree. I refuse to be run out of town by some nutzo."

"Raymond, do me a favor. You and Stella try to stay away from public places for a little while. Give me a chance to find out about this 'Enforcer' character. I have good friends on the South side who will tell me straight stuff."

"Hang out on campus for a few days, until you hear from me. OK?"

"OK."

CHAPTER 58

I need to talk to Gabe Sanchez

Once back at the office, I found Alma and went over the lunch meeting with Raymond III.

Alma was concerned. "Hey boss, I live in South Tucson. Everyone down there knows who the Enforcer is–the worst kind of bad news. First of all he possesses every bad characteristic that a human being can have. Secondly, he is young enough not to care. Thirdly he is massively involved in the drug trade on both sides of the border.

You know that South Tucson is the battleground for the illegal narcotic business. You may think you know what it is like down there from reading the daily paper, but you don't live there.

The Enforcer is the worst of the worst. He is responsible for murders, torture, and home invasions. No one messes with him."

"Thanks, I'll think about it. I need to talk to Gabe Sanchez."

"That's easy. He hangs out with my uncles two or three nights a week at the Marine Corps League Club, along with the other 'borrachos' from Company G.

"Boss, why do I have this sense that you are going to do something stupid? Be careful, I do need you around here."

Truth was, I wasn't really sure what I was going to do. I knew Gabe knew his way around South Tucson, though, so it seemed like a good place to start.

Chapter 59

Just grease the son-of-a-bitch

The Marine Corps League club house, a sharp looking building flying both the American and Marine Corps flag, is located in the middle of South Tucson, just off South 6th Avenue. It is mostly a social club with a nice bar, comfortable and well furnished. It opens at 3 in the afternoon and closes when the last Marine leaves. The league club was started by a group of Marines from the Korean era as a place to hang out together. Over time, it came to include new generations of Marines.

I entered the door, clearly marked for members only.

"Are you a Marine?"

"What's left of one."

This drew chuckles from those at the bar and nearby tables.

"You a member?"

"Yes, sir."

"Why don't I know you? I haven't seen you in here."

"I live on the far east side and don't want to drink and drive."

Gabe had entered and was standing behind me.

" It's OK, Frank. He is one of us. Another poor broken down Marine from Korea. Give him a beer."

Chapter 59

As Gabe poured my beer, he took a little heat from the bar and tables. "Tell us the truth about Gabe's Korea experience!"

"Gabe, are you still telling people about the Purple Hearts you got from cutting yourself on the lids of C-ration cans? Guys. The Silver Stars—all I know is that he was seen going in the tent of a gay lieutenant and coming out with Silver Stars. As far as I remember, Gabe never heard a shot fired in anger."

"Guys, this is Smart Mouth. I may have told you stories about him and later I will tell you more." He turned to me, "So, Smart Mouth—what brings you to South Tucson?"

"I need to talk to you about something—privately." We headed to a back table, where I filled him in about Raymond's grandson and the drive-by shooting.

"Shit! Smart Mouth—you read the local paper. South Tucson is full of people like that. Who is the guy who is after him?"

"All I know is that he goes by the name 'Enforcer' and that he attended Pueblo High School until he dropped out."

"Jesus, Smart Mouth! That Son-of-a-Bitch is one bad kid. A terrible human being. He has every bad characteristic a person can have and has added a few of his own. He is part of straight shootings, drive-by shootings, and drug killings. Stay away from him. Christ—he has all of South Tucson hiding behind locked doors at night."

"Gabe, the boy had nothing to do with anything connected to him. One way or another he is going to leave Raymond's grandson alone."

"Shit!!"

"I knew Ray. He was one helluva Marine. Tell me what you want me to do."

"I need to talk to this Enforcer guy."

Gabe asked, "Do you know Richard Solano, the South Tucson police chief?"

"I read his name in the paper, but I never met him."

"His uncle was Hector Solano—one of the Company G Guys."

"OK. Sure. I knew Hector Solano—he was at Inchon with Company G and got killed going north toward the Reservoir. I played ball with Hector at Tucson High."

"I will talk to Richard. See what he can find out."

"Gabe—keep in mind that there is to be no police involvement."

* * *

Three days later, I got a call from Gabe.

Gabe said on the other line, "Richard can contact the Enforcer through an informant. Do you want to do it?"

"Yes, Gabe. . . . See if the informant can set up a meeting with the Enforcer."

Gabe spoke, "I am in for whatever you need. South Tucson would be a much nicer place for us and our families if you just greased the son of a bitch instead of talking to him."

"Gabe! . . . that is not part of the plan."

CHAPTER 60

First Platoon Baker Company headed to Tucson

The search for the members of first platoon that Herman, Charles, and I started had taken an unexpected turn.

Each member of the old platoon was informed about the situation with Raymond's grandson. The essence of individual responses had been the same. We needed to act. Not surprisingly, each member of the platoon had ideas of their own about how to solve Ray's problem. That certainly hadn't changed. Those ideas included one similar to Gabe's—grease the bastard.

Sifting through ideas we found our best opportunity to get together was the annual reunion of the 1st Battalion, 7th Marines. It was scheduled in Tucson. Originally Charles had been the only one attending the reunion—this reunion was also to be held at another one of his hotels.

When we had parted back in the hills of Korea, none of us had given it much thought. We had left each other physically, but without knowing it we would always be together. Each had simply had gone off in a different direction.

Strange, but true.

Now when they were informed of this problem each response had included "Tell me where and when. I will be there."

First squad, first platoon Baker Company was headed towards Tucson and the Battalion reunion.

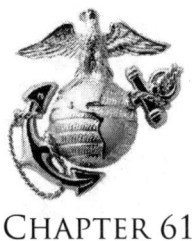

Chapter 61

No stronger bond can exist

For those headed to Tucson, time had deadened some of the pain. So many started out with us. Others came and fought beside us. Too many did not come home.

Some of that pain will always remain.

Everything in Korea had not been pain. Korea had not been only the firefights, assaults, and other nasty things that go with war.

There had been so many great laughs, jokes, and just plain funny things. We had shared day to day drudgery, the rains, and the awful living conditions. All of those things, in their own way, brought us closer together.

In this day and age it is common to use terms of connecting, fellowship, and bonding quite freely. Some of these men coming together now might not understand the precise meanings of those terms. They only know how it feels.

An outsider might not recognize the simple look and greetings between any two of these men as they meet again. Only we understand the depth of that feeling.

The connection between each of us was formed under the worst of conditions. Without knowing it then we had grown so close.

No stronger human bond can exist.

CHAPTER 62

First Platoon fall out and fall in

Charles' sleek corporate jet taxied up to the Executive Terminal at the Tucson Airport. One by one its passengers came down the stairs. This fancy Learjet had crossed the country and gathered Goat, Boost, Doc, Moose, Hack, and Jose.

Hard to tell when they deplaned if the luxury transportation or seeing each other took first prize. Either way, it was a jovial group. The bar on the plane may have helped.

Charles, Herman, and I were waiting in the terminal and had missed each of the individual meetings of these men. Only a blind man could have missed our anticipation as we waited for the plane's passengers.

To say that the individual meetings were like finding a long lost brother, would be a gross understatement. Each individual relationship was special and carried great intensity. The shared nature of that year had never left any one of us. Not as individuals nor as a group.

After a huge round of hugs and emotion, we stood back, all looked at each other and then hugged again. The last time we had seen each other was over 50 years before and thousands of miles away.

On the tarmac was a huge stretch limo with a big hand painted sign on the windshield.

"DOC MOBILE"

Charles had his arm around Doc's shoulder and directed him to the large vehicle.

"Doc, the special transportation is for you. It is my thanks for the piggy back ride you gave me a long time ago. It is up to you if you want the rest of these lowlifes to ride with you." Otherwise they can take the city bus."

"Thanks Charles."

Doc stroked his chin, paused briefly to think and said "Well, if I remember correctly, they always invited me along when they went on those wonderful hikes in the beautiful Korean countryside. I guess if would only be fair to invite them along now."

Like a bunch of kids, we piled into the limo and headed across town to the hotel. Poking, laughing, and giggling. Another bar, full comfort, and each other.

The site of the hotel was a spectacular setting at the foot of the Catalina mountains. The limo was expected. The general manager, concierge, and three executive staff members were waiting with a team of bell hops as the limo pulled to a stop.

When we checked in, our group found we were assigned the penthouse Presidential Suite and the floor immediately below it. The accommodations were passed off as being fully complimentary. Not so, it was going on Charles tab.

The Presidential Suite covered the entire top floor with several balconies, a Jacuzzi, a lap pool, and a fully stocked bar.

As first platoon moved about the top two floors there were many comments comparing this hotel to the Kansas Line, the Jamestown Line, and No Name.

CHAPTER 63

We had never left each other

When people form groups, they always follow it up with the formalities of meetings, committees, planning, and all with minutes taken. That kind of stuff would never fit in with 1st platoon Baker Co. We are a more earthy type.

The timing of the official reunion of the 1st Battalion 7th Marines, Korea 1950–1953 was fortuitous for us.

The group having this reunion in Tucson had been formed by the men of 1st Battalion, 7th Marines that had served together at the Korean Inchon invasion and the march north to the Chosin Reservoir. Those that fought at that reservoir on the northern border of Korea had their own name. The Chosen Few. These were men with steel balls. When the Chinese entered the war in late November of 1950, their troops had poured over the border between China and Korea. It was not expected. The Army divisions collapsed on both sides of the 1st Marine Division and the division was left completely surrounded by the Chinese Army.

Douglas MacArthur had assured President Truman and the entire world that the Chinese would not enter the Korean War.

Wrong!!

'Dug Out Doug' MacArthur was eventually recalled by the President and fired from his post as Supreme Commander. Too late, however, to help the men of the 1st Division.

The Army units protecting their flanks had been overrun and destroyed by massive numbers of Chinese troops. The 1st Marine Division was left to fight their way out of the encirclement. An epic battle in Marine history resulted. Against a multitude of Chinese divisions and a bitter cold North Korean winter they fought their way to the sea and rescue.

Their group was later expanded to include all Marines who served in 1st Battalion, 7th Marines during the three years of the Korean War.

Charles, Herman, and the Professor had previously discovered the group and were members.

The group's annual reunion this year was to be in Tucson at the El Puente del Montes Resort—one of those gorgeous destination-type hotels. The hotel looked as though it were simply laid down at the foot of the Santa Catalina Mountains. Not a single rock nor saguaro cactus seemed to be disturbed. Like all mega-resorts, the hotel came with multiple golf courses, spas, many restaurants, pools and walking trails. A standard room during the fall, winter and spring seasons ran in the $300 to $400 range without the golf. Golf was extra.

Windows on all sides showed the beautiful mountains and the natural beauty of the desert. At night the hotel looked down on the lights of the city. Every piece of the furniture, especially in the luxury suites, was exquisite. The atmosphere was soft and perfect.

The Presidential Suite had been reserved for 1st platoon and was designated as the room for the Professor and his wife as well as our gathering place.

The next floor down had the executive suites—not ordinary hotel rooms. Each had two bedrooms and included every amenity that could possibly be thought of for a hotel room. First platoon occupied the entire floor. Each member of 1st squad found his room stocked with a full bar, bottles of wine, baskets of fruit, and a variety of fancy food.

Not a single room door was closed. The guys moved in and out of each others rooms. The hallway served as a meeting place and

Chapter 63

the gatherings moved constantly from room to room. The laughter at the old jokes and jabs at each other was ongoing. Things seemed to pick up right where they had left off. A half century had not elapsed.

Goat and Jose kept running out into the hallway with something new that they had found in their rooms. Two school kids on Christmas morning.

Jose brought a bottle of fancy wine into the hall and Herman offered to get him a screw cap and a paper bag to make him more comfortable.

Fifty years and it was as if not a week had passed. We were more than happy with each other.

It was hard to tell that this was an impromptu meeting and impossible to tell that we had no contact all these years.

The reality was that this group did not need a reunion. We may have parted a long time ago but we had never left each other. We had been together the entire time.

CHAPTER 64

Ready to move out one more time

Time makes physical changes to the human body. Men that have passed their seventieth birthday show it.

Looking at this group roaming up and down the halls of this fancy hotel, those changes were apparent.

Two or three wore hearing aids. Most likely, a couple of others could have used one. Each blamed the multiple massive explosions in Korea. None seemed to accept the simple fact that the hearing loss might have been part of the aging process.

Most had also added beef, especially around the middle. The good life. Not one would have attempted to get into the old standard dungarees with the 32-34 inch waist. During the Korean years, stripped to the waist, the ribs could have easily been counted on each and every one of us. Those ribs were now lost from view.

Goat blamed his weight gain on the long hours behind the wheel of his 18 wheeler freight truck. He attributed hemorrhoids to the same source. All these years and he was still humping his big truck all over the USA.

Naturally when Goat told us about his hemorrhoids, he got the full treatment about no longer being a perfect asshole.

And the joint replacements—hips, knees, and shoulders . . . high blood pressure, high cholesterol, and even some breathing problems.

Chapter 64

Then there was sleep. It didn't come as easily as those nights in Korea when the watch was 50 %. There, when it was your turn, you slept instantaneously and deeply. When you woke up you were rested, fully alert, and ready to go.

Herman talked about years of sleep problems and his recurring nightmare. Being back on the top of 673 and all alone.

Baker Company, 1st Battalion, 7th Marines. Baker Company no longer exists. Somehow, somewhere in time, the Marine Corps changed it to Bravo Company.

Doesn't seem right.

There was full agreement on one issue. Alcohol had been the reason that each of us had lived this long and this well. Unlimited beer rations. Amen brother.

Doc made an attempt to explain the scientific part of that issue. He tried to point out that there were some negative aspects to the role of alcohol. The group politely refused to accept his thoughts on the subject.

The intense search for 1st squad was special—we had found Jose.

Jose.

To a man, we thought he was dead. When Raymond had carried his little brown broken body off the slope of 673 everyone who had seen him brought in, totally believed he was gone.

Jose.

Physically you saw no evidence of permanent injury. A slight limp, but no damage that kept him from walking a mail route for over 40 years. It was an amazing thing considering the massive amount of shrapnel taken out of his body. Whatever it was that destroyed Los Hombres, had to have been something big. Those that were on the left flank going up the hill heard a single large explosion and the Hombres were gone.

Raymond was making a last sweep under heavy fire on the forward slope of 673. On the far right flank he had spotted a flicker of movement in the area where the four members of Los Hombres had been. Ignoring the intense fire, the mortars, and mines, he had moved next to Jose. Our platoon sergeant, doing his job as he saw it, came down that hill with Jose's loose and bloody body. Somehow, the Corpsmen stuffed enough blood into him to keep him alive and the rest was, as they say, history. God made sure that nothing touched the world's friendliest open smile.

Those people on his postal route had a bright spot in their lives day after day.

Looking at the full group, there was a complete irony. Each put in the full year of heavy duty fighting in Korea. It would take a shoe box to hold the Purple Hearts earned. Several had multiples of that award. Everyone here had at least one, except for Herman. Herman, the one guy who made it to the top of 673 all by himself on the first day of a five day assault. Go figure. Maybe God took care of those with a pure heart.

This group loved the expression "Not as lean, not as mean, but still a Marine."

Being part of this group and doing nothing but sitting in a soft chair looking at each of them, was an awesome experience.

There was a lot of wear and tear and a lifetime of miles on each of us. At this moment our full interest in life was getting reacquainted.

We now possessed a combination of quiet resolve and a full knowledge of consequences. The flicker of the flame of youthful bravado could and would burn again with a white hot heat, if ignited.

Being a Marine had never been being the biggest, the strongest, nor the fastest. Inner strength, singleness of purpose, and heart remain the essence.

We'd had many years of sorting through what we learned. Those lessons had by now had time and opportunities to be tested.

The Slot was a lifetime maximum challenge. 'The first step' on 673 ruled out forever any intimidation of task or situation.

Anyone looking at us gathered in the hotel rooms could easily miss what was under the surface. Pure forged steel.

Chapter 64

In a few hours the greetings would stop and we would be face the task at hand. First squad, 1st platoon, ready to move out as a group one more time.

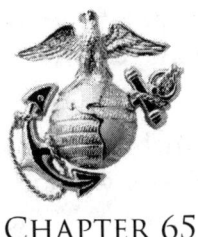

CHAPTER 65

South Tucson

The city of Tucson has grown dramatically since its days as a small western cow town in the high Sonoran desert. At the end of World War II, Tucson had 40,000 people and a single high school. Now the University of Arizona alone has almost that many students. A city pushing a million people.

The Mexican border is 65 miles due south. As Tucson developed, most of those of Mexican descent settled on the southwest side of the city.

Even as the city of Tucson grew around it, South Tucson voted to maintain its borders. The mostly Mexican-American residents refused to give up their neighborhood.

The proximity of the Mexican border has made Tucson a highway for illegal drug traffic. Tucson has become known for redistribution of marijuana, cocaine, along with the entire spectrum of drugs in the narco-traffic business. The bulk of that action is located in South Tucson.

People involved in drug trafficking are not only sensitive to competition, but anything else that interrupts their business activities. They take their work seriously.

Most of the drug-related murders are committed execution-style; though sometimes innocents who get in the way also die. When that happens, it is front page news. The run-of-the-mill

Chapter 65

drug-related killings can be found in the back sections of the local papers or not at all, depending on what else is going on in the outside world.

The city of South Tucson had been massively influenced by this movement of illegal drugs. The main street of the city, South Sixth Avenue, and the closely adjoining streets are a war zone. The fierce struggle for control between the heavy duty cartel influence, the street gangs that migrated from Los Angeles and El Salvador, and the local amateurs has reached a level of violence that leaves casualties on a regular basis. The forces of drugs, money, and testosterone at work.

The shootings and paybacks commonly spill over into the neighborhoods. While the target may be a single individual, often the fallout touches unintended victims.

Fast food places, Ace Hardware, parking lots and the like are not exempt from shootings and—are often used as body dumping grounds.

South Tucson has become a battlefield.

The majority of residents stay at home at night. They hope the war will someday end and their teenagers will survive.

Chapter 66

No award or honor equals being made a sergeant in the United States Marine Corps

The official reunion of 1st Battalion 7th Marines was scheduled to last three days. Like most reunions, there were a variety of outings and activities.

Golf, tennis, and hiking on the trails near the hotel. Trips were offered to view the Arizona Sonora Desert Museum, the San Xavier Mission, or a 65-mile trip to the Mexican border town of Nogales.

The opulence of the hotel and the side trips were not a consideration for the men of first platoon. We had a job to do.

We gathered in the spacious room on the top floor.

Charles, Herman, Smart Mouth, and Gabe Sanchez had been in heavy contact prior to the gathering in Tucson. They took turns and covered the situation as they saw it.

The demeanor of the men in the room had changed dramatically. Each was quiet, attentive, and focused.

A basic plan was put forth for the face to face meeting Gabe had now set up with the Enforcer.

Charles spoke up. "Before we discuss that we need to decide how to handle the Professor and his wife. The Professor has Alzheimer's. I have talked several times on the phone with Mrs.—or rather, Dr. Harris. I tried to call her by her first name several times and was curtly reminded that she was Dr. Harris."

Chapter 66

Boost said "Harris? Wow. I couldn't have told you the Professor's last name or his first name if you had a gun to my head. I never thought of him as anything but the Professor."

"The Professor is Dr. Harris and his wife also holds a PhD—a doctoral degree, so she is also Dr. Harris. She told me that our Professor had a shit load of honors and honorary degrees from a wide variety of universities, including all kinds of awards for academic excellence. Spoke several languages, the whole works.

According to Mrs. Dr. Harris, the professor's Alzheimer's is complete. He has zero recognition of anyone or anything that goes on around him. He requires total care."

Goat jumped in. "Jesus, Charles, why is she bringing him here?"

"Good question, Goat. The same one I asked her. I had told her that all of us from the platoon would be here at the reunion. She said she was coming and bringing 'Dr. Harris.' Through the whole conversation she called him that. She told me that she has never understood the part of his life as a Marine. She admitted that she is coming for herself. She told me that no matter what award or honor he received, his private response to her was always the same.

He would say, "My dear. No award or honor will equal being made a sergeant in the United States Marine Corps. No real or spoken respect from academic colleagues will ever match the respect given to an odd ball like me by the men of 1st platoon."

Still a pretty quiet guy, Moose spoke up. "They are staying in this suite. We may not want her to hear what we are doing."

By his side as they had been in Korea, Hack turned to Moose. "Moose we don't even know what we are going to do yet. So, don't worry, we can decide on that when the time comes."

Herman laid out his version of the basic plan. "We have set up a meeting with the Enforcer to get him to lay off of Ray and his girlfriend."

Charles then went over what he had obtained in the way of equipment, supplies, vehicles, and weapons."

He moved on to explaining the substance of our offer. "We are going to offer big money and/or large quantities of legitimate prescription drugs. We only want the contract lifted on Raymond's grandson."

Doc looked concerned. "Hey Charles old boy—what if he accepts our offer of money or drugs? Where are we going to get enough money or prescription drugs to satisfy someone like this?"

"Doc, the only thing I have been good at in my life is making money. For some reason it is a natural talent. I have fucked up every human relationship in my life except the ones with the men in this room. I have ex-wives and children in bunches. They all have an intense dislike for me and I have earned it. Sgt. Got Balls was a special man in my life—just like you are Doc. I won't miss the money but I sure could not live with myself if I let Raymond or anyone in this room down."

"As for the prescription drugs. . . Smart Mouth has been in the pharmacy business all these years. Really, Doc, he has never been as dumb as he looks or sounds."

Doc's head snapped towards me. He looked at me intently. The question about illegally using prescription drugs as a bribe was written all over his face.

As we looked at each other, we did not exchange, or need to exchange, a single spoken word.

My only response was a shrug and body language that clearly said "So?!"

That settled, I went over the local scene. I told the group about Gabe Sanchez, the men of Company G, and a local businessman, Mr. Kim. "Gabe has a contact who has set up our meeting with The Enforcer."

Jose took notice of this part. "Is Sanchez that the crazy Mexican from 2nd platoon with a million Silver Stars and Purple hearts?"

"The same."

Herman said, "Say! Speaking of crazy Mexicans! Will someone tell Boost to quiet down? He talks too much!"

The small smile appeared below a beautiful full head of wavy white hair.

CHAPTER 66

Now that he had the floor, Herman added, "Yeah, by the way Smart Mouth, how have you know when to take a pee all these years without Boost telling you it was OK?"

Nothing had changed.

CHAPTER 67

Honey Harris

The day had been long and intense with lots of give and take. New ideas were brought up and some were added and accepted, some rejected. The plan was taking shape.

Mr. Kim's role was explained. The owner of a chain of dry cleaning outlets, Mr. Kim was a successful business man in Tucson. He was a Korean-born naturalized American citizen. Gabe had approached him and Mr. Kim's response had been a simple one. He would have been offended if we had not included him. He told Gabe that whatever was his, belonged to us.

It was about time for a break. The valet appeared at the door with luggage and both of the Dr. Harrises. She held the Professor's hand and led him into the room, not knowing that the room was in use.

"I'm sorry. I was told that this would be our room."

Charles had risen to his feet. "Please come in Dr. Harris. I am Charles. This is your suite. We were just using the sitting room before you came."

She led the Professor into the room by holding his hand. A gentle pull, but there was no question. It was the manner of directing him. It was our Professor, but his eyes showed nothing.

She introduced herself to the group. "I am Dr. Harris and," she added, looking fondly at her husband, "this is Dr. Harris."

Chapter 67

Because Charles had briefed us, 1st squad was showing the appropriate sensitivity to the situation.

Each of us stood and an air of formality took over. The men of 1st platoon were careful to avoid what they wanted to do—touch and hug the Professor.

Charles continued acting his part as host. "Dr. Harris. Pick which bedroom you want. This suite will be your quarters while you are here. I think that the master bedroom with its adjoining sitting room will give you plenty of privacy while we meet out here. . . . If that is OK with you."

She protested that her reservations were for a regular room, but Charles assured her that we wanted both of them with us. Both the room and the offer to be with us seemed to please her. She guided the professor to an easy chair and accompanied the bellhop to scout out the master bedroom and deal with the luggage.

It was a choker for all of us. Deep breath time. Without realizing it we found chairs, couches and places on the floor. We formed a semi-circle in front of the Professor's chair, much like the days in the hills of Korea when the Professor would deliver his wisdom and knowledge of the world. Jose placed himself at the Professor's feet and gently put his hand on his knee. Goat sat on the arm of the chair and put his arm around the Professor's shoulder.

Goat spoke quietly to Jose as they sat there.

"Jose. Do you remember the afternoon on the side of that hill in Korea when the Professor, explained all about the Marine Corps and what made it special?"

"Yeah, Goat. I could almost tell you word for word what he said. Over the years, I have gone over it a million times in my mind."

"Jose, do you think he ever figured it out?"

"Sure, Goat, he figured it out."

Goat looked around the circle at the rest of the group and asked, "Anybody here ever come upon the answer? I remember big Ski asking him if there was a single thing that made us different. The Professor said he hadn't figured it out but was going to continue to search for it."

After a few moments of silence Boost spoke quietly.

"Marines learn to trust each other. It can't be any more complicated than that."

Jose and Goat were talking quietly to the Professor when Dr. Harris returned to the room. She stopped just inside the doorway and looked at the men sitting in their small circle around her husband. For a moment she stared and then she lost it. Tears streamed down her face. If she had not shown emotion, she would have been the only one in the room.

Hack moved next to her, put his arm around her shoulders and said in his clipped New Jersey accent "Honey, welcome to 1st platoon."

She wiped the tears, got it under control and smiled. She was the first to speak.

"I have been married to this man for over 40 years. I have never understood how he felt about being a Marine. After 10 minutes in this room, I understand."

Boost put out his hand and introduced himself. "Dr. Harris, I am Frank Bustamante."

She reached up and kissed him on the cheek and said. "I know you. You are Boost and that is 'Honey' to you big boy."

'Honey' Harris had just joined 1st platoon Baker Co., 1st Battalion, 7th Marines. She was now one of us.

The bar opened.

The group then moved, as one, to the hotel's fancy main dining room. A large circular table formed a natural perimeter. With Honey's permission, Jose and Goat got feeding instructions and flanked the Professor at the table.

There are special moments in life. This was one of those. Every one of the most positive good feelings was in place, every fulfillment seemed to be there. Everything was as it should have been.

Chapter 68

Not as lean, not as mean, but still a Marine

The huge picture window to the east revealed the sun coming up over the beautiful Sonoran desert, accentuating the saguaro cactus. Dawn with its fresh desert air and brilliant show of color.

Daybreak found Herman, Gabe, Charles, and I hunched over a map of South Tucson and the meeting spot Gabe had selected. We had been at it hard for over an hour.

Gabe's contact had done his job. The Enforcer had agreed to meet us.

We had timed the meeting for 7:30 in the evening. Perfect for the cover of darkness—and it left adequate time to return to the hotel for the formal reunion gathering.

The rest of first squad had awakened and was assembled around the table.

Gabe carefully went over the details of the plan.

The corner he had chosen was an empty one near the center of South Tucson—one block away from South Sixth Avenue, but not visible from that main street.

An empty two story building overlooked the entire vacant lot. The diagonal corner had a used car lot with a second story office. Gabe had secured access to both buildings.

There would be four riflemen—each with high powered rifles that had full night vision and range far beyond what was necessary.

The view from the upper floor of both buildings was open and clear; each spot would have a Marine armed with a sniper rifle and a spotter.

A third rifleman would be in the cab of a large 18-wheeler truck parked on the street across from the lot. A slightly open window of the sleeping quarters of the truck would give a full view.

To complete the protective rifle coverage, another truck was parked on the street itself. A tar covered roofing truck. The lift of the truck would be in the elevated position with the side rails installed, giving an opening for vision out, yet protected from others seeing in.

These four spots, with the high powered night vision rifles, were easily within range to cover the entire open lot and protect those that met with the 'Enforcer.'

Gabe explained that the guys who would meet with the Enforcer would need to move away from the sidewalk and onto the vacant lot. By moving into the vacant lot they would insure clear vision for the each of the Marines with rifles. The 'fields of fire' principle did not need to be explained to Sgt. Got Balls disciples.

Gabe finished and was complimented on the completeness of his work and his placing of each rifleman and spotters.

Coverage was perfect.

"Gabe's positions," I explained, "allow us quick and easy departure routes. We don't have the agility we once had. Mr. Kim will have his dry cleaning trucks parked on the street a half block away. One will point towards 21st Street set to head south. The second will point towards South Sixth Avenue ready to go east."

Gabe continued the explanation of his simple exit strategy.

"Two shooters and their spotter will go to the smaller of the trucks and the second pair of shooters, their spotter, and the guys who are meeting with Enforcer will go to the full-sized dry cleaning truck. On signal, two old junkers manned by men from

Chapter 68

Company G will have engine failure in the middle of the two main streets. Traffic going north and south on South 6th Ave will be held up, allowing the two dry cleaning trucks to pass through the openings. Once they pass, the stalled junkers will start and traffic will resume."

"Twenty minutes later Mr. Kim and his brother will disperse their passengers singly and in pairs at various locations on the hotel grounds where they will easily blend in with the other hotel guests."

"Everything will be left in the trucks. It will be sanitized and then all disappear as if it had never been there."

Charles said approvingly, "Jesus, Gabe, that is a good job. We can make it work."

Herman reviewed the communication plan. We would use multiple disposable, pre-programmed cell phones on vibrating mode, and satellite radios with headsets and earpieces.

Hack shook his head. "These radios and phones are awesome stuff compared to those damn World War II SR300 radios we used in Korea. No dragging those rolls of phone wire up and down hills."

Everyone had been attentive and absorbed Gabe's briefing. Not a word was spoken.

Gabe Sanchez had been platoon sergeant of 2nd platoon, but his reputation had spilled over to the rest of Baker Company. He had a 'don't fuck with me attitude,' and his reputation for bravery under fire was well known.

Formal introductions all around. . . . then Gabe took additional questions.

Hack asked, "How are you getting the streets blocked so we can cross?"

"Those will be Company G. They are a bunch of South Tucson guys who were in the Marine reserve unit here in 1950 when the war broke out. Mostly high school kids then. When Korea hit they were picked up as a unit and landed at Inchon. They were also at the Chosin Reservoir. They left a lot of friends over there.

Now they are a bunch of old grey haired buzzards like the rest of us."

"I went to them and asked for help. They were told they could not ask questions. They won't. They are still Marines and will get their job done."

Moose asked, "Gabe, I am from Minnesota. I don't understand about the roofing truck."

"Most of our houses in Tucson have flat roofs. The roofers strip the old roof, down to the wood, lay down tar paper and then cover the whole surface with hot tar. The trucks lift the tar and roofers up to the roof on a platform."

There was no way Gabe would get off easily with these guys.

Goat. "Hey Gabe. What we always heard about you was that you had a horrible temper and the Chinese pissed you off a couple times by knocking you on your ass with grenades. True or false?"

The flash of Gabe's eyes alone gave the answer. "It was those god-damned concussion grenades they used. Lifted my rotten ass off the ground and threw me against a big rock. No way I take that shit."

I added, "All his citations were similar. Something like, 'Sgt. Gabriel Sanchez, after being badly wounded by enemy hand grenades, completely disregarded his own personal safety and single-handedly attacked and destroyed the enemy bunkers.' The third Silver star had a more elaborate wording."

Charles took over. "Guys. We have a lot to do before tonight. We need to decide who is going to do what."

Doc spoke up for the first time that morning. "Here is my idea. We get a wheelchair and put one of us in it. We rig something that looks like an oxygen tank and make the guy in the chair look pitiful. It should give us a edge. One guy in the chair, one pushing and I will walk beside them beside them with my little medical bag."

I objected. "Hey Doc. You are a non-combatant. You get to be a look out."

Chapter 68

"Jesus, Smart Mouth, you haven't changed! You are talking and not listening. I walk beside the chair. Two reasons. One, you guys never let me take the point and it is now my turn. Two. This time, I will be armed and ready. For the past 15 years I have been in the top five nationally at the U. S. Pistol championships."

That settled, Hack turned to look at Moose. "I will get in the chair and Moose will push." End of that discussion.

Charles continued with the next order of business. "We will now pick the shooters. Raymond is not here so I will speak for him. Raymond never finished eating Smart Mouth's ass about his prowess on THE sniper patrol. If <u>he</u> were here, he would say something like he once did on a volunteering thing. 'We will have a show of hands, and Goat, if Smart Mouth raises his hand, break his arm.'"

The laughter subsided, but Gabe had to hear the 'sniper patrol' story, which somehow got told despite everyone talking over one another. Gabe's eyes twinkled and I knew I would live forever in Tucson with the fall out.

Back to business, the shooters were chosen. Boost, Jose, Charles, and Goat.

Gabe and I ended up as spotters.

Herman would coordinate communications. A recent hip replacement left him less than mobile.

I drew on my memory and reminded Herman of his phoney radio experience that got him off the line and a job at Division.

Honey had been listening at the door of the master bedroom.

"I'm in. What is my job?"

The room went quiet. And then more quiet.

Finally, Hack said. "Honey, I am glad you asked. We DO need you. Here is what we need. We do not want anyone to know that we have left the grounds of this hotel. You man the door of this suite and the phone. You answer any calls that come in for any of us and also cover the door. Then, if needed, you lie for us. We may be at the main pool, in the bar, or just chasing girls. The critical time is about an hour and a half before the main reunion banquet. You can say 'They are in a meeting and can't be disturbed or something.'"

Honey smiled. "How about, 'I can't bother them, they are having a prayer meeting?'"

With this, she drew chuckles from the group. Boost said "Honey, I like you better every day."

After lunch and short naps we all needed, we gathered again and reviewed items of business. Timing, attire, transportation.

Charles and Doc were assigned to familiarize everyone with their assigned equipment. Hack and Moose would each carry a 9 mm Glock in the small of their back. Doc would have one of the same in his medical bag.

Charles took Boost, Jose, and Goat off to review the function of the high tech fancy night vision weapons and then to the open desert to squeeze off a few rounds. Doc took charge of Hack and Moose and their new weapons.

Herman set about getting the disposable cell phones charged and ready to communicate with one another.

Gabe and I went to South Tucson to take another look at the lot.

Chapter 69

First Platoon—Move Out!

First squad, 1st platoon, Baker Company went into the night together one more time. This time into the streets of South Tucson. Each of us had a clear mind and purpose. We each have had a full life. The firm foundation for that life came from a true professional—Sgt. Raymond Gotshall. His message: "Do the job and do it right." Plain and simple.

As we reach the empty lot, one block off South Sixth Avenue, it is just barely dark. Especially in this corner of South Tucson the homes are very old and run down and the lot is cluttered with weeds and debris.

Four men with modern rifles equipped with super scopes and night vision adaptors have moved quietly into their places. Each is totally motionless in the full prone position. Jose on the raised bed of the roofing truck; Goat hidden behind the sleeping compartment window of the large semi cab; Charles and Boost patiently watching from windows of the two empty buildings. As spotters, Gabe and I continuously scan the area with night vision binoculars.

Crouched down, there I am looking through my binoculars out of the dirty window of a second-story window of a dilapidated South Tucson building, scanning the empty lot below. To my right, another gray-haired man is peering through the scope of a high-powered rifle.

It is one of those moments in life when you stop and wonder, "What twists and turns in my life put me in this place, at this time?"

Ours is to act and repay.

At this point in our lives the structures of society no longer command us. We have reached an age where we know fully what we do. Not as lean, not as mean, but still Marines. The reality. We are better Marines now than when we roamed the countryside of Korea.

We apologize to no one for what we are about to do. Not family, friends, authority, or God.

Those who know us will understand. The rest. . . . Fuck'em.

Herman has set us up so that we are all connected with wireless headsets and ear pieces. We can all hear each other. We have agreed on a single command communication. 'Hold' or 'Shoot.' Hack will be primary to issue that command; we spotters only will do so if needed.

Herman also has coordinated with Company G and set communications for the exit strategy with a disposable cell phone system. A simple code signal has been agreed on for traffic control.

Approximately fifteen minutes before the appointed time, from several blocks away, a man in a wheelchair approaches the empty lot. A large, stooped man is pushing the chair. Another man, who appears to be a keeper or guardian, is walking beside the chair. The man in the chair does not sit erectly and seems to be attached to an oxygen device strapped to the wheel chair. The old men move slowly down the street.

From the chair Hack says to his 'attendant,' "Moose give me that Rolex watch you have on."

Without hesitation, Moose hands over the watch to his old buddy and watches as Hack straps it to his wrist.

At exactly the agreed time they arrive at the deserted lot.

Momentarily, a large Hummer pulls up to the curb. The first person to exit is an enormous man, clearly the bodyguard. Gabe had briefed us. This would be Elefante. Two men who accompany the Enforcer at all times, come out of the vehicle next. They are another pair of bodyguard types and are known around town to be proficient with knives. The three look the area over and view the three old men with disdain. The obvious leader of the group then gets out from behind the wheel of the big vehicle and walks slowly toward the wheelchair.

The small man in the wheelchair straightens up and clears his throat. In a raspy voice he tells the newcomers that he appreciated them for coming and being prompt.

The man in the chair speaks with difficulty and seems to be gasping a bit for his breath.

"We are here because we have something we wish to talk to you about."

I see the two cutters smile contemptuously, but they do not speak. This is obviously a one man show—and that one man is the Enforcer.

The Enforcer, appearing slightly impatient, asks "What do you want?"

"We are here to make an offer to you. It is our understanding that there was a recent drive-by shooting. We hear that there is still a contract on the young man who is Stella's friend."

The Enforcer replies. "That is true, but it is a matter of a personal issue and I do not negotiate things of a personal nature."

Gasping between sentences, from the wheelchair Hack rasps. "At least listen to our offer. We would like that contract lifted. We are prepared to offer a substantial amount of money. . . . Or, we have access to large quantities of pure pharmacy-controlled prescription drugs to offer."

The Enforcer is dismissive. "I have lost respect. Money or drugs do not replace that." With a nod to his companions, he adds "No deal. We are leaving."

Hack lifts his arm a little so the Rolex is visible. The Enforcer spots the elegant watch and commands his cutters to take it.

As the two bodyguards take a step toward the wheelchair Elefante and the Enforcer reach for weapons.

Hack quietly says the magic word.

"Hold."

Hack rises from the wheelchair as if to hand over the watch. He makes a small turning motion and the first cutter goes down with a red slice across his throat. The second cutter is knocked toward the ground by a compact swing of Moose's huge arm. The second motion of Hack's knife almost took his head off.

Elefante's first step forward ends as a hole appears between his eyes. It matches the one in the middle of Enforcer's forehead. The silenced weapon in Doc's hand has made almost no movement or sound. Pfft. Pfft.

Herman triggers the traffic control. Traffic jams stop the cars on two major streets at the exact moment each truck arrives. As each dry cleaning truck passes through the created openings, the streets return to their normal flow. One vehicle heads east and then north; the other west and then also north.

Doc, Hack, Moose, Jose, and Gabe are sitting on the floor in the back of the larger truck heading toward the hotel.

Hack says simply, "Moose, here is your watch back. That prick sure wanted it. Say Moose, I can get you some big money for that thing. Nice piece."

"Thank you Harold, but it was a gift from all of my sons and their families on my seventieth birthday."

"Jesus, Moose, why didn't you tell me that when you gave it to me?"

"Harold, you didn't ask."

Silence.

"Harold, I have to tell you something."

"What?"

"Harold, I believe you have lost a step over time."

CHAPTER 70

The gratitude of the Korean people is forever

The final event of this year's reunion of 1st Battalion, 7th Marines is being held in one of the huge banquet rooms of the elegant hotel. By the podium two sharp young Marines in dress blues are guarding the American and Marine Corps flags. Grey hair abounds, much of it congregated in the vicinity of the bar.

There is a notable difference between the people in this room and a regular cocktail party. Here you can see many small knots of men. No general mingling. The individual groups of men have been together in a different place and another time. You could feel their closeness.

They are no different than the men of 1st squad, 1st Platoon, Baker Company—each of us has cleaned up, made ourselves presentable, and reported one at a time to the gathering place. None of us would leave the Presidential Suite until everyone was ready and we could go together. Honey has dressed the Professor and brought him in.

Being together tonight is something none of us had expected. What has happened in the last couple hours wasn't something any of us could have foreseen. For 1st squad it is just one of those things that needed to be done.

The strength and intertwined feelings that had existed between us many years ago are still there. At that point in time we had separated one or two at a time. We had not realized how much had passed between us during our time in Korea. We will remain together for all of our days. Being here, together in one room, after all this time is almost unreal.

When each pair of us met up this time, it was with a long warm hug—a hug that was held and felt. When we had parted so many years ago, none had any thought of the future. Each of us left a bit of himself behind when it was his turn to leave Korea.

Seeing each other again is special, but nothing compared to the individual reunions with Jose. Some of us had not seen his broken and battered body leave 673. Those that did were certain that he would not make it to the rear quickly enough to do any good. When Raymond had made his last sweep of the slope on 673, he had seen Jose and a flicker of life. In our minds he never made it. To see him alive and showing the Jose smile warmed each of us.

Before we came downstairs, Charles had ordered Champagne brought to the suite.

"God gave us Jose back. Jose will make the toast."

Jose stood in front of the group. After thinking for a minute, he confesses that he has never given a toast before.

"I feel like someone from the Wizard of Oz. I am among the men who gave me heart and courage. I am with the Professor who gave me a brain." At this, Honey smiles.

"My toast is to Sgt. Raymond Gotshall, United States Marine Corps who gave me and all of us a long life. To Raymond, wherever you are. Hear! Hear!" Raised glasses all around.

Once in the ballroom our perimeter forms out of habit.

Someone pointed out a group of the Chosin Reservoir Marines. "The Chosen Few." Strange how our guys gawk at them. Hero worship. It would not have been surprising if 1st platoon went up and asked for autographs.

You need to understand the United States Marine Corps and its mentality. The older you get the more it comes into focus.

CHAPTER 70

Marines revere the Marines who came before them.

First squad looks at the "The Chosen Few" like they are gods. Everyone knows the story of how they had fought off the entire Chinese army in temperatures well below zero. After they had fought their way out, in the last mile into the final perimeter their commanding officer had moved up and down their column and told them, "We went in like Marines, we are coming out like Marines. Straighten up those lines, get in step, look sharp!"

They did him one better. They formed up the ranks and came through the line singing the Marine Corps Hymn.

Soon the evening's events are almost over. The last event of the reunion has a formal tone.

The speaker is introduced as a man who had immigrated from Korea to the United States as a child.

"This Korean-born man is now an American citizen and a successful business man in Tucson."

First platoon is getting ready to tune out until we see that the speaker is 'our' Mr. Kim.

"I was born in Korea. It is my native land. I came to this country with my family as a child and I am an American citizen. I am proud of my Korean heritage and I am proud of my country, The United States of America. The men in this room made that possible."

"The Korean people truly appreciate the freedom you gave them and will be forever grateful to each of you. You are too young to have fought for the freedom of your own country. You were not too young to have fought for the freedom of the Korean people."

"Many of you left your blood on Korean soil. All of you left friends and tears. The gratitude of the Korean people is forever."

With a small bow to the crowd and a second imperceptible bow in our direction, Mr. Kim starts to leave the podium.

As one, the entire room rose to their feet. Mr. Kim has touched us.

Chapter 71

The police official indicated also that robbery was not a motive. Each of the victims had substantial amounts of money and jewelry on their persons. When the South Tucson Police arrived at the scene their vehicle, a high end Hummer, was still there.

The homeless man who discovered the bodies was not a witness and the police official stated that they had not yet found any witnesses. The officer also indicated that in past instances of a similar nature, witnesses in South Tucson were difficult to find.

CHAPTER 71

The following morning a small article appeared in *The Arizona Daily Star*, section 2, page 2. It read:

TUCSON, ARIZONA

Late last night, four bodies were discovered by a homeless person on an empty lot in South Tucson.

The bodies have not been officially identified, but are believed to be individuals known to be involved in the war over drug traffic. An unidentified source said the four were the top people in one of the most powerful local gangs. The same source indicated that one of the bodies was the leader of that group. That man is known with a street name, The Enforcer. The other dead men were reported to be a bodyguard named El Elefante and two men always in his company. According to the same source, those men were known as "El Cortadores," so named for their ability and propensity to use knives.

In a statement at the site, a South Tucson police official stated that a full investigation had begun. That official stated that the killings did appear to be related to the illicit drug industry. He added that generally these types of killings are based on a payback or territorial issue.